Jothen detected a vague shimmer and stir in the blue water about him. The glimmering motion in the depths rose upward with an eddying motion and resolved itself into a school of barracudas.

Jothen, Kim, and Ruvani looked on in fascinated horror as the deadly fishes began an exhibition of precision swimming in formation. The barracudas patrolled back and forth, back and forth, and it seemed that even their tails and fins moved in unison.

They swam to the left, then each fish pivoted and did an about-face as if in response to a silent command, and swam to the right. Each time they repeated the motions, they drew a little closer. The manuever was purposeful and deadly, a deliberate and sadistic prolongation of trial by terror. As the predatory creatures glided past, a host of cold, appraising eyes was cocked at Kim, Ruvani, and Jothen, as if each barracuda was thinking, "Will these three be enough for all of us?"

Then, when Jothen heard Kim shriek, he knew the final confrontation had begun.

# A TORRENT OF FACES

## JAMES BLISH & NORMAN L. KNIGHT

ace books
A Division of Charter Communications Inc.
A GROSSET & DUNLAP COMPANY
1120 Avenue of the Americas
New York, New York 10036

# CONTENTS

"For that man cannot exhaust or lessen the powers of nature follows from the indestructibility of matter and the persistence of force. . . . That the Earth could maintain a thousand billions as easily as a thousand millions is a necessary deduction from the manifest truth that, at least as far as our agency is concerned, matter is eternal and force must forever continue to act. . . ."

Henry George: *Progress and Poverty*

This novel makes the assumption—suggested by the epigraph from Henry George—that the world will support a population of about one trillion (one thousand billions, or 1,000,000,000,000) by the year 2794. The part of the assumption contained in the word "support" is admittedly the wildest sort of fantasy.

It is of course likely that world population will continue to double itself each century, though the rate may flatten out toward the end of the second millennium. It is also likely that by that time most of these people will be starving to death, and the rest will be scraping desperately.

We chose to examine an alternative. Physically, George is right; given a huge cooperative endeavor, the Earth *could* support such a population. But a human society of this magnitude will never develop if the race does not organize itself into some uniform political and economic unit before the population has expanded much beyond its present numbers.

What sort of unit? We concluded that nothing less than a Utopia would do. We realize that Utopias are out of fashion lately; on the other hand, the picture of the future as a universal Asiatic despotism atop the starving masses has been painted to death by all the modern dystopians from Huxley on—and we could not believe that a population of this size could be a slave society. For one thing, a tyranny is too indifferent to individual human lives to undertake the colossal engineering effort involved; for another, the existence of so enormous a population even under very mean circumstances would require a citizenry capable of intelligent cooperation—it could not be run as a multibillion horde of sullen yes-men.

It will surprise some readers, and perhaps horrify a few, that the economic system we settled upon for our Utopia is a form of the corporate state, or what was once called fascism. We were interested in the fact that this kind of economic system has actually never been tried (Mussolini's version was a clumsy and indifferent fake, and that of Jerry Voorhis, though eminently sensible, suffered the usual fate of any political notion born in California). We thought it might be workable, and perhaps even inevitable, in a high-energy economy; and while we would agree that the notion of an even quasi-democratic fascism is unlikely, we don't view the possibility of a democratic socialism as likely either.

Our future world requires one hundred thousand cities in an area as small as Puerto Rico, about twelve to sixteen miles apart, if the cities are spaced evenly all over the globe in a checker-board pattern. Yet even these close-set megalopoli could not contain an uncontrolled population for long. By the time the population reached 4.56 trillion, the cities would be shoulder to shoulder, covering the whole Earth and reaching well under the seas; so our solution of George's challenge is strictly transitional.

Our World of One Trillion did not spring full-blown from Henry George and the present-day population explosion, however. In many important ways it is a logical outgrowth of two previous novels by one of us (NLK): *Frontier of the Unknown* (*Astounding Stories*, 1937) and *Crisis in Utopia* (*Astounding Stories*, 1940; *Five*

*Science Fiction Novels*, Gnome Press, 1952), to which this book is a sort of sequel. We began speculating about the population side of the problem in 1948; the intervening time was consumed mostly by endless pages of calculations, several dozen drawings and diagrams, about thirty thousand words of notes, and many fat letters almost completely covered with stamps—during which time the essence of the problem has not changed a bit, but has come to seem a great deal more immediate.

We are indebted to Frederik Pohl, editor of *Galaxy Magazine*, for much valuable criticism.

JAMES BLISH
NORMAN L. KNIGHT

*Alexandria, Va.*
*Silver Spring, Md.*

*1948-1967*

Cast of characters in order of their appearance

Biond Smith, chief, Disaster Plans Board
Jothen Kent, senior water engineer, Gitler, Missouri
   (Unistam)
Deban Tod, chairman, Communications Corporation
Chen U, chairman, World Resources Corporation
Dorthy Sumter, chairwoman, Submarine Products
   Corporation
Marg't Splain, chairwoman, Transportation Corporation
Storm, chief of Tritons, and executive chairman, SPC
Kim Wernicke, ecological surgeon, Starved Rock Bio-
   logical Preserve
Umiak, an aircraft steward
Ruvani, a Triton girl, Storm's daughter
Defabio, a Barrier-hilthon monitor
Tioru, a Triton, and deputy chairman, SPC
Dr. Kemal Matouf, an entomologist
Squid, a Triton-Drylander hybrid boy
Limpet, a Triton girl
Neratino, a Triton technician
Alva McGee, assistant chief, Disaster Plans Board
Fongaváro Jones, technician, Tananarive, Madagascar
Thaniel Brewster, chief of Tenants' Services, Philadel-
   phia (Unistam)
Piscetti, chief of operations to Jothen Kent
Guivrec Krantz, a corpse
Dr. Helga Auer, a physicist for Transcorp
Willy Naujack, an amateur biophysicist
Flavia, an asteroid


Computers, Preserve visitors, Barrier-hilthon staff,
dolphins, Joneses, spacemen, Philadelphians, World
Forest rangers, precinct guards, Gitler staff, Prime Center staff, and the unemployed.

The dove descending breaks the air
With tongues of incandescent terror . . .

**T.S. Eliot:** *Four Quartets*

## BOOK ONE

## 1 Biond on Edge

The city inside the picture frame in Biond Smith's office was standing on edge.

Biond, of course, couldn't see it, since he had his back to it. Only a tiny mirror set into the banked, horseshoe-shaped console before him hinted at what was in the frame. But that didn't matter. The perpendicular city was for his visitor to look at; Biond had seen it often before.

While Biond read his way through the last few projected frames of a filmstrip, Jothen Kent, his visitor, studied the city with obvious interest. It was, after all, Jothen's city: Gitler, Missouri, of which he was senior water engineer. Its peculiar name, Jothen even knew, derived from its founding by a group of Ukrainian refugees after World War III, in honor of an obscure politician who had led an earlier, unsuccessful attempt to destroy the Soviet state.

Biond knew this equally well, but it had no significance for him. To Biond, and to the Disaster Plans Board in general, Gitler was just City 2,103, World Zone 6 (Union of Occupied Classes).

"Looks funny, seen all at once that way," Jothen said. "I'm used to thinking of it from the inside—in terms of the sluices and penstocks and so on. Where's the view coming from?"

"VIGIL Eighteen, part of the Relay satellite net," Biond said, flipping the viewer to the last frame of Jothen's protocol. "The focal plane is about three miles up."

He turned in his chair to look directly at the picture. At once he could feel himself falling sidewise out of his seat, his feet being plucked out of the treadles of the console, his ears singing. Biond's orientation was heavily biased toward the visual end of the sense triad; he sometimes felt a moment's vertigo even while looking down at a map. Had it not been for the presence of Marg't Splain on Prime Center, he would have reported himself for therapy long ago. Now he simply clung unobtrusively to the smooth, motherly forearms of his chair.

The process was reversible: he could look at the picture as a map, hung on the wall. The whole area in the frame was uniformly green, except for the dead square of the flyport exactly in the center of the city. A muted black tracery made another square around the flyport, just one and a half miles out from the margins of the paved area. There was another such square surrounding that, at the same distance farther out; and finally—five miles from the mathematical center—the city came to an end, a pyramid with ten miles to a side. That final square had four immense, interrupted ellipses cut into each side, like bites out of a monstrous wafer. A closer look at the bites would even reveal tooth marks: eighty-story tiers of apartments arranged in ten one-hundred-foot-high setbacks.

The Chinese walls that wove back and forth sinuously over the surface of every level of the city showed the same setback system, as did the margins of the individual levels. The thirty-two ziggurat-like towers reared above their levels at the corners of each square, as well as along each side in the ratio 1/2/1/0. The towers were conspicuous because, like the flyport, they were gray-white against the general background of the greenery; otherwise the small concentric circles that they made in the picture would have been invisible from a height of three miles.

Except for its regularity and its comparatively small size, Gitler, Missouri, could have been any city in the world—any one of 100,000 such cities. And only its regularity, its perfectly rational shape, marked it out to the trained eye as a Disaster City.

After a moment, Biond had to turn away from it, with a slight involuntary lurch as his muscles tried to react to the illusory shift in the gravity plane. He had set the scene up for Jothen, and it was downright foolish to become involved with it himself. It was too good a mirror of his own perturbations. Even in this year of rationality 2794, most people had some small insecurity that might be called forth by exposing them to something very familiar in an unfamiliar context. The city standing on edge was one move—far below the level of conscious argument, and by no means the most unfair in Biond's armamentarium—in Biond's campaign to persuade Jothen Kent to stay home.

Jothen did not seem to be at all disturbed. He was smiling faintly. He was a tall, heavy-boned man with red hair cropped close to his head in conventional style. His craggy but mobile face showed marked traces of some emergent Caucasoid strain and was decorated with rather thick red-gold eyebrows. One rarely saw body hair these days, but Biond had to admit that the streaks of rich light over the blue eyes had a startling and not unpleasant cosmetic effect. The contrast of red-gold and blue was picked up in an irregular pattern in

Jothen's dress half-cloak, which, however, he wore without the popular exaggerated shoulders. With them, Biond thought, he would have looked like a delta-winged air infantryman out of the pages of the Third War. The rest of Jothen's costume was flatly utilitarian: sandals and white boxer's shorts.

"You've got a case for a vacation, Jo," Biond said finally, turning off the film projection. "Admittedly Gitler's never been occupied since it was built, and you've been on duty there the whole time. But now you know the other half of the story. We may need to occupy the town at any moment."

"The chances," Jothen said slowly, "look pretty low to me, Biond. Otherwise I wouldn't have asked permission to leave. None of the cities Gitler is set up to serve is in or even near the Zone of Fire. As for an epidemic, that's even more unlikely than an earthquake—your own plague section admits that it hasn't had so much as a sneeze reported to it, from anywhere in the world, since the winter of 2742. The storm season is over for my zone, and anyhow it's my theory that modern cities, even the oldest, are one hundred percent weatherproof. And I've got a vacation coming to me."

"I know you have," Biond said. "But I still think you ought to spend it in your own city."

Jothen shrugged. "I've had my fill of that for a while," he said. "There's not much to do in Gitler. It's different if you live in an occupied town. A Disaster City is a damned dull place to be, Biond."

There was certainly no countering that proposition. Biond wondered whether it would be worth trying to persuade Jothen that Novoe Washingtongrad and even York Basin were also damned dull places to be. He shelved the notion as too last-ditch to bother with.

"Where do you want to go, then?"

"It's all in the protocol. I thought one of the planetary resorts—"

"Out," Biond said flatly. "Suppose your city did have to be occupied on short notice—and you were in the twilight zone of Mercury, watching the sun come up and go back down again over the Antonaidi Range? That'd be a nice mess. Why don't you go to one of the Preserves? There's one near you, as I recall."

"Sure," Jothen said. "Starved Rock Preserve. Kim's an ecological surgeon there. I don't think she'd warm to spending her vacation at home either."

Something cold ran quickly down Biond's back and vanished. There should have been no need for Jothen to remind him of that; it was in the film dossier Biond had just finished reading. The fact that he had set up a block on it was fresh warning, should another be needed, of how deeply the thought of Marg't Splain was disturbing his judgment, even in apparently unrelated matters. The crass directness with which his unconscious had operated was unpleasantly fascinating: *Jothen has Kim Wernicke. Kim Wernicke equals Marg't Splain. I cannot have Marg't Splain. Therefore: Kim Wernicke does not exist.*

"Well, there's still the seaside, the floating hotels, the highlands, the poles," he said. "But I don't think you'll have much of a chance at any of them. They're booked up solidly for years in advance. Got a reservation anywhere?"

"No," Jothen said. "I was waiting until you—"

"Good grief, Jo. You're wasting your time, then."

"I don't think so," Jothen said. "If the planets are out, I'd like next best to go on a sort of busman's holiday. I'm not interested in sightseeing or swimming, per se. Suppose I go to one of the big coastal cities, or even undersea, to study their water supply plants? I hear that something special in the way of new techniques had to be evolved for Triton Reef, for instance."

"Hmm. Do you speak Triton—or pidgin dolphinese?"

"I don't speak anything but Basic," Jothen said composedly. "Kim speaks a lot of languages, since she's in contact with the public most of the time. Besides, if you okay the trip, I can get conditioned in any language I need, you know that. As an employed citizen I'm allowed machine education in any subject essential to my specialty—and I think a trip like this would be ruled into that category."

Jothen leaned forward, bracing his hands on his thighs. "Look, Biond," he said, "I've known you for some time, but even a stranger would have spotted that language question as the purest sort of quibble. As far as I can see, there isn't a single good reason why I shouldn't be allowed to leave Gitler for three weeks, except for this general policy of discouraging traveling. And I don't mind telling you that I think that policy's asinine."

"No, it isn't," Biond said, with the unconscious sigh of a man who has been given an unexpected lead out of a maze. "It's essential. Let me ask you a question, Jo. When we have to put a disaster plan into operation, what's the minimum number of people we have to move?"

"I follow the Maneuvers Census as closely as you do. About a hundred million. A hundredth of one percent of the world population, whatever that is at the time."

"Right. That's a lot of people, I think you'll agree. Now then, suppose one percent of the present world population elects to take a monthly traveling vacation each year—people for whom we have to provide transportation, sure, but for whom we also have to provide transient housing, food, recreation. No, don't get out the slide rule, because I know the figure like the back of my hand. It comes to about one point six billion people *every month.*"

"I had no idea," Jothen admitted.

"It's only the beginning. The figure is hypothetical, because we can't figure on that percentage going on vacation annually—we don't have that many people employed! Most of the world is idle. We don't dare encourage them to move about as they please."

"Are you sure there are so few people on jobs?"

"If I'm not sure, who would be? Look, Jo, you live in a city designed for an average population, but it's an empty city, staffed with a maintenance crew, every member of which has a job. That's a rare and highly artificial situation. Ever since the Cybernetic Revolution the number of employable people has been falling on an exponential curve. We literally have no use any more for anyone but creative and administrative minds, of a caliber our grandfathers would have thought very high indeed. Furthermore, the leaching-out of the gene pool, which took place while the population was reaching its current peak, has left us with a high majority of pure thumpheads. All but a tenth of one percent of the world is living on the dole—as is their right, of course. And next year, you and I and an appalling number of other employables may find ourselves outclassed by some new think-box—and then we'll be living on the dole too."

Jothen pulled reflectively at his nose. "Then you don't really have a vacation problem," he said at last.

"Of course we don't. We have something far worse. We have a population that has nothing to do with itself *all the time.* Obviously we can't allow the whole world to be constantly in transit, just because it's bored. We're barely able to keep our essential transportation running as it is. We must keep people at home. We do it in dozens of different ways. We keep language barriers up, for instance. We could give the world a common language overnight if necessary—after all, everyone who has a job can speak Basic now, and Basic doesn't *have* to be a privilege—but instead we go out of our way to create language rivalries. On that point alone, we've Hispanized the Earth."

"I don't know the term," Jothen said.

"Sorry. In old Spain, the man who spoke Catalan had a vast contempt for the man who spoke Basque. Now we've made it a point of honor for every man but the man with a job to speak no language but his own. We've encouraged local customs and cultural matrices in the same way. If you can't sing the songs that are sung by everyone in a given city in a given year, you're a fool and an outcast in that city—you may be torn to shreds by children. And so on.

"There used to be a song in this part of the world, just about a millennium and a half ago, that summed it all up nicely. It asked how you kept the farmer down on the farm after he'd seen Paris."

"You gave him orders," Jothen said wryly, "as you would me."

"No, because agriculture was a private industry then, fragmented—not a corporation. Our problem is even worse. We have no farmers, only managers. We have to keep the Parisian himself in Paris, though there's nothing there for him to do, and nothing for him to do anywhere else either."

"Then why," Jothen said quietly, "are you chewing up all this valuable time trying to keep one single man 'down on the farm'? Why did I have to come to Novoe Washingtongrad to see you, if the only reason for turning me down is the general policy? You don't try to keep every single applicant at home by making him travel to a personal interview. Why me?"

"I didn't say that the general policy was the only

reason. I'm explaining the policy because you called it into question—now you can see that it makes sense. The reason I'm trying to keep *you* home is that I'm chairman of the Disaster Plans Board, and I don't want to find myself evacuating a horde of people into a Disaster City that has no water engineer!"

Biond calmed himself down hastily. There was absolutely no reason why he should be shouting at Jothen. After a while he added:

"Which brings up another matter. The Jones Convention is scheduled for Gitler this year, starting two days after you've asked to leave. You wouldn't know about it, but the Chavez Convention last month wasted water at such a terrific rate that Resources considered discontinuing convention years entirely. I had to release half the staff of the city it was held in as unemployable."

"Where was that?" Jothen said interestedly.

"I can't say. It was a violation of the declassed men's dignity to give you the name of the convention, even. Don't trace it, please."

"Certainly not. But don't worry about the Joneses. They're a dwindling clan—we don't expect more than a million of them to show up. If we'd been assigned the Singh Convention I'd have worried, but I think we'll be able to quarter all the Joneses in the second level, northeast wing. The boys can handle them."

Biond shrugged. "On that your assessment is final, of course."

"Thanks. Well then, Biond, what's the verdict?"

"You have a job. That makes you a free agent. If in your judgment you can leave Gitler safely for three weeks, neither I nor anyone else in the world can prevent it."

"Hell, Biond, I know that," Jothen said. "Naturally I want your approval, so I won't be declassed if my judgment turns out to be faulty. Biond, please don't spar with me. This trip is important to me. Just between friends, I hope to persuade Kim to marry me. So far I haven't made a dent, but I have the feeling that with three uninterrupted weeks to work it out, things might be different. At least she'd have the chance to see what living with me on a twenty-four-hour basis would be like."

A small, cold shock wave launched itself in the pit of Biond's stomach. Someone in Prime Center had been talking, someone had violated his dignity—perhaps Marg't herself. How else could Jothen have known so precisely where he was most vulnerable? And given that knowledge, Jothen's stroke was itself outrageous, as invasive as a parlor psych-analysis. Seen in this suffused orange light, the Triton Reef vacation, too, appeared to have been in Jothen's mind as a prime goal from the beginning—he had accepted the impossibility of visiting any of the usual resorts with suspicious quickness . . .

Biond was interrupted by light—two of the clear tabs on the console began to glow. As calls came in to the console, they were computer-screened and shifted into specific, coded, ultrahigh frequencies, depending upon their general content and point of origin. Afterward the wave-guided signals passed through a dividing network into temporary storage, while the code went to the proper tab on the console; which tab lit, and what color, gave Biond an instant visual report on the nature of the call and its probable degree of urgency. The development of the system and a few simple adjuncts had thrown no one knew how many myriads of receptionists onto the dust heap; it had all happened long ago.

One of the calls was from Prime Center; the tab light was green, indicating official business. Since most of the calls received by employed people on the job fell into that category, it was probably routine. Transport Corporation's tab was yellow—moderately urgent. As Biond eached for the console, it turned scarlet—a rare signal, and one that had needed no explanation since the beginning of modern history.

Biond's hand hesitated over the button labeled TAPE, which would take off both messages for later inspection. Then he pressed it. No emergency that Transcorp could have discovered could affect the Disaster Plans Board intimately enough to demand action now, rather than five or ten minutes from now. Besides, emergencies are not met best by a distracted mind.

The lights went out. Jothen watched Biond with alert expectancy. The shock wave spent itself in a series of small tingles in Biond's fingers and toes. The diversion had given Biond's reasoning, too, a chance to shake down. Clearly Jothen had spoken in confidence, not attacking Biond, but exposing his own dignity as an act of friendship. To turn him down would seem to Jothen an unfriendly act, or, at the worst, an unfeeling one. For Biond himself, it would be an act of envy; Jothen would not know that, but Biond would.

Damn Marg't Splain. And damn Chen U, for that matter.

"I'll stretch a point," Biond said with sudden energy. "I think you're right, Jo. DPB can spare you for a fortnight or so. And good luck with Dr. Wernicke. Why isn't she with you, by the way?"

"She's on a field trip, otherwise I would have brought her to plead, of course. There's been an epizoötic of something or other in her area—false monarchs, whatever those are. Thanks for the wish—I'll need some luck."

"The gene pool needs stock like yours and hers."

"That," Jothen said, "is what I keep telling her, but somehow it doesn't seem to be the right argument. None of the others seem to be either." He stood up, smiling, and held out his hand. "Thanks again. I'll keep posted, of course. I wouldn't keep the poor old town standing on edge much longer, though, if I were you. My water system's efficient, but that's one strain it wasn't designed to take."

Biond could not repress a tight grin. "It was an experiment," he said. "I'll file it under negative evidence. . . . And—you're welcome, Jo. 'Find the deeps at peace.' "

" 'And the darkness quiet,' " Jothen said, also in Triton. It was not until after the door had slid shut after him that Biond remembered that Jothen had claimed to know no language but Basic. The water engineer from empty, remote Gitler, Missouri, had had his boss outgunned from the beginning, and had known it.

## 2   To Run a World

Deban Tod took the package out of the delivery well and opened it. His huge, bland face fell theatrically. "This appears to be plankton chowder," he said. "I had left special orders for all of us tonight, ladies and gentlemen, but they appear to have gone astray. I myself am damn tired of boiled brit."

"I've no objection," Chen U said, shifting comfortably in his chair. The small-boned, neatly articulated man looked even smaller against Deban Tod's outsize furniture, but he handled himself with such perfect assurance that it did not seem to matter. As chairman of World Resources Corporation he was effectively the president of the Earth (officially there was no such office, for the Union of Occupied Classes was an oligarchy with no single head, and Prime Center—the rulers of the world, now meeting here tonight—a committee with no chairman). Nevertheless, Chen U allowed no sense of this to pass from himself to other persons, no more than he allowed others to notice that his wife, Marg't Splain, was a head and a half taller than he was. Chen U made himself neither great nor small; in repose, in speech, in gesture, in act, he let it be known that he was of a proper size for Chen U.

"Nor I," Biond said quickly. "By luck, I haven't been served the stuff in a month."

"Very well," Deban said. He thumped down beside Biond on the viewing couch. "Dip in, everybody."

Biond dipped in, although his appetite was puny. Like everyone else, he ate with his fingers for the most part, using the spoon only for foods not solid enough to pick up, and rinsing his fingers and lips periodically. The dining table, which had risen from the center of the floor, was provided with finger bowls sunken into its top. Induction valves, actuated by the approach of a hand, kept them half filled with tepid sea water containing a trace of citric acid. Everything loose on the table, including the almost indestructible napkins, was community property, and would be returned at the end of the meal to the neighborhood distribution center, where it would all be flamed clean.

Late afternoon sunlight slanted in across the carpetment from the porch. Biond would have preferred to have taken his meal out there, but when Prime Center met in Deban's apartment everyone had to eat indoors, even when the wind was right. In addition to being the elected head of Communications Corporation, Deban was an ardent amateur gardener. He belonged to a world-wide organization of such amateurs and faithfully followed every issue of the 3-V magazine devoted to the hobby.

The flowers seemed to delight Dorthy Sumter, the slight, blond representative of Submarine Products Corporation. Submarine had originally been a wholly owned subsidiary of World Resources, and had been split off by its stockholders into an autonomous company only recently; hence Dorthy had not been seated on Prime Center long enough to have seen Deban's growths before.

"Are they dangerous?" she said, peering through the silicoid at the ordered riot of color on the sunporch. Her Basic pronunciation was tinged with an accent Biond found hard to identify. It seemed almost Polynesian, but there was also enough agglutination in it to suggest that it had been influenced by Welsh. Suddenly Biond had it, and wondered how he could have missed it before—the accent was Triton, of course.

"Yes and no," Deban said. "Some people can develop sensitization reactions to some of them—allergies—given enough time. But I keep my garden sealed only for the same reason that the Biological Preserves are sealed—to keep my pets from seeding the World Forest. I imagine Chen U would be mightily irritated if some of these plants turned out to be cross-fertilizing some crop of his."

"It's happened before," Chen U said, ducking his chin politely to his chest in order to tuck in a biscuit.

Marg't Splain was looking thoughtfully at Dorthy's back. The younger woman was wearing a scintillating emerald cincture that complemented her hair without making her tanned skin look sickly. Though she was extremely slim, her figure was delicate and interesting; her reason for wearing clothes indoors, therefore, was not immediately apparent. Most people wore clothing outside their apartments, either for specific protections if they worked, or for casual protection otherwise, but at home nudity was the rule.

Biond was almost sure that Marg't was wondering what kind of physical defect Dorthy had to conceal. He knew better; he had several times visited Dorthy's home office at the Reef, while Submarine was being split off from Resources, and there, where she had been on her home grounds and quite certain of herself, her slight body had flashed unencumbered, unflawed, and singularly gracefully from task to task.

The cincture, instead, was probably a measure of her new insecurity. She was still a little awed to be a member of Prime Center, and more than a little in awe of Marg't, who bossed Transport Corporation. Biond guessed that she was simply avoiding having to observe the elaborate code of manners that applied to formal nudity—at least until she had learned to observe the far more elaborate code of precedence that prevailed on Prime Center.

Biond had to admit that the precaution was wise. He loved Marg't Splain, but he was under no illusions about her magnanimity. She would be quick to take offense should Dorthy inadvertently do something gauche for a nude woman, like running or bending over—to take offense, and make political capital of it. The simple clothing enabled Dorthy to stop worrying about that, at least.

He also knew that speculative glances were occasionally coming his way as well. He was the only other clothed person at the meeting. He could only hope that the rest would take his formal breeches as a politeness to Dorthy. Most particularly, Chen U.

Luckily, there was another distracting person present. Dorthy had brought a Triton with her—one of those miracles of tectogenetics who could live underseas or on the land with almost equal facility, who tended Submarine Products' dimly undulating crops, and rode in partnership with its dolphins. The Tritons were a new human species, the first since *H. sapiens* himself.

This one was called Storm; he was Dorthy's executive vice president over his fellows. He was tall, with a dappled dark skin—though the colors meant nothing, for the Tritons could change their markings better than any chameleon; it was a subsidiary form of communication among them—and the long flat muscles of the swimmer. Storm was young, with a quietly handsome face. Though his intercostal spiracles were invisible now, his race could be told by the webbing of his fingers and toes, his crest, the tubercles that pebbled his hairless crown, and by several other more subtle signs.

Of these the most striking was that he wept, constantly. This defect of the Tritons had thus far defeated every effort of the tectogeneticists, though they had bred out others far more complex. The Tritons' body fluids necessarily shared exactly the tonicity of sea water, which meant that they were 1.5 percentage points saltier than the body fluids of land dwellers. This was also true of their tears; and as these evaporated in air, they quickly became too concentrated for the tissues of the eye to tolerate. As a result, a Triton on land wept two tears, quite automatically, each time he blinked.

Though Storm had thus far said nothing at all after the introductions, and listened to the others with a face polite but remote, the mechanically falling tears rattled Biond. Nor did he think he was alone in this. Several times he saw Marg't looking speculatively from the Triton to Dorthy, and then back again.

"Speaking of the Preserves," Marg't said abruptly, "has anybody ever wondered what it'd be like to eat real eggs? Or even real bacon?"

"Marg't!" her husband said. "What a subject for mealtime!"

"Isn't that the most pertinent time?" Deban Tod said. "Though the question does seem a bit academic."

"Why is it academic?" Marg't twisted her magnificent shoulders toward her husband. Her aristocratic, perfectly chiseled face was gradually becoming animated under its helmet of fantastically sculptured blond hair; not even this coiffure could distract attention from the way her features came to life when she stopped thinking about internal politics. "That's why I mentioned the Preserves. One could get the proper animal there. The Preserve staffs have to dispose of an animal now and then, don't they?"

"Yes," Chen U said. "Not often, but now and then."

Marg't's head came to rest facing Chen U, considerably after the protracted sinuous turning of her coppery torso had stopped. "Then it shouldn't be difficult," she said. "The stacks could tell you which animal bacon came from, and the Preserve could supply it. Isn't that so?"

"No," Chen U said. "Not even a person on Prime Center could take an animal out of a Preserve, dead or alive. Any carcasses the Preserves have to dispose of are destroyed inside the Preserve, and destroyed utterly. No one could take one out."

"I could," Marg't said. Biond looked sidewise at her. He thought she could.

"I was talking to a young man today," he said, "whose current fiancée is head ecological surgeon for one of the Preserves. I did him a favor. He might be moved to return it."

Marg't turned her speculative glance to the Disaster chief. "But wouldn't that be in bad taste?" she said, her voice melodious and innocent.

There was a brief moment of silence. Then Deban said, "Well, U, what's on the agenda for this evening?"

"Food, by coincidence," Chen U said. "Briefly, World Resources is considering cutting the basic ration—in fact, the decision's already made."

"But how is that possible?" Dorthy said. "I thought the

ration was down to the minimum recommended level now."

"It is. But the recommended level and the minimum daily requirement are two different things. We aren't planning any changes in the carbohydrate, fat, bulk, vitamin, or trace-metal levels, though, just in the amino acid. Right now the daily per-person allotment is a little over fifteen grams of ten aminos. The average minimum daily requirement is less than half of that, but we've been maintaining it at the present level because occasional individuals require more than the average minimum, and we could spare it."

"How big a cut do you plan to make?" Deban asked.

"First of all, we're going to cut two aminos out of the diet entirely—histidine and arginine. They can be synthesized by the body itself. We included them in the present diet because we had them to spare, and because Paul Argus and the Genetics Board wanted us to. But we can afford to drop them. Secondly, we propose to cut the amount of the other eight aminos back to MDR level as a general policy, with an additional credit symbol on the card system allowing extra rations for all persons whose metabolisms require more."

"I hate those cards," Biond said gloomily. "The first thing people do with them is lose them."

"The record-keeping requirements of the new system will be extensive, without doubt," Chen U said smoothly. "But the saving in food will more than cancel out the increased energy budget."

"Not the heart of my complaint," Biond said. "Oh well. What I really want to know is why Resources decided to do this. Surely we're in no danger of a shortage?"

"Not yet, but we will be soon."

"I thought dinosynthesis—"

"We don't have production fully adapted yet, Biond. Only about a quarter of our photosynthetic industry has been converted to dinosynthesis yet, even though the machinery for the two processes are partly compatible. It takes time to apply a new process on a world-wide scale, after all. In the meantime, consumption's rising—consumption always rises, that's axiomatic—and the computers say we're to have a pinch in the year before we finish conversion. The proposed ration cut anticipates that. We're being Joseph the Provider, as it were."

"How will the cut affect what we get, in terms of meals?" Dorthy said hesitantly.

Chen U smiled at her. "You'll never notice it," he said. "You'll get the same variety of foods as before, in the same quantities as always. We'll even continue putting skins on the bananas, silly though the procedure is. The amino acid content of your meals will be lower, that's all."

"And you're sure that there's no danger of malnutrition?" Biond said.

"None at all. Eight aminos, in quantities of a gram or less each, are all the human body needs per day to make protein—the other fourteen it synthesizes. There are individual variations, as I mentioned before, but we'll see to it that all those people are given the additional amounts they need."

Deban picked up his phone and said, "Local. Kitchen. Instrument 29–1, 012. Endit." At once the plates and cups and gear rose straight up and soared into the disposal tunnel. Deban put down the phone and stared thoughtfully out at his garden.

"There's something you've left out, U," he said slowly. "You mentioned the Genetics Board. It's a pity Paul Argus couldn't make it tonight. I'd like to know what the board's angle is on this."

"I can tell you," Chen U said. "They asked us to keep histidine in the diet because it's a necessary amino in every other animal except man. They felt that omitting it from the human diet might have some long-term effect that we've been unable to detect so far. Similarly, arginine is necessary in the diet of rats and some other animals. They can live without it, but they don't attain proper growth. Again, omitting it from the human diet has no detectable effect, but Genetics hates to take chances."

"So do I. Does Genetics oppose the new amino schedule?"

"They do," Chen U admitted.

"Then I oppose it too," Deban said promptly. "I see no harm in cutting back the actual amounts, but let's keep histidine and arginine both in the ration."

Dorthy said, "May I make a suggestion?"

"That's what you're here for, Dorthy," Biond said.

"My company's growing very rapidly. The Caribbean Hatchery is already producing on an enormous scale, and we're opening deeper and deeper frontiers all the time—we're no longer limited to the continental shelves since the Tritons and dolphins began to exploit this Deep Water Safari technique. If there's going to be a shortage, why not make it up from the sea?"

Chen U smiled indulgently. "We've computed the rate of expansion of your outfit," he said, "and while it was astonishing enough to give you a place at Prime Center, Dorthy, it doesn't begin to match the consumption curve. Natural foods, including those from the sea, can never meet more than a small fraction of our needs. No, we're going to have to cut the ration, and take our chances with Genetics' assorted misgivings. Frankly, I don't put much stock in them. Our experiments show absolutely no effect from the omission of histidine and arginine, and they've been conducted over more than thirty-five years."

"I won't ask where or how," Deban said. "But let's have a vote, just for the record. Biond?"

"I don't know enough about it. I'll just go so far as to say I don't like it. Call mine a *no,* pro tem."

"Transcorp?"

"I think it's necessary," Marg't Splain said. "It's only to cope with one lean year, anyhow."

"Dorthy?"

"I—I still think you're underestimating Submarine Products." She hesitated and looked around the rest of the circle; then, apparently seeing no overt hostility in her confreres' expressions, drew in a deep breath and burst out eagerly:

"It happens that SPC is concentrating a special effort on a high-yield natural process for making aminos and proteins in quantity. We have a research team of about twelve hundred people—twelve hundred seventeen, if I remember correctly—working on it. Most of them are Tritons. The technique is being tested at twenty-five different stations throughout the world, in different seas, in different latitudes, at different depths, but all well down into the Dark Water—"

"Dark Water!" murmured Biond, like an incantation. "What is the Dark Water?"

"That's SPC argot for all the underseas where no light penetrates," Dorthy said, embarrassed perhaps, but forging on all the same. "There are bacteria living in the bottom ooze that synthesize nitrogen compounds in the absence of light. They live by oxidizing manganese. The oxidation releases energy and the energy makes the syntheses possible. You might say that these bacteria eat manganese. With a little tectogenetic tinkering we've produced several strains that put out ten to a hundred times the quantity of mixed nitrogen compounds the natural strains do—still not much, but there's a good prospect of improvement. One of these strains is an excellent arginine producer. The crude product is a sheet of jelly-like slime loaded with aminos. We don't know how many. We're still separating them."

"A very gratifying and unexpected development," declared Chen U, his eyes sparkling with an animation Biond did not quite trust. "But why have we not heard of it until now? And what volume of production have you achieved?"

"It's very new," Dorthy said. "We've been working on it only five months, changes in technique are made almost daily, and it was just last week that we found we had a hundredfold jump in production by one of the new strains. But the output of partly refined aminos is low. This morning we had about one point three kilograms of arginine, ninety percent purity, and smaller amounts of the others.

"Our chief trouble is the low concentration of oxygen in the water. The deeper you go, the smaller the concentration that prevails. But we can lick that.

"There's a Triton team at Great Barrier Reef setting up a pilot plant for synthesizing aminos and proteins at a depth of three thousand feet. They're laying a pipeline along the bottom from shoreline water level down to the culture area—about one square kilometer. Oxygenated surface water will be pumped down this pipeline to the culture. The pipeline project, and harvesting the slime for fractionation and purification ashore, gives them a wonderful opportunity to demonstrate the usefulness of the Deep Water Safari—"

"Deep Water Safari!" Biond interposed again, helplessly. The occasional irruptions of poetry into Dorthy's statistics distracted him every time. "I'm sorry, but you mentioned that before, and I intended to ask about it. I've heard a bit here and a bit there, and it sounds fantastic."

"It does at first," admitted Dorthy, "but it's straightforward enough. The Tritons are at home under water."

(Storm permitted himself a faint Mona Lisa smile.) "Skin-diving humans, even with Scuba, become uncomfortable if they stay down very long at one hundred feet or more. They're aliens in a submarine environment. Then there's always the limitation of the oxygen supply—the tank becomes empty, the batteries for the gills run out. But Tritons are water people. They believe that even the greatest deeps are accessible to them without benefit of Scuba or bathyscaphe. They've been down to two thousand feet, traveling by easy stages and resting every hundred feet to allow their internal fluid pressure to equalize with the pressure outside. In one instance twelve Tritons descended to two thousand feet and stayed down for forty-eight hours. The return was made in stages, like the descent. They felt no ill effects on surfacing. Tritons are naturals for underwater construction, surveying, salvaging, or rescue operations. Think what a Deep Water Safari could mean to a bottom-stranded bathyscaphe! A Deep Water Safari can move about freely, observe, explore, collect—"

"I wouldn't dispute it," Marg't Splain said, somewhat coolly, "but I'm sure all of us would like to hear more about the aminos."

Dorthy flushed. It began at her shoulder blades and flowed up into her ears and cheeks. Evidently she had not heard Marg't's faint emphasis on the word *all,* or if she had, had not identified it as a shaft aimed at Biond alone.

"I should tell you that our tectogenetic tinkering has produced a *thing*—I suppose it's a plant, and someone has suggested calling it a sarcophyte. It looks like squirmy chocolate-colored spaghetti. It has a rich meaty flavor, and it's nontoxic."

Dorthy glanced at Chen U, and said, "If a crash program were authorized I believe that we might be producing aminos by the kiloton at the end of twelve months. And sarcophytes as well, if they prove to be nutritionally acceptable. It would take some of the burden from the other processes during the conversion to dinosynthesis. Eventually it might take over amino production entirely. There are millions of square miles of ocean bottom, down there in the cold and the dark . . . waiting."

Unexpectedly, Biond shuddered. But apparently nobody noticed.

"This is all very well," Chen U interposed gently, "and I'm sure our colleagues here are surprised and pleased by much of it. But Dorthy, this is not exactly the time for it. What we need from you now is a vote, not a prospectus."

Dorthy returned to dry land with an almost audible plop. "I'm sorry," she said, flushing slightly under her tan. "I'll vote yes, then. On a temporary ·basis only."

"Quite. Then it's three for, three against," Chen U said. "The cut will proceed, of course, but the opposition is duly recorded. Now is there anything else? Biond, any catastrophes up your sleeve?"

"Neither sleeve nor catastrophe on my person."

"Biond, did you get that red message my observatory chief sent you?" Deban said. "I'm curious to know what it was. He hasn't had anything to say to anybody up to now but 'no report' since he went into office. If it wasn't personal—"

"I got it, but I haven't studied it yet," Biond said. He had, as a matter of fact, forgotten it. "I was tied up at the time. I'll send you the gist later, if you like."

"Dorthy, anything else new—any problems, I mean? . . . All right. Marg't, when do we go to the stars? It seems to me that it's about time to let that crew on Ganymede out of exile and give up."

"You can't give up," Marg't said, with quiet, cold intensity. "The interstellar drive is our only real hope, and you know it as well as I do. Besides, we're making real progress at last. Another year's work—"

"And another fiasco," Biond said, more drily than he had intended. "Marg't, we've been hearing this story ever since the announcement of the Weinogradsky scholium. Our top space-flight speed is still only a bare fifteen hundred miles per second. Let's face it, old Milne was right, and Einstein before him. Weinogradsky's equations are elegant, but there's no conceivable way that they can be tested."

"They've been tested. Before Weinogradsky."

"I know—phase velocity in wave-guide theory, and the rest of that. Skipping the good possibility that Weinogradsky's examples are illusions—I'm not a physicist and won't pretend to be one—I deny that the interstellar drive is the hope of the race, even if it is obtainable. As a matter of conjecture, I'd be more inclined to call it a curse."

"Excuse me," Chen U said, "but I haven't time to listen to the ensuing debate. If I feel the need I'll replay it from memory, from one of the last dozen or so meetings. I'm due at the flyport right now, and in Seattle an hour from now. Good night, all—and Marg't, stand your ground."

He went out, smiling. Biond stood with the rest as he left. So, of course, did Marg't, halfway, her hands still linked gracefully in her lap. But the moment that Chen U was gone she swung on Biond, the corners of her lips deepening.

"Are you going to give me the Marching Chinamen again?" she demanded.

"Of course I am," Biond said contemptuously. Every word cut him like knives, but he was still too good an officer to allow his emotions to fog a matter of public policy. But he was also enough of a human being to see that he was coming closer to being a flagellant at each new meeting. "It'd be utterly impossible to export people from this planet fast enough to keep up with the birth rate, even if everybody in the world wanted to go."

"What in the world are we talking about?" Dorthy said. "The last I heard, the Ganymede project was a study of extraterrestrial bacteriology, out to make operational tests of the old Arrhenius idea that life went from world to world by light pressure. What has that to do with an interstellar drive?"

"Nothing," Marg't said, "and the Ganymede project isn't any more interested in xenobacteriology than you are. The publicity about it has been deliberately misleading."

"But why?"

"Because," Marg't said, "stupid people like Biond are afraid of the very idea of an interstellar drive. They can't see that the only way we'll ever relieve the Earth of its overcrowding is to have new earths to occupy. They think that human dignity should be subject to more and more restrictions, so that we can stay home and become stagnant. They want to revive the old, old birth control campaigns, in the face of the plain evidence that such campaigns never work and setting aside the infringements upon human dignity that campaigns of that kind are founded on. They see human fertility as nothing but a menace. They're incapable of seeing it as the driving force that it is—the force behind human destiny. . . . Are you married, Dorthy?"

"No," Dorthy said, startled.

"Marry. Have children. Drive the Bionds out of their shells. Help increase the population pressure on this planet to the explosion point. Nothing else will serve. And nothing else needs to serve—because it can't be stopped. Sooner or later the human race is going to burst out of this little egg, and spread to—to where?

Is there any limit? To the eight corners of the universe, perhaps!"

"Bravo," Deban Tod said.

"Bravo indeed," Biond said, "but Marg't, your eloquence is outrunning your sense of justice. The reason the Ganymede project was classified secret isn't quite as you paint it—though I thank you for the public analysis of my role in the matter."

Marg't looked back at him with magnificent iciness. "I apologize," she said. "I had no right to invade your dignity. I'm entitled to a low opinion of your common sense, all the same, Biond. Suppose that the populace does learn that we're on the threshold of the drive? And suppose the knowledge *does* produce a spurt in the birth rate? When we get the drive, the population problem will be solved. We'll own the galaxy—and the increased birth rate will have all the justification it could need. Is an adequate amino ration the only goal this lazy, malingering race has? Are we fertile for nothing? The sky is full of stars—does nobody here want them but me?"

Deban Tod stood up. "To be continued at our next meeting," he said. "In the meantime, I'd like to get away from the cares of state in time to practice a little horticulture." He went over to Dorthy and took her hand. She looked up at him, obviously awed. The two of them made a most curious couple, to Biond's form-sensitive eye like a sentimental father-and-daughter grouping out of the immediate pre-atomic era, or perhaps a burlesque of the heroic sculpture of an era even more primitive. Deban was nearly twice as tall as Dorthy.

"Would you like to join me, Dorthy?" he said. "I'd be happy to introduce you to my flowers."

Unaccountably, the girl looked away to Biond. Biond looked back, puzzled. Did Dorthy think that seats at

Prime Center had to be paid for with an oath of chastity, ritual mutilation, or some similar barbarity? After a moment he was forced to produce a slight smile and an even slighter nod—though why Dorthy had asked him for approval at all was also mystifying.

Nor did it seem to satisfy her once she had it. Her lips paled, and several tiny muscles just above her chin went into obvious tetany, momentarily adding ten years to her apparent age. She looked away.

"I'd like that," she said to Deban.

The Triton, Storm, rose smoothly. He bowed slightly to no one in particular, and went out, still without having said a word to anyone. It was not exactly an exit; it was more as though he had just evaporated, like his unheeded tears. Damn the man. What was there about him that made him so disquieting?

"That leaves nobody but you to go home with," Marg't said. "If you're not otherwise busy, Biond, let's continue our argument in the tubeways. I'm going to get through to you somehow. If you please?"

"Certainly," Biond said. Warning waves of scarlet stormed through his body at every blow of his heart. He could not, he must not go with Marg't. It was wrong. He must not go. He would not go. "If you still think it's worth the effort."

"But of course I do. Fine. Goodnight, Deban, Dorthy."

"Goodnight." "Goodnight."

"Goodnight," Biond said.

"Goodnight." "Goodnight."

The door irised shut behind Biond. Goodnight, all. Goodnight.

## 3   A Red Message

Before the period immediately after the Third War, when most of the world's megalopoli were still under construction, the corridor walls of the monolithic cities had been completely covered with a form of compulsive scribbling called "ads," the purpose of which had been to increase the consumption of goods. Like many of the customs of that age, the practice seemed insane; fortunately, it had become extinct with the advent of the completely controlled economy.

Not all the "ads" had been wiped out, however, as the section of Novoe Washingtongrad that included Deban's apartment testified. The early planners of the great cities had profited by the experience of the ancient Baron Haussmann, and where they had been revising an existing city rather than raising a new one, they remained careful not to eliminate all traces of the old. Many people liked living in the small, time-dimmed sections of the cities where the walls still winked with color and with invitations to buy (or, more usually, "enjoy") mysterious products that seemed to duplicate each other endlessly and to be useful for nothing at all.

"I wonder what it was like before they eliminated the popeyes," Biond said, scanning the glowing corridor speculatively.

"What were those?" Marg't said. She did not seem to be much interested.

"Ads that reached out physically, grabbed the customer, and held onto him until the message was delivered," Biond said. "Spelled *p-o-p-a-i*. I don't know

the derivation. But they must have made getting from
place to place pretty hazardous."

"Maybe. It's a dull business now. At least the Beth-
esda T does have a certain quaintness."

A capillary feeder line took them, via a moving hall-
way that transformed itself smoothly into a spiral escalator, to the base of the eight-apartment tier, where they
caught the more swiftly moving carpetment of a secondary feeder line. At this hour of the evening, and indeed
all around the clock, the tubeways were crowded and
did not encourage private conversation—and not only
because of the noise, which was minimal. Since any
crowd made some eavesdropping impossible to avoid,
forcing the opportunity upon a fellow traveler was as
serious a breach of dignity as the eavesdropping itself
would be.

While they were in transit, therefore, Biond offered
only an occasional inconsequential remark, which Marg't
answered with a monosyllable or not at all. She seemed
suddenly morose, or at least much withdrawn. Even the
admiring turning of the heads of passengers around
them—for in addition to being extraordinarily beautiful
in an age when physical perfection was commonplace,
Marg't was a popular public figure, like most First Ladies—failed to brighten her up.

The feeder line brought them into a local secondary
utility stack. There they took an express elevator down
to the base of the Chinese wall and into the neighborhood distribution center. This housed, among several
dozen other functions, an express transfer terminal.
From there on across the city the trip was by pressure
car, through one of the main trunks that radiated from
the municipal center. Once they had reached Marg't's
neighborhood terminal, the entire procedure had to be
gone through in reverse; its complexity explained why
long trips through the cities were undertaken only for

the most compelling reasons, and why any work that could conceivably be done at home was done there, not in an office.

Biond was getting an object lesson in what unexpected kinds of reasons might turn out to be compelling.

"Come in," Marg't said.

Biond followed her in. The apartment, unlike Deban's, was wholly standard, even to the furniture; evidently Chen U had no bulky hobbies, and perhaps even had made a deliberate effort to avoid giving his home any personal character. In this setting, Marg't's physical opulence gave an effect of tropical exuberance kept under control only with the greatest difficulty. It would not have surprised Biond to hear that Chen U had planned exactly that, too.

"Make yourself comfortable."

"Thanks." Biond sat down warily. He was at once trembling with deliberately nonspecific anticipation, and in a state of acute guilt shock. "At this point in the evening, Marg't, an Age of Waste hostess would be offering me a drink. It was quite a fixed ritual then."

"Oh, are you thirsty? I'll order some water—"

"No, I'm not, it was just a random thought. Besides, water had no value in those days. They drank coffee, tea, alcohol—vegetable beverages with virtually no food content, but slightly stimulating, or narcotic. They even grew one plant solely to smell the smoke it produced when it was burning. Tobacco, it was called. They had thousands and thousands of acres tied up in the stuff."

"I never heard of any of them," Marg't said, "except the alcohols, of course, and I didn't know they were potable. But I've always supposed that the Age of Waste earned its name somehow—I'm no antiquarian, the details don't interest me. But the time is coming eventually when we'll be able to do wasteful things again if we want to. A great deal more wasteful than just tying up five hundred pounds of good river-bottom soil in exotic plants, like Deban does."

"I doubt it," Biond said gloomily.

"Biond, please consider. How long are you and the rest of mankind going to be content with just one earth, when out in space there are two earthlike planets for every hundred thousand stars? What could possibly be more wasteful than letting all those planets lie fallow—while we go to seed here, and eventually suffocate in the sheer mass of humanity?"

"I shouldn't be surprised," Biond said, "if many of those worlds already had tenants of their own."

"Nor should I—but how can we possibly find out without going there? And what other possible solution to our present problem is there? Birth control has been a miserable failure, you know that as well as I do. The campaign of 2500 was as thorough as any such campaign could possibly be. Every living adult got ample, free supplies of the new pill, access to more at demand, and clear, easy instructions on when to swallow it. The compound itself is germicidal, mildly aphrodisiac and habit-forming, in addition to being contraceptive—an ideal combination. And what happened? This year the population is almost half again what it was in 2500!"

"That's perfectly true. If it hadn't been for the campaign, the population now would be *double* the 2500 figure. The trouble, Marg't, is that in 2500 it was already too late for such a campaign to be more than palliative. It should have been started several centuries before that, even before the Third War—which it might even have prevented. Back then, they had a real chance of reducing the rate of growth to a safe level. But the people who saw that clearly at the time were howled down."

Marg't was waiting impatiently for him to finish. "That may be true and it may not. I haven't the exact figures in mind, but it's my opinion that the decline in the rate follows the Pearl curve—"

"No, indeed. I don't think we've seen any Pearl-curve effect yet, and Paul Argus tells me we should pray we never will—I don't know why. The depressant effect of the 2500 campaign was real enough."

"And yet you admit that it was only a palliative in those days, three hundred years ago! What conceivable good could such a campaign have now? And how would you go about converting people to the Pill these days? We've already reached saturation point on per capita intake!"

"A new program would have to involve compulsory mass sterilization, I'm afraid," Biond admitted. "Mass executions would be just about as easy to put across. But what the hell, that's the very nature of our trouble— that we have no solution. And that's the whole of my case against the interstellar drive, Marg't—that it would be a great achievement, but would do nothing to solve the overcrowding of the Earth. Forcible mass deportations would be out of the question, just as forcible sterilization is, and any response you'd get to a plea for volunteers would be feeble, to say the least. Most people now are perfectly comfortable. They live well, feel secure, and have freedom of opinion and action. Tell them that sooner or later some future generation is going to suffer a world breakdown, and they'll tell you to let the next generation worry about it. Pull up stakes and go pioneer on some planet a dozen light-years from the nearest vidphone? Not a chance."

"Nonsense. They'd go in hordes, given a properly conducted propaganda drive. Let the corporations pass a few deliberately restrictive laws, suggest to the people that they're unduly crowded and that their lives are dull, then break the discovery of the interstellar drive . . ." She broke off and sighed. "I can see that I'm going to get nowhere with you, Biond. But thank you for the opportunity of trying."

She rose gracefully, her every line expressing gentle regret. For an instant after she was fully on her feet, she seemed to be continuing to rise from the Earth. Her chin tilted, her elbows rose above her head, her spine arched, her whole body seemed to poise upon the balls of her feet.

She was stretching.

It was a direct, egregious violation of the nudity code. The woman was cold-bloodedly bribing him—with the offer of stolen goods. Such a compound social crime was sometimes committed in fiction, but to be actually involved in one stunned him; he was as thoroughly a child of the antifertility taboos as anyone in his society. In his mind he rose simultaneously to embrace her and to break for the door. The result was that he sat frozen where he was, even his breathing suspended.

The vidphone rang.

Marg't stiffened, her lips thinning. Then she swung on the tall cabinet, her finger jabbing at the RECORD button.

"Marg't, wait," Biond said shakily. "It's—it's a red message."

She'd turned again and looked at him, incredulously at first, then with gradually increasing anger and contempt.

"So it is," she said. She picked up the phone. "Marg't Splain here. . . . Yes, he is. One moment."

She held out the handset to Biond; the screen remained blank. He took the phone with care. He already knew, in a general way, what the call was. Already that gleaming red tab seemed to have fastened itself on his forehead like a brand.

"Biond Smith here."

"Your office, Mr. Smith. In reviewing the recorded messages for the day, we found one which seemed to justify invading your privacy. We therefore exercised Discretion Level One and traced you here. Mr. Deban Tod expressed disapproval of this course. Please give us your opinion for our future guidance."

*But I haven't done anything wrong yet. I don't even know whether or not I would have.*

"It's all right," Biond said. "Deliver the message."

"Digested, it is as follows. The Astronomy section of Transport Corporation reports a nondivertible meteor of significant size will fall in the Hudson's Bay area forty days from today. Immediate consultation is requested."

Biond closed his eyes and swallowed. "Is the arrival size of the meteor reported?"

"Yes, sir."

Biond felt a faint flash of his old irritation at the literal-mindedness of even the best computers, but it was gone almost immediately. "All right, then, how big is it?"

"One mile in diameter, sir."

*"One mile!"*

"Yes, sir. Does the message justify our exercise of discretion at this level, Mr. Smith?"

"Yes," Biond said hoarsely. "Yes, it does. Clear my calendar and make me an immediate appointment with the section involved. And send an alert for a full-dress board meeting at zero nine hundred, day after tomorrow."

"Biond, what is it?" Marg't said. "You look positively ill. Maneuvers again? Or has somebody developed a slight cough in Indonesia? Or are we all going to die tomorrow?"

Biond looked at her. He did not see what he had been seeing only a few minutes earlier. He put down the phone.

"Die?" he said softly. "I don't know. No . . . no, we shall not all die. But we shall all be changed."

## 4  Jothen Aloft

From the air, Starved Rock Biological Preserve looked
not unlike a lichen. The view never ceased to startle
Jothen, simply because the colors were all wrong.

In the near distance there were at least five cities
visible from the helicopter, all of different shapes, most
of them far smaller than the Preserve; but they were all
of the same color as the World Forest, simply because
the forest marched right over them, from tier to tier
and back down again. No forest crossed the acres and
acres of silicoid that roofed the Preserve, however. Instead, all the growing stuff was underneath, with sun
highlights glinting over it.

Each of the seven major sections of the Preserve
was a different shade of green, not a one matching the
green of the forest. The reason was simple enough: each
sector maintained a different artificial climate and contained a different kind of ecological complex, all of
them strangers to the climate and exiles from the ecology of the world at large; but the contrast was nevertheless jolting to the eye. The seemingly meaningless
differences in the sizes of the sectors, so different from
the obviously planned extensions of the cities, also
were disturbing, because they were not governed by the
iron laws of expanding human populations, but by the
extent of the feeding ranges needed by the fauna in
each sector. Additionally, the Preserve did not pyramid
toward its central flyport—which otherwise was usual

52

enough—in any rational way, but simply sprawled irregularly over the landscape, hugging the contours.

Inside each sector, Jothen knew, sector compartment bulkheads broke each major division into hundreds of smaller ones, most of which were about four square miles in area and hence not visible from the helicopter. All that could be seen at this altitude was this immense, foliose, varicolored excrescence hugging the land, its longest leaf about thirty miles in radius, with sector headquarters and flyports at its edges like bulging sporangia.

This whole monster was Kim Wernicke's baby, and it was at the moment the only one she seemed to want. It was hardly odd that the Preserve looked like a parasite to Jothen. He could almost sympathize with the anticonservation faction, which wanted to do away with the Preserves and put the land they tied up into production. That would solve one of his problems, too—or would it?

The closer the shuttle copter dropped toward the silicoid roof, the less detail Jothen noted. He saw only the glare of the sun on the transparent sheeting, the tiny pinwheels of the aircraft warning beacons on the tips of the fire lookout stations, and the caterpillar-like movement of the highway that ran around the edge of the Preserve. What went on under all that glastic became more blurred and less interesting the closer it brought him to Kim.

Nevertheless, as always, he was forced to take in some of it. Although rapid transit tubes for Preserve personnel ran all through the foundations of the structure, Jothen as a visitor was denied access to them, and very strictly. They were full of booby traps for the unwary: airlocks a visitor would not know how to operate; side-shoots that might lead one abruptly into the Preserve proper— and perhaps face to face with a wild cow or a tiger;

germicidal, fungicidal, and viricidal chambers that could
kill a man, too, without a protective suit. To get from the
central flyport to the HQ of Kim's sector, Jothen had
to take the sightseers' highways, like any other tourist.

There might have been a time when he would have
found it fascinating, but today it seemed maddeningly
circuitous. The highway wound from one subsector to
another, sometimes at ground level, sometimes halfway
up the sector wall, along a path designed for the maximum of sightseeing and the minimum of speed. The
visible surface of the highway was smooth and uniform;
it consisted essentially of continuous metal strips, each
about an inch wide, covered with a heavy elastic web
that stretched as the highway went around a curve.
Portable revolving chairs were scattered over it more or
less at random; anyone who wanted to linger in a particular subsector could step off the highway onto one of
the numerous stationary "overlooks" and take his chair
with him.

"Ma, Dad, lookathere. Look at that thing with all the
hair along of his neck. Now he's running. I betcha that's a
horse."

"Yes, well . . . yes, the placard says there are horses
in here."

"Almer, is it true that—that we used to drink *milk*
from those beasts?"

"No-o-o, I don't think so. The milk animal was called
the ox."

"What does a ox look like, Dad?"

"Well, it looks rather . . . we'd better move on, there's
a lot to see yet. Come along now."

Abruptly the highway swooped toward the ground,
its arched vitrolith roof seeming to dive into a mass of
undisciplined greenery. For a moment Jothen could see
nothing but close-pressing leaves, all odd, all utterly
unlike the spicules of the bamboos, giant sugar cane,

hybrid poplars, and Monterrey pines that made up the World Forest. Then there was an interval of darkness, followed by a roar against the roof of the highway; they had passed through an interior wall between one sub-sector and another, directly beneath an air blower.

When Jothen could see outside again, the way was running along the ground, and was at the moment passing over a small brook that flowed through a port-cullis in the interior wall he had just passed through himself. Above the concrete apron of the wall, glassy sheets rose to the Preserve roof, broken here and there by sets of jalousies that could be opened to permit bird migration from one climate to another—a habit of birds, Kim had once said, which the Preserve geneticists had been able to attenuate, but not breed out entirely. Nearby was one of the supporting girders for the roof, with a downspout from the rain gutter running down beside it, heavily overgrown with glossy-leaved vines.

In the near distance a rain distributor, three times as tall as its surrounding trees, revolved its three conch-like blower casings lazily. These rotors, Jothen remem-bered, had a positive drive rather then depending upon the Newton reaction of the ejected air and water, so that the distance the rain was thrown could be con-trolled directly by the force of the air blast; it was the kind of thing in which he took a professional interest. The leaves in this sector sparkled brilliantly, indicating that the machine had been operating only a little while ago.

"Look, Dad, a yak. What a big old nose on him."

"I don't see how anybody ever rode on those things. They're too jumpy."

"You'd never get *me* on one, not for a second."

A yak? No, it was a deer. This must be Kim's sector, then—North American Temperate, the only remainder of that once vast, bluely sylvan, raptly still ecology anywhere on Earth, the last fragment of the realm of deer and bears and wolverines and wild tobacco and sugar maples and oaks, and quiet everywhere under smoky skies. Here, at least, it would never change, and for that reason Kim clung to it—not for the rainbow trout in the brooks, or for the snow that fell every year or the squirrels that sat in the crotches of unfamiliar trees chiseling away at black walnuts, but because this was all of it that there was or ever would be, and it was permanent and immune to man in its glittering silicoid womb.

Or so—cloudily, to be sure—Jothen saw it. He stepped off the highway at the base of the sector HQ tower, and finally was allowed the use of an official elevator to the sector surgeon's office.

Kim came forward at once, holding out her hands. "You're as prompt as ever," she said, smiling. "Nobody's prompt any more. But for once I'm almost ready."

"Good for you. We'll need to stay on schedule—I have rocket passes."

"I know, that's why I hurried. I'm all packed. But, Jo, where are we going? Is it still a mystery?"

Jothen grinned. "No, not anymore. We're going to Australia."

"Australia!" Kim clasped her hands together like a child. "Oh, Jothen! To the Barrier-hilthon?"

"No," Jothen said, drawing out his surprise to the last. "Nowhere so commonplace. Guess again."

"I can't. Tell me before I kick you."

"We're going to Triton Reef," said Jothen, who in his heart of hearts hoped to see the Barrier-hilthon too before this trip was over—but without suspecting that it was a wish he might unwish, had he been given the foresight.

"Triton Reef! You mean—we're going to live *on* the reef—with Tritons?"

"Don't look so distressed. The Tritons welcome Drylander visitors. They have dry and comfortable guest quarters available, with all the modern amenities. You won't live twenty-four hours a day in a scuba rig or sleep in a tidal pool. And don't bother to take a camera. The Tritons have cameras galore—all kinds. They start clicking shutters before they can talk, I'm told. You can borrow any sort of photographic equipment you may want. Probably they'll give you some pointers on improving your swimming, too."

"H'm. Somehow I felt they were pretty standoffish—except with their own kind."

"Well, they're not. They're as gay as dolphins. You'll meet dolphins, too. The Tritons will act as interpreters. But you'll find out about all that when we get there. We had better get started if we're going to make connections at Chicago with the plane to Cedros Island."

"Where's Cedros Island?"

"Off the coast of Baja, California. It's the takeoff point for the reef rocket."

"Must we go by rocket? What can we see from three hundred miles up? It would be more fun to fly lower and see more."

"Don't worry about that. The rocket people have something new called zoomvision. It's a sort of telescopic TV. The zoomvision camera scans through a port on the underside of the rocket and each passenger has his own viewer—you wear them like goggles. You can even see people on the ground if there are no clouds in the way."

The telephone chimes sounded three musical tones in sequence. Kim turned toward the instrument.

"Kim Wernicke here."

"This is the switchboard computer at the Barrier-hilthon. If you wish this conversation to be private please make the necessary preparations."

"It isn't necessary. Proceed."

A click and a series of *pings* followed. Another voice spoke.

"This is the computer in charge of incoming mail. The parcel that you sent to Dr. Matouf arrived eight days ago. Dr. Matouf was absent then and has not yet returned. Shall I refer the material to outgoing mail to be forwarded to his Istanbul address?"

"Is someone caring for the specimens?" Kim said.

"Yes. We summoned an entomologist from the Kooka-burra Biological Preserve. He has had them in charge since then."

"Don't forward them then. Dr. Matouf was very specific that he wanted them held at the Barrier-hilthon until he returns from his current field trip."

"As directed," said the voice of the computer. Came a silvery *ping*, then silence.

"What's all that about?" asked Jothen.

"An entomologist from Istanbul, Dr. Kemal Matouf, a very eminent man. He's revamping the classification of the *Thysanura*—silverfish to you. Maintains that the structure of their blood proteins reveals new facts about their evolutionary relationships. He's asking for specimens from everywhere."

"Sounds very exciting," Jothen said ironically.

He was dead right.

When Jothen had been flying toward Starved Rock Biological Preserve some hours previously, his attention had been focused on the Preserve itself, his thoughts wholly with Kim. But now Kim was with him, they were flying to Chicago, and the Preserve lay far behind on the southwestern horizon, gleaming under a late afternoon sun.

Now he was scrutinizing a puzzling phenomenon that had appeared on the skyline ahead. It resembled a low range of mountains, grayish mauve in the distance, that lay along the entire northeast quadrant of the horizon. Mountains? In Illinois? As they drew nearer he could see the usual forested terraces, but the bluffs that separated the terraces were bands of pastel colors. He turned to Kim.

"I'm surprised to see mountains here. I thought that all this region was flat as a tabletop."

"Jothen!" Kim laughed. "That's Chicago! Or rather, it's one corner of it."

Steadily churning across the sky, the helicopter bore them nearer still to the terraced ramparts of Chicago, and Jothen stared, fascinated, as they seemed to rise higher and higher and extend themselves endlessly on either hand. Even before the first architectural mountain range was overpassed, still other ridges, peaks, chasms, and buttes rose beyond it. Soaring towers and masts, great glittering domes, and skeleton frameworks of new construction materialized in the blue distance. As they advanced farther, the monolithic city spread beneath them from horizon to horizon, a bewildering tracery of green terraces and tinted walls.

Jothen roused himself from the semihypnotic fixity of his concentration on the unrolling panorama below.

"I suppose I shouldn't be astonished. I've seen some of this in photo books. One has to see it from the air, oneself, to appreciate the real bigness of it. I've been holed up in a Disaster City for so long that I've forgotten how jammed the rest of the world is."

A great climactic pyramid reared itself before them, a Mount Everest towering above the lesser peaks. The sun, low in the west, lighted its terraces and walls with a mellow coppery glow. The forefront of a convoluted, lowering, gray cloud ceiling was gliding above it, carried toward them on the wind off Lake Michigan. As Kim and Jothen watched, a rippling misty curtain of rain descended from the cloud, blurred the outlines of the pyramid as with a veil of pearl-gray gauze, and magically bloomed with a giant rainbow ring. The circle of spectral colors formed a softly glowing frame around the pyramid.

"Now there's a perfect symbol of our endless argument," he said thoughtfully. "A circular rainbow. I could follow it around and around forever, and never find the pot of gold at the end. There is no end."

"If this is the preface to another of your periodic proposals of marriage, it's no go," Kim said. "In the kind of world we're in, no one has the right to marry and beget children. Take another look at your symbolic rainbow! That overgown pyramid beyond it is the Municipal Services Center. It serves a population of three billion—plus a million or two by the latest count. You see only a fraction of the pyramid. Most of it's out of sight, like an iceberg. It goes down to bedrock, and deeper.

"Somewhere inside is the headquarters of the Civic Medical Services. I was born there. Every day approximately fifteen thousand babies are born there. The nine outlying regional centers produce about the same number daily. Conveniently next door, there's a branch of the Municipal Crematorium. Their total daily output is about one hundred forty thousand cremations—a net daily population increase of ten thousand. And for what? So that this frightful human termitary of vitrolith and glastic and metal, of pipes and cables and computers, of myriads of escalators and elevators and moving floors, can grow forever bigger and bigger, higher and higher, deeper and deeper, forever!"

"Take it easy," Jothen said.

The helicopter flew into the curtain of rain and the rainbow circle vanished. Kim plowed on without noticing.

"Do you realize how huge Chicago is? It extends

northward to Sturgeon Bay and westward halfway across Wisconsin and Illinois. From some of the high points on the west wall you can see the Mississippi River on a clear day. And you discovered for yourself that, a few minutes out from Starved Rock, the rim of Chicago showed itself on the horizon. It spreads fifty or sixty miles southward into Illinois and Indiana, and then up into southern Michigan. Recently it annexed Lansing. The east wall of Chicago is only about fifteen miles from the west wall of Detroit. It's an ugly tumor on the face of the earth—and we're the viruses that created it. I don't fancy the idea of increasing the virus population. There are too damn many now."

The helicopter veered around the pyramid. Only the higher pinnacles of Chicago's jagged roofscape still smoldered in the orange-red light of the fading sunset. The rain had ceased. Venus shone like a pale emerald in the blue-green ribbon of unclouded sky in the west. Along the eastward rim of the world, constellations of colored lights flashed into being—some shining steadily others blinking a coded rhythm. They marked the far-flung flyports along the lake front.

"I don't like to think of myself as a virus," Jothen said quietly. "Let me be something constructive, like an enzyme or a spore. And my constructive suggestion for now is that we begin to think about getting off. We'll be landing soon."

The flyports of Chicago were vast expanses of smooth gray-white vitrolith extending into the lake from ten to fifteen miles. They were bejeweled with big lights and little lights, alive with moving lights and the shapes of service vehicles and taxiing planes. They stood upon a labyrinth of Cyclopean columns and arches, in whose cavernous underspaces were water-processing installations, wharves and drydocks and shipyards. From the air the fringe of flyports resembled a row of stubby teeth that bordered the lower lake from Manitowoc, Wisconsin, to Grand Haven in southern Michigan. The shuttle copter descended toward this teeming immensity—diffidently, it seemed—and settled into a berth at one of the heliports along the shoreward side of Airport 42, unofficially known as the Lincoln Park Flyport. The "park" had been engulfed by inexorable urban expansion nearly seven centuries before; only the name remained.

As Jothen followed Kim from the helicopter he emerged into a dazzle of light and sound. He had a fleeting glimpse across three miles of flyport of the sparkling blue delta-winged javelin that would take them to Cedros Island, then found himself whisked into an elevator along with Kim by a politely insistent attendant. The elevator hummed downward, halted, opened its doors. Another brisk attendant guided them into a tube-train that hurtled through the substructure of the airfield to a station beneath their plane. Then out of the train, into another elevator, up, and out into a short passage with a moving floor that discharged them at the plane's entrance.

Jothen experienced a transient illusion of being an inanimate object on a production line.

They were greeted at the door of the plane by a stocky, ivory-skinned steward uniformed in ultramarine blue. He had glossy black hair and a ready smile that compressed his cheeks into two fleshy folds, thereby reducing his eyes to a pair of oblique slits. When he spoke it was with animation and gestures.

"I am Umiak," he said formally. "I shall accompany you on this flight. You are wondering about my name but are too polite to ask so I shall tell you. It is an Eskimo name. Your compartment is number thirty-two. Please follow me."

He indicated the interior of the plane with a sweeping motion of his arm. After they were settled in their compartment, Umiak said:

"If you desire information or anything not supplied by the autoserver, press the blue button on the service console and I shall come. Takeoff time will be in fifteen minutes."

The plane rose vertically until it was above the highest pinnacles of Chicago. Then it soared, jet propelled, on a long slant into the evening sky.

Kim touched Jothen's arm. "Look! There's the afterglow again. We're overtaking the sun."

Umiak returned and offered each of them a small graduated cup of mint-flavored liquid with the request that they drink it immediately.

"Your dossier indicates that you will begin your firsttime rocket flight at Cedros Island," he explained. "Many people are apprehensive of the first flight. This medication will prevent that. By the time we touch down at the rocket terminal you should be well tranquilized." Then he added deferentially:

"I could not avoid overhearing your remark about the afterglow. We have overtaken the sun only a very little. We see the afterglow now because we are five miles higher than we were on the flyport. But after we have passed St. Louis you shall see more than the afterglow. I promise you a sunrise in the west."

Umiak raised both hands, palms upward, as if he personally were lifting the sun.

Jothen asked, "Then we'll have daylight again for the last part of our flight?"

"That is correct," Umiak said, bowing himself out.

"A sunrise in the west," Jothen said. "Like hope long lost and then regained."

Kim regarded him speculatively. "If you're looking for another symbol," she began in a tone of mild annoyance, "don't. There's no use repeating the same tired old words."

"That's not my intention. I'm thinking of your description of Chicago—'a frightful termitary made of vitrolith and glastic and computers,' and so on. You emphasized its bigness and the overwhelming mass of its architecture and machines. You mentioned people only twice—first they were termites, then they were viruses. But you left out something, Kim.

"Granted that Chicago is an unsightly excrescence on the face of the earth, the important fact is that it's full of people. People aren't viruses. People have brains and minds. Chicago has a three-billion-plus population, which is another way of saying that it possesses more than three billion minds. You think that only a small percentage of these minds are producing new ideas, and that the rest are just contented animals, dreaming on warm cushions. But that's not the whole story. There are degrees of creativity. Most people are creative in some degree. Their ability may range from a simple knack of making up stories and jingles for children or for decorating an apartment, up to the genius level. If one estimates the number of minds of genius caliber in Chicago at one hundredth of one percent that's—m'm, what is it now? —three hundred thousand. On the basis of the world population, that's one hundred million high-level productive minds.

"Well, what *are* they doing? Sure, only a relative handful is keeping us fed, housed, healthy, and literate. But that's only part of the answer. There are millions doing imaginative, original work—some of it revolutionary, some of it trivial—on their own initiative simply because they can't endure idleness. There are amateur mathematicians, astronomers, potters, botanists, historians. There's a group in Paris that's revived the art of printing. Instead of paper they use silicose, the silicone analog of cellulose. They produce printed books, beautifully bound and illustrated, just for the joy of it. There's Dr. Matouf and his silverfish. Never underestimate the Dr. Matoufs. I shouldn't have made fun of him. Out of all this amateur activity, and spare-time just-for-fun pro activity, can come the precise theory, the precise data, that will put the capstone on something big next year or next century."

"Jothen, what led you into this line of thought, and where did you happen to get the information?" Kim said.

"My work occupies only part of my time. Mostly, it's a matter of routine inspection and reports. If a leaky valve needs replacing it's an event. So in the long stretches when there is nothing to do I dial the library. I have a library projector in my apartment and after going through the usual grist of technical reports on hydraulic engineering I turn to other things, sometimes microfilm, sometimes photo books and 3-V magazines . . . just for fun, if you like."

"How does this relate to 'Hope long lost and then regained'?"

"You cited Chicago as a sort of scale model of the world and the human race—a malignant growth running wild. You feel that the future holds little hope. Maybe it would help to think of the world as a hive of creative brains. The very multiplicity of human beings may solve the problems that their multiplicity has created. Have we the right to *refuse* to marry and beget minds? The world needs all the minds it can get, even if ninety-nine percent do little more than vegetate."

"For your information, Jothen, you have a one-track mind."

"If that's your argument in rebuttal, I can't give it a very high rating."

The discussion might have become acrimonious if Umiak had not returned.

"How are you feeling?" he inquired. "Any headache?"

"No headache. I'm all right."

"We are about to overpass St. Louis," volunteered Umiak. "You may wish to see it."

The greenish-blue afterglow had increased in brightness so that the world beneath was in semitwilight. St. Louis was visible as a gigantic dark disk with scalloped edges. The red sparks of aircraft warning lights outlined the terrace rims. Alternating vertical stripes of vivid red and white light flooded the upper tiers of the truncated central pyramid.

The city stood athwart the Missouri and Mississippi rivers above and below their confluence. Parts of its north and west walls formed two dams, each retaining an artificial lake. The waters of both rivers flowed into St. Louis through internal penstocks, yielded their tithes of water and energy, reappeared as smooth torrents that poured from the mouths of sluices in the south wall and swooped down the catenary curve of its surface into the downstream reservoir. The reflected light of the twilight sky transformed the three reservoirs into immense luminous pools. Jothen knew that these pools were part of a giant's staircase of dams and lakes that mounted from the Gulf to the headwaters of both rivers—rivers once turbulent, mighty, and at times vastly destructive, now flowing tamely in vitrolith channels.

As the flight continued southwestward from St. Louis the terraced contours of the universal Forest slowly emerged from dusky obscurity as the light of the reversed sunset crept up the sky. Everywhere were the chains of lakes and dams that marked the river courses. Everywhere were the endlessly diversified patterns of the terraced cities—wheels and stars, snowflake designs, labyrinths of polygons within polygons, interlaced circles, three-dimensional lattices of arches piled one above the other like Roman aqueducts. Many of these shapes were still a-building and therefore unsymmetrical. At times flotillas of clouds allowed only glimpses of the tapestry of cities and forest.

While the plane was crossing the southeast corner of New Mexico the edge of the sun appeared above the western horizon, throwing the topography of the land into high relief. A sprawling, gleaming flat structure was revealed below. Kim sat upright and exclaimed, "There's a Biological Preserve!"

Jothen said, "It's hard to be sure of colors from this altitude, but it doesn't look like Starved Rock. Everything around it is lush and green. The Preserve is a drab greenish-brown."

"It should be. It's the Staked Plain Preserve of Desert Life. Naturally it isn't oversupplied with greenery. In some sectors the rain sprays are turned on for short periods only once or twice a year. There are sectors with wind machines that can make sandstorms."

"No mirages?"

"I don't know. If they do occur it's not by design."

Southwest of the Staked Plain Preserve the city of Juarez-Elpaso, formed like a ten-petaled flower, lay across the Rio Grande between an upper and a lower reservoir. Beyond the Rio Grande the contour terraces became narrower and climbed the flanks of range after range of mountains, stopping only at the timber line.

Half of the sun's disk was now above the horizon.

"Something's wrong," Kim said. "This country down below—it's unnatural. There aren't any big cities. Just mountains and forest and an occasional tiny square settlement with a flyport. Why is that?"

"*That* I can tell you," replied Jothen. "This is earthquake country, the land of volcanoes and restless strata. It's part of a U-shaped zone around the Pacific basin from the west coast of South America to southeast Asia. When it began to fill up with big modern cities it was plagued with one disaster after another. It was not far from here that a new volcano burst through the middle of a city with a population of thirty million—in the latter part of the twenty-sixth century, I think. After that the cities in the earthquake zone were progressively abandoned and dismantled. This increased the density of population elsewhere, but there was nothing else that could be done. The 'little settlements' are stations for fire fighters and foresters. There are fire watch towers on the ridges and seismic observatories buried inside the mountains, but most of them are unmanned and automatic."

Baja California slid away from under them and the Pacific Ocean came up over the curve of the green earth. First it was a gray-blue line edging the green; then it expanded until there was only sea and sky, with the copper disk of the sun poised on the horizon at the end of a ribbon of orange light.

A remote blue mound seemed to rise from the sea as the plane approached. Wisps and banners of vapor slanted up from it in a crooked streamer across the sky.

"That must be Cedros Island!" exclaimed Jothen, beginning to feel a stir of excitement.

"Cedros Island is smoking," Kim said. "Does it have a volcano, or is that the smoke from geobenthic mines?"

A line of blue-white flame sprouted vertically from the island and grew steadily upward. Higher and higher it climbed, became attenuated, dwindled to a cobweb strand of fire, tapered off into invisibility. The line of flame became a fuzzy trail of vapor that disintegrated into shreds and tatters, drifted aside on the winds of the upper air, and joined the other dissolving wisps.

"There's your answer," said Jothen. "No volcano. No lava mines. Just the remains of rocket trails. There's a launching every twenty or thirty minutes, I've heard."

"We're coming down," Kim said. "You can see the landing areas, one at each end of the island. There are a few planes on one but no rockets on the other. Where are the rockets?"

"In launching pits, the travel counselor told me. The rockets let down into the sea in a horizontal position and float there. Hydrofoil tugs come out and tow them in."

When the plane landed it maneuvered onto a square outlined in yellow. The square sank on hydraulic pistons, lowered the plane into an underground hangar. A sliding cover rumbled into place and closed the opening through which the plane had descended.

The rocket compartment was shaped like the inside of a drum lying on its side. It ceiling was a curved glow-panel radiating a soft white light; the rest of the interior was enameled a pale jade green. Jothen and Kim lay side by side, strapped down in reclining contour seats padded with foot-thick green plastifoam.

"That was fast," Kim said. "Plane to tube-train to elevator to rocket. The attendant who strapped us in—what was she saying about monitored air?"

"She said that the air over and around Cedros Island is full of rocket exhaust gases, mostly hydrofluoric acid," Jothen said. "The rockets burn liquid hydrogen and fluorine. That's why the plane went underground as soon as it landed. We've been breathing filtered air ever since we left the plane. If a trace of exhaust gas gets into it an alarm goes off."

There was a short silence. Both of them were listening, trying to detect some faint sound, some clue as to what was going on outside. But their compartment was well insulated against outside sounds.

A voice spoke from a grill near the ceiling glow-panel: "This is your launching computer speaking. It is now fifteen minutes to blast-off. Erection of the rocket has begun."

"We're moving!" said Kim. "I can feel a slight tremor. But I still feel as if I were right side up."

"The compartment is mounted on rollers. It rotates as the rocket comes up vertical, but it will lock in position so that we'll be flat on our backs."

Another silence.

"This is a Spartan type of travel," Jothen said. "No autoserver. A container of water and a tube of food paste for each of us. Well, I guess that's enough. It's a quick trip. No viewing port. And they closed the cabin door after we were strapped down."

"How many other compartments are there?"

"Nine. All occupied."

"Five minutes to blast-off," announced the launching computer. "Booster now being coupled to rocket."

Came a series of light jars and vibrations.

Jothen said, "Brace yourself. It won't be long now."

"Where are our zoomvision goggles?"

"In a recess in the chair arm, under your right hand. But you can't get them out now. The lid on the recess won't open until after we're in orbit."

The computer began its final announcement:

"We are approaching the last ten seconds before blast-off . . . *Ten* . . . *Nine* . . . *Eight* . . ."

"What is it, Kim? Frightened?"

"*Five* . . . *Four* . . ."

"No. I'm floating on a cloud of tranquilizer. I feel . . . as if . . ."

"*Three* . . ."

"As if I could fly without wings. Silly, isn't it?"

"*Two* . . ."

"Not silly. Euphoria. Tranquilized exaltation."

"*One* . . ."

Jothen never heard the word "*Blast!*" A slow-motion

pile driver descended on him. He was being flattened into the plastifoam cushion. He felt rather than heard the vibrations of the ultrathunder of the hydrogen-fluorine blast that was rushing them skyward. The luminous ceiling dimmed and went dark. He felt no fear. He was flying away from everything. He had outstripped the rocket and was on his own. He had left even himself behind. Jothen had traveled faster than Jothen. That surpassed the speed of light, didn't it?

Then the darkness was gone. He was suspended in an infinite void of white light. It was utterly silent. He felt a supreme sense of peace. He could solve any problem.

How about your own problems? Do you have any problems, Jothen? Yes. Why can't I make any headway with Kim? Everything I say seems to be the wrong thing. Of course it is, you damn fool! You try to do it all by logic. You try to be eloquent and persuasive and it comes out sounding like a tract or a lecture. This is no engineering problem. Well, what should I say? What *are* the right words? There you go again--words, words, words! Don't think so much about the words. Consult your emotions, then express them. How do I do that? That's your problem. It's *still* your problem.

He became aware that the luminous white void was merely the white glow-panel above him. The sense of crushing pressures had passed. Instead he had a sense of disembodied lightness. Kim was shaking his shoulder.

"Jothen! What happened to you? I think I was unconscious for a bit, but you were out for several minutes. You were mumbling things."

"I was? What did I say?"

Kim hesitated. "All I could make out was one word—my name. You kept saying 'Kim.'"

"That's not surprising. You're on my mind most of the time."

"So you keep saying, in various ways, most of the time. How about trying out our zoomvision?"

"Oh, all right," Jothen said, not quite without a sigh, "why not?"

## 5 The Shipwrecked Hotel

The Great Barrier Reef is a vast platform of coral extending southward from the coast of New Guinea along the eastern shore of Australia for over one thousand miles. Parts of the platform are submerged under relatively shallow water; parts are awash at low tide and parts rise above the high-tide level as atolls and islets. The outer rampart of the reef is a wall of coral as dense and hard as concrete, an impregnable break-water against the battering waves of the Pacific.

Inlets along the barrier give access to the maze of channels, atolls, shoals, islets, and sandbanks that lie behind it. This inner zone varies in width from twenty to a hundred and fifty miles. Seaward from the outer rampart the water depth increases rapidly and finally plunges precipitously into the oceanic abysses.

The reef is an intermediate realm; a bridge between the two dissimilar worlds of dry land and open sea; the natural symbol of the Tritons who colonized it. The reef colony is the most populous Triton community in the world, surpassing even the West Indian settlement that extends from the Bahamas to the coast of South America. It is a community more dispersed, more self-sufficient, less mechanized, and less regimented than the megalopoli of the Drylanders.

The Tritons are not, however, so self-sufficient as to be indifferent to the good opinions of the Drylanders, whose tectogenetic creations they were: a new human species, to exploit the sea—with their coevals the dolphins—as the Drylanders could never hope to do. Triton Reef could never afford to ignore the Barrier-hilthon.

An observer on the outer escarpment of the reef near the inlet known as the Lark Passage would have seen the upper portion of the Barrier-hilthon as a varicolored dome riding on the sea about five miles offshore. Actually, the Barrier-hilthon is an artificial island, with its base planted in the bottom ooze at 315 fathoms. It is an enterprise of the Transportation Corporation, which provides hotel accomodations for two million guests and a service staff of twenty thousand. Externally, its architecture is severely simple and compact—a steel globe 3500 feet high, with its surface divided into twelve segments of alternating colors—red, white, blue, white, red —that converge toward the yellow disk of the flyport at its summit. As seen from the air it suggests a gigantic beach ball afloat on the sea.

A projecting flange four hundred feet wide girdles the Barrier-hilthon at water level. The inner zone of this flange has been converted into a "beach" of white coral sand, complete with sea shells and picturesquely contorted fragments of weather-bleached driftwood. A sea-water swimming pool occupies the zone between the beach and the upcurved outer rim of the flange. This outer rim excludes surf, sharks, and barracudas, while its curvature and overhang discourages venturesome swimmers who otherwise might be tempted to climb over it. Direct contact with the open sea, of a sort, is provided by large stainless-steel grilles set in embrasures spaced equidistantly along the curved sea wall. Rollers that dash themselves against the grilles enter the pool as showers of spray and smooth surges of water.

Internally the Barrier-hilthon is an automated labyrinth of guest rooms, entertainment halls, service salons, escalators, moving floors, and elevators. Twenty levels, each containing ten stories, are reserved for these facilities; four more levels are for service installations. An indoor beach and pool encircle the hotel at the same level as the outdoor pool. Seen only by the service staff is another, hidden labyrinth between the walls and beneath the floors—a labyrinth of pipes, cables, waveguides, and conveyor tubes radiating from the complex of service mechanisms and their controlling computers that are stacked in a cylindrical column along the vertical axis of the Barrier-hilthon. Except when medical or dental attention is necessary the guests very seldom see members of the service staff other than the lifeguards and swimming instructors on the beaches.

Situated on the second level beneath the flyport is the Master Computer that co-ordinates and supervises the subsidiary specialized computers that direct the automatic services of the Barrier-hilthon. But the Master Computer itself is supervised. In a circular control room at its core, a twenty-five man team of monitors keep constant vigil in four-hour shifts. They work in a twilight obscurity lit by only the vidscreens and the winking luminous dots and squares on their consoles. Here the human mind impinges on electronic circuitry. Here the monitors receive reports on matters specified by them. Here decisions are made and actions initiated in situations in which the Master Computer finds itself incompetent to act without instructions.

The Master Computer speaks with a manifold voice. It can carry on twenty-five different and simultaneous conversations with the monitors.

"The tropical storm over the Solomon Islands is increasing in intensity," announced the Master Computer to Monitor Nine, at the same time displaying a weather chart on the vidscreen. "It is centered over Bougainville, moving south-southwest at twenty miles per hour. Central wind velocity, fifty-five miles per hour. It may develop hurricane force. We are feeling peripheral wind and wave effects. Hurricane Advisory Alpha has been issued."

"Wait twenty-four hours before issuing any further advisories," replied Monitor Nine. "By then we'll know more about the force of the storm and its probable path."

To Monitor Fourteen the Master Computer said, "A report has been prepared on the alleged appearances of arthropods in guest rooms. Do you wish to receive it now?"

"Proceed."

"Two reports have been received, claiming that arthropods were seen in guest rooms. The investigator interviewed the complainants and showed them life-size 3-V movies of various arthropods with a portable viewer.

"Complaint Number One: Madame Renee Lamotte reported seeing a scorpion in her bath-spray compartment. Stated that she knew it was a scorpion because, quote, it had a sting on its tail, unquote. When shown the movie of a scorpion she denied that it resembled the creature that she saw. Her comment on the movie of an earwig was negative also. By this time she was in a highly agitated condition and refused to look at any more pictures. Her husband privately advised the investigator that Madame Lamotte has had an insect phobia since seeing a so-called historical 3-V drama of life during the Age of Waste, with emphasis on the prevalence of insect pests.

"Complaint Number Two was filed by Mulaka Ouagadu, who reported finding a centipede in a slipper. He failed to identify the pictures of a centipede with the creature that he claims to have seen. After viewing three other pictures he refused to go on because he found them emotionally disturbing. He does not know Madame Lamotte but had heard the rumor about the scorpion.

"Investigator's conclusions: Madame Lamotte is a neurotic woman who imagined that she saw an insect-like creature and called it a scorpion. Ouagadu heard the scorpion rumor, became alarmed, and also had arthropod delusions. It is the investigator's opinion that neither of the complainants, quote, is capable of distinguishing an ant from an angleworm, unquote.

"No other complaints in this category have been received. End of report."

"Make a general announcement to guests and service personnel," directed Monitor Fourteen, "that rumors of scorpions et cetera in the Barrier-hilthon have no foundation in fact."

The Master Computer said to Monitor Three, "The party of Tritons and dolphins is approaching Sector Twelve as scheduled. The necessary announcement is being made via the beach PA system."

The multitude on the beach halted their activities and listened to the resonant synthetic voice that rolled from the concealed speakers on the colorful dome that towered above them.

"This is the Voice of Barrier-hilthon. We have made arrangements with the Tritons of Great Barrier Reef whereby you are about to receive visitors of a most unusual nature. In a few minutes some of the grilles in the sea wall of Sector Twelve will open and Tritons and dolphins will be admitted to the pool. No doubt each of you has heard many tales of various degrees of accuracy regarding Tritons and dolphins. Now you shall see them, talk to them, and obtain your information at first hand."

There was a general exodus from the pool and a

babble of voices rose from the beach in agitated crescendo, subsided, and was followed by an expectant silence punctuated by the rhythmic swashing of water through the grilles as billows broke against the sea wall. Abandoned beach balls and plastifoam rafts bobbed about in the pool.

Three grilles slid aside with metallic clashes and disappeared into slots in the sides of their embrasures. Through these openings the spectators on the beach saw the glistening curved front of a massive turquoise-green billow upheave itself, fling itself toward them, and pour into the pool in three hissing cataracts. Three dolphins plunged through on the crests of the cataracts, their sleek arched bodies momentarily half out of the tumbling foam-flecked water. A bronze-skinned Triton child lay prone on the back of each dolphin between its head and dorsal fin, arms and legs clasping the dolphin's body. Dolphins and children vanished in a white smother of foam.

Then, midway between beach and sea wall, the dolphins surfaced explosively in a tremendous power leap that carried them ten feet into the air. At the apex of their parabolic flight the three Triton children slid sidewise from the dolphins' backs, and children and dolphins dived into the pool in unison. A burst of applause rose from the beach.

With the arrival of every billow more water gushed into the pool bringing more dolphins, more Tritons. Some of the Tritons had skins of a rich brown color, some were purplish-black, some were like brown-tinted ivory, others were dappled. The pool became alive with swimming Tritons and leaping dolphins.

The three grilles clashed back into position.

The dolphins were quick to perceive the possibilities of the floating beach balls and butted them into the air, aiming so that the balls fell into the throng on the beach.

At first this created flurries of surprise, but the onlookers rose to the occasion and flung the balls back into the pool. A lively two-way beach-ball bombardment began.

The crowd commenced to move back into the water. Soon everyone was in the water. Even the nonswimmers were in waist-deep. Several haphazard games of water polo were organized. Triton children were instructing children from the hotel in the sport of dolphin riding. Tritons and guests raced each other to the sea wall and back—an unequal match, it should be recorded. There were experiments in conversing with dolphins. The air rang with shouts, laughter, and a tumult of splashing.

A Triton girl hoisted herself from the water onto a plastifoam raft, stood erect, her black skin glistening like mobile obsidian, and emptied her gill chambers by ejecting multiple jets of water from the slits on her sides. A ring of swimmers collected around the raft, clung to its edges, and plied her with a barrage of questions.

"Why did you squirt spray like that?"

"I can't breathe air unless I empty the water out of my gills."

"I don't see any gills."

"They're inside, where you have your lungs."

"How long can you stay out of water?"

"I've been out as long as twenty hours."

"What's your name?"

"Ruvani."

"Do you eat raw fish?"

"Raw fish! No! Mostly we eat from an autoserver. Sometimes we catch fish, or crabs, or lobsters, or dig clams, and cook them with a fire outdoors."

"A *fire! Nobody* is allowed to make a fire! You might set fire to the Forest!"

"There isn't any forest where we make our fires. We

78

make them with driftwood on little islands behind the barrier. Most of them are sandbars or bare rock. Some of them have a few wild trees. They're too small to bother planting a forest on them."

"What's that little rod fastened to your belt?"

"That's an electric shark prod. It pulls out into a long rod—like this. When a shark comes too close I touch him with the tip, give him a shock, and he goes away."

"It's such a thin little rod. Where's the battery?"

"There isn't a battery. The electricity comes out of me. Like an electric eel."

"Out of you! Oh, really! I don't believe it. Prove it."

"All right. Put out your finger. Now I'll touch my finger to yours. I'll try to make the shock as light as I can. *Now!*"

"Ouch!"

"Convinced?"

"Yes! My arm hurts clear up to my shoulder. Could you kill a person?"

"I don't think so. I've never tried. I *have* killed moray eels."

"Don't you feel the shock yourself?"

"Not the way you did. It feels—it's hard to say how it feels. It's a sort of thump between my shoulder blades, like being hit with a rubber hammer."

"Why do you use a rod? Why don't you just touch the shark with your hand?"

"Too risky. When a shark feels a shock he may lash around with his tail or bite blindly in all directions. Or he may take off like a rocket. One can't be sure what he may do."

Ruvani's ordeal—though she bore it very well—might have gone on for an hour, as it had often before; but this time she was interrupted. A siren wail from the PA speakers rang over the pool.

"Your attention, please," a commanding voice boomed. "Your attention, please. A tropical storm is approaching from the northeast. Clear the beach and pool. Clear the beach and pool. Guests will please return to the hotel and remain indoors until further notice. The grilles will be opened and Tritons and dolphins will kindly return to their homes. That is all."

There was a general stir of movement on the beach, but it was not a scramble. There had been something vaguely reassuring in the tone in which the computer had said "That is all," as though tropical storms were no novelty to the Barrier-hilthon.

As indeed they were not; but the computer's "That is all" had not been quite candid. In fact, hazardous conditions on the beach due to the approaching storm were not likely to occur for another twenty-four hours. The object of the warning had been to move everyone to a safer location, without causing a panic, to avoid a danger of an entirely different nature.

Ten minutes before, the Master Computer had stunned the monitors by announcing:

*"The Barrier-hilthon is sinking."*

From the moment of the Master Computer's announcement, the monitors were tied up in emergency actions and in trying to locate the malfunction in the computer that had generated the announcement. It *had* to be a malfunction. But it was a first-magnitude malfunction, and the monitors were taking no chances.

The check-out of guests was proceeding as usual. Guests en route to the Barrier-hilthon had been halted in transit. The watertight doors of all entrances had been closed and secured. Only the check-out exits remained open. Transportation Corporation had been informed that evacuation of the hotel might be necessary.

The reports relayed by the Master Computer indicated an increasing loss of co-ordination of its subsidiaries. The Barrier-hilthon was sinking. . . . The Barrier-hilthon was not sinking; it was still securely embedded in the bottom ooze. . . . The aquaphone switchboard had ceased to function, thereby blocking underwater communication with submersible ferries and shore installations. . . . Computer 5B (in charge of ballast) had activated all pumps at full capacity and was emptying the ballast tanks. . . . Communications were broken between the Master Computer and Computer 5B.

All off-duty shifts of the maintenance staff had been recalled and the combined force was searching for the malfunction. One task force had been ordered to stop the pumps manually. The series of doors leading to the Manual Pump Control Center had been closed by Computer 5B and had to be manually opened—only to be closed again by Computer 5B, doggedly following the electronic command, "Activate all pumps and keep them going until ordered to stop."

As the technicians checked and counterchecked the multimillion components of the Barrier-hilthon it became evident that there was not one malfunction but several. The hotel was afflicted by the computorial equivalent of schizophrenia.

The monitors by-passed the Master Computer and issued a directline order to Maintenance Supervision: "Kill Computer 5B and stop the pumps."

Killing the computer was a simple matter of shutting off its power supply. Stopping the pumps was a more complex operation. There were two thousand pumps and they could be shut off only in sector units. To maintain the Barrier-hilthon's axis in a precisely vertical position it was necessary that they be stopped in a definite sequence. It was an operation that never before had been manually performed. When the newly built Barrier-hilthon had been lowered into its present position, the ballast tanks had been filled under the control of the computers. Since that day only slight automatic adjustments in buoyancy were necessary to compensate for the daily tidal cycle. The possibility that the Barrier-hilthon might spontaneously attempt to become free-floating had not been anticipated; the designers had envisioned nothing more than local flooding due to structural failure. Now, during the first stages of the manual shutdown of the entire ballast-pump installation, great volumes of water continued to be discharged and the Barrier-hilthon's buoyancy increased.

The guests of the hotel, still happily unaware of the disaster that was taking shape, paid little heed to the transient shudders that quivered through the steel fabric of their automated microcosm. The few who noted them ascribed them to the impact of breakers on the windward sea wall. But the monitors knew otherwise. The steel globe had detached itself from the adhesive bottom ooze and was just barely afloat in its bowl-shaped emplacement.

The technicians manning the pump controls lacked the smooth co-ordination of Computer 5B. Their eyes were fixed on the tilt gauges, watching the axis of the Barrier-hilthon for slight departures from the vertical. Repeated minute tiltings and hasty compensations created an atmosphere of growing urgency tinged with panic. The result was a jittery, exaggerated caution and increasing slowness in their operations.

Meanwhile the Barrier-hilthon floated higher and higher. The jutting flange that supported the beach and swimming pool was more than one hundred feet above water level, exposing its underside and a zone of the spherical hull encrusted with sea growths. The water from the pool poured through the grilles in noisy cascades. The docks for hydrofoil and submersible ferries, which transported guests to and from the mainland, were likewise above water level. Hotel guests were ordered to retire to their rooms, to remain there until called, and to prepare for departure.

During these events a high-speed colloquy was taking place between the Barrier-hilthon's Master Computer and the Master Computer at the Triton-operated base known as the Lizard Island Complex, inside of the reef.

"Barrier-hilthon to Lizard Island. Emergency. We are about to become free-floating due to computer malfunctions. Ferry docks are above water level. Evacuation is proceeding via flyport only, imposing ten times normal load. Need all available helicopters and hovercraft."

The same appeal was transmitted to Transcorp by way of Prime Center.

But the Lizard Island Tritons had further plans for speeding the evacuation.

"Lizard Island to Cairns' Reef. Emergency. Relay to satellite reefs. Barrier-hilthon will soon be adrift and is being evacuated. Send all submersible ferries to cooperate with aircraft. Sea is too rough for hydrofoils. Evacuees will be transferred from flyport to submersibles via rescue slings."

"Lizard Island to Snake Reef. Emergency. Relay . . ."

"Lizard Island to Osprey Reef. Emergency . . ."

The first flights of aircraft from Lizard Island and Snake Reef arrived at the flyport an hour ahead of the flight dispatched by Transcorp from the mainland. At the same time the Barrier-hilthon swam clear of her emplacement crater. Under the mounting force of the southwesterly wind, her enormous mass yielded sluggishly and began a creeping, reluctant drift toward the northeast and deeper water. All of her more massive installations—power plant, sea-water distillery, fresh-water storage, sewage processing—were in her lower levels. The major part of her mass as well as her center of gravity were still below the water line. She moved with the ponderous steadiness of an iceberg, ignoring the increasing roughness of the sea.

Maintenance Supervision reported to the monitors that one malfunctioning module had been located and replaced, and the automatic pump control was restored. The pumps were stopped and the hotel continued her drift with the elevation of the outdoor beach and pool—now completely drained—at slightly more than three hundred feet above their normal level.

Lizard Island received another distress call from the hotel's Master Computer.

"Barrier-hilthon to Lizard Island. We have been hit by a fifty-mile gust. Aerodynamic force on outdoor-swimming-pool flange tilted vertical axis two tenths of one degree, causing oscillation of water in indoor swimming pool, which overflowed into adjacent halls. We are draining indoor pool. Increasing wind may cause dangerous rolling. We must resubmerge partly or completely to normal level. Take a fix on our position and give us probability of sunken crags or reefs in our extrapolated course."

There was a momentary pause while the Lizard Island computer consulted its electronic memory and triangulated the Barrier-hilthon's position with radio direction finders.

"Lizard Island to Barrier-hilthon. Existing depth charts for your location are obsolete. Recent collapse of submarine cliff and extensive mud slides have drastically altered bottom contours. Resurvey incomplete. There was a submerged basalt peak very close to your extrapolated course. If its position and depth are the same as before, you may collide with it whether you resubmerge or not."

The removal of evacuees by aircraft and rescue sling was proceeding from the outdoor beach as well as from the flyport. The operation was hampered by the rough-

ness of the sea and rising wind. The transfer from swaying rescue slings to rolling and pitching submersibles
had to be made in the water by swimming Tritons, who
removed the occupants of the slings in a welter of waves
and foam and swam with them to the submersibles,
where Triton hands hauled them aboard. The rate of
transfer was frighteningly slow. In four hours approximately five thousand had been evacuated, and darkness
had fallen. The tossing navigation lights of submersibles
clustered around the Barrier-hilthon like a swarm of
red and green fireflies. The beams of their searchlights
played over her striped dome, probed the air above for
descending aircraft, swept to and fro over the tumbling
waves.

"ATTENTION ALL OCCUPANTS. PLEASE RE-
TIRE TO YOUR ROOMS. WE EXPECT A COLLI-
SION WITH AN UNDERWATER CLIFF WITHIN
THE NEXT HOUR. REPEAT, RETIRE TO YOUR
ROOMS. ALL WATERTIGHT DOORS WILL BE
LOCKED IN TWENTY MINUTES."

Since she had not been designed as a navigable sea-
going vessel, the Barrier-hilthon possessed no motive
power, no rudder, and no sounding devices, obstacle
detectors or other navigation aids. The monitors were
kept advised by the Lizard Island computer of their
position and course with reference to the last charted
position of the sunken crag. Everyone was waiting. The
steel globe had become, in effect, one vast, blindly listening entity.

The basalt crag, studded with uneven rocky fangs,
was the visible portion of a larger mass that lay buried
in mud and coral sand—one corner of a great block that
had been detached and upended by some ancient earthquake. Its total bulk, had it been visible, would have
dwarfed the Barrier-hilthon. And it had changed in
neither depth nor position.

The Barrier-hilthon bore down upon it with deliberate, inexorable slowness. Her rounded side grazed its spiked and saw-edged summit. The basalt plowed with grinding and crunching din through her outer and inner skins, inflicting a monstrous diagonal wound 1100 feet long. The rending metal emitted a jagged, rasping scream, then trailed off into a quavering squeal. Rumbling torrents of bubbles erupted from the gash and raced upward. The Barrier-hilthon reeled, and the people in her rooms were thrown upon the sloping floors.

At the first impact the hotel computers reacted with lightning swiftness. Each sector of every level was sealed off from the others. The axial service stack was sealed off from the rest of the structure. The doors to the beach and the flyport were closed. Sectors of the eighth, ninth, and tenth levels were flooded; the unbalanced globe changed its direction of tilt.

The hotel went under swiftly. The sea poured over the sea wall and flooded the beach. The picturesque driftwood fragments floated away. A narrowing ring of foam climbed the red, white, and blue dome until the summit of the radio and video aerial atop the flyport control tower disappeared in an eddy of foam and driftwood. The pumps shifted ballast at top speed; the hotel gradually righted herself and came to rest on the oozy bottom with the top of her control tower 150 feet below the surface.

Those who had been waiting on the windswept airfield of the flyport and on the outdoor beach had been washed away and left floundering in the stormy nocturnal sea. Each felt that his last moment of life had come. But the sleek flanks of dolphins rose on either side, pressed against them, and bore them up. The hands of Tritons reached up from below, supported them, and towed them toward the wave-tossed submersibles.

A preliminary report on the number of known casualties, the extent of the damage to the Barrier-hilthon, and the state of its automatic services had been delivered to the monitors by the Master Computer. The flood of telephone calls from terrified guests was being handled by computers in the lower echelons of the electronic hierarchy. A moment of silence prevailed in the control room. The submergence of the flyport aerial had closed that avenue of communication with the outside world. The thoughts of all twenty-five monitors were essentially, "What now? What do we do next?"

The Master Computer spoke to Monitor One:

"You have a call from the flyport control tower. Do you wish to receive it?"

"The control tower! But there's no one there! We ordered everyone out just before we went under."

"There is someone there now. Will you take the call?"

"By all means. Put them on."

The face of a blond young woman appeared on the vidscreen in front of Monitor One. A light-weight scuba mask with miniscule oxygen tanks on either side was pushed back on her forehead.

"Hello, Control Room!" she called. "What has happened down there? Is it very bad?"

"Bad enough, but better than we expected. But who are you? How did you get into the control tower?"

"I'm Dorthy Sumter, head of Submarine Products Corporation. I came in an UWS—an underwater speedboat—with a Triton rescue team. They're going to inspect the damage to your hull and take measurements so we can put a patch on it. We got in through a hatch in the roof of the control tower."

"That's the access hatch to the aerial. How did you open it without flooding the place?"

"We put a scapelock over the hatch and came in."

"A scapelock?"

"A prefab escape airlock. Do you mind if we come down? We'd like to take a quick look around and talk to whomever is available."

"I'll talk to you. We're just about to change shifts. My name's Defabio. I'll be in the Monitors' Lounge. All our transport systems are operating—except in the flooded sectors. Watch the location maps along the way. If you get lost use the nearest house phone and ask for Guide Service. The Level Computer wil give you all the information you need."

When Defabio greeted Dorthy in the Monitors' Lounge she was accompanied by a Triton whom she introduced as Tioru. Dorthy was sheathed in an insulated, heat-retaining, all-over suit of fluorescent orange-yellow plastic, with webbing between the fingers. Tioru, like his fellow Tritons, was not chilled by prolonged exposure to water temperatures down to fifteen degrees centigrade and was clad only in a yellow cincture. A green fiberglass cylinder with closed ends was suspended from a nylon cord around his neck.

"What's in the case?" asked Defabio after they had seated themselves.

"Video tape," replied Dorthy. "I suggest that it be shown on your intercom system to everyone in the hotel. Then they'll know what we propose to do. It should raise their morale, and I supect that it needs raising."

"And what do you propose to do?"

"Since this will be a Triton project, Tioru should tell you."

"Thank you," said Tioru, bowing slightly to Dorthy, then to Defabio. "There are two things that we can begin to do at once. First, to get all your people out of the Barrier-hilthon. Second, to repair the damage to your hull. You have something more than two million people aboard and the only way out, at present, is through the scapelock. We won't consider trying to get everyone out through that. It would be like draining a thousand-gallon tank through a pinhole. You'll need more scapelocks."

Defabio interrupted. "That scapelock on the control tower—how did you attach it without letting in water?"

"A scapelock is an eight-foot dome with an airlock on top. We cemented the dome to the roof with a metal-to-metal adhesive that hardens rapidly even under water. You couldn't pull it loose now without taking part of the roof with it. A built-in pump empties the water out of the dome and the airlock. We went through the airlock and opened the hatch. No problem.

"We estimate that we can install five hundred scapelocks on your flyport landing field without crowding."

"Five hundred! Where can you get five hundred scapelocks on short notice?"

"We have a plant on Lizard Island that makes them, and a number of other things. We have a stock of about one hundred there and have begun making more around the clock. There are fifty more stored at Cairns' Reef. We've ordered others to be brought in by unmanned rockets from Fiji and the Andaman Islands. Still others are available in the Bahamas. Perhaps we won't need five hundred. We won't know until we've clocked the operation. We'll have to cut a hole through your airfield under each scapelock. We've requested permission from Transcorp to do this. It came through half an hour ago. I have a transcript for your files."

"Hold on!" protested Defabio. "The top of the control tower is one hundred and fifty feet down, the airfield, about four hundred. You can't shove people out through your scapelocks at that depth. The water's cold, and the pressure is around twelve atmospheres. They'd drown before they reach the surface if they didn't die of fright first. This is the first time in their lives that most of them have been outside of their native cities. Many of them have never been more than a few miles from their apartment until now. And about ninety percent of them can't swim!"

At this point Dorthy broke in:

"The video tape will prepare everyone for the escape routine. And we'll put miniscubas on them. Like I'm wearing now. The little cylinders hold twenty minutes' oxygen supply. They were made for Drylanders' use during brief underwater activity—when transferring from one sub to another while both are submerged, for example."

Tioru continued, "Each person will receive a five-minute air-pressure build-up in the spacelock. Outside there'll be a Triton or a dolphin waiting. When each person emerges he'll be hauled up to a sub and through its airlock before he can count ten. He won't be exposed to the cold and pressure for long, and he won't have to go all the way to the surface. The subs will be only forty or fifty feet above your airfield. It's fortunate that you're down as deep as you are. It's blowing fifty miles an hour up above.

"As soon as one sub has a capacity load it will move out and another one will move in. There'll be a traffic control system for subs set up in your control tower. We'll bring our own aquaphone T and R equipment. And we're setting up receiving centers on the mainland for your people.

"Now—casualties. How many casualties do you have?"

"The casualty check is still going on," Defabio said gloomily. "We have twenty-three deaths that we know of. And a list of fractures and dislocations a yard long. Over two hundred when I came off duty. We can't get to the ones in the flooded sectors. The rooms there are tight but the halls are full of water under twenty-eight-hundred-foot depth pressure. We can feed them via the autoservers as usual, and send in first-aid materials through the parcel conveyor tubes. We can give them first-aid instructions by vidphone, provide music and 3-V movies, and that's all."

Tioru said, "We'll take out the accessible casualties first. The inaccessible ones will have to remain inaccessible for a while. We can't open the rooms in the flooded sectors until we can pump the water out of the halls, and we can't pump the water out of the halls until we have repaired the hull."

"There's another thing," said Defabio. "Small children and babies. We have forty-seven newborns in our maternity ward—which is in an upper level and not flooded, I'm happy to say—and swarms of older juveniles."

"We've thought of them. We have something special. You'll see. Don't worry."

"Don't worry!" Defabio said with a wry gesture, but of course he had to trust Dorthy, if not the Triton. He stood up. "This will take a full-scale meeting of the monitors to make it official, but I'll take it upon myself to approve the whole project. No one in his right mind could object. We too would like to get out of here alive. I'll put your video tape on our intramural network at once. You notify your Triton HQ to get the rescue operation rolling."

Then he paused, looking momentarily nonplussed. He said:

"How does one say 'Thank you' on behalf of two-million-plus people?"

Tioru said gently, "To begin with, you wait until there's something to thank us for."

The rocket carrying Jothen and Kim had traversed five time zones and was entering the sixth. During the first half of the flight they had seen little other than the immense expanse of open sea—a world of blue water and armadas of clouds that, seen from an altitude of three hundred miles, were shreds of white fluff that seemed to rest on the blue.

In the latter half of the flight they viewed, from an apparent altitude of five hundred feet, mile after mile of ocean that was churned into transient rosettes of foam by leaping fish—a minute fraction of the incalculable horde beneath the surface. The sea twinkled with the flashing myriads of silver-scaled bodies. A floating fish-processing plant cruised slowly through the agitated waters, reaping a living harvest. Once they sighted a herd of whales, fringed by dolphins—a curiously pastoral sight.

Now the zoomvision viewers showed irregular green shapes embossed upon the blue field, each bordered by a white line of beach and surf. Scattered among the lush islands were the white rings and crescents and filigree patterns of reefs and atolls.

"If we're on schedule we should be near the Solomon Islands," Jothen said. "I think I can see a few of them strung out along the horizon. And there's something a bit more spectacular. Take a look, Kim."

"I see some elongated islands," Kim said, "and a whirlpool of clouds coming up over the rim of the Earth. It's like a scale model of a spiral galaxy."

"It's the topside of a typhoon. This one must have built up so fast that it got out of hand before the Weatherwatch boys could spike it. I hope Osprey Reef is well out of it, on the other side."

"Is that where the Triton family's to meet us? What do you know about them?"

"Very little. There are three of them. The father's name is Storm, which I hope isn't prophetic. He's an assistant to Dorthy Sumter, the head of Submarine Products. Their home is on a coral islet they call Seahorse Reef. It's part of the outer barrier. I . . . I'm afraid I told Storm we might be on our honeymoon."

"You," Kim said, "are absolutely incorrigible."

"I've been practicing," Jothen admitted. But he was given no chance to pursue the subject further.

"My viewer's gone dark," announced Kim.

"So has mine. We must be starting re-entry."

"I'm sorry to have to tell you this," Storm said, "but something has happened that alters all our plans. We are not going to be very good hosts, I'm afraid, and your vacation may not be very restful."

Jothen found it difficult not to stare at Storm's rhythmically falling tears and his fleshy, plume-shaped auditory antennae, constantly aquiver. He did not seem to disturb Kim, but then she was used to biological oddity.

"Nothing personal, I hope?" she said.

"No. A disaster at the Barrier-hilthon. Let's board the sub and then I'll tell you the whole story."

Storm's *Sea Dart* was a slender five-man craft propelled by centrifugally driven water jets. He took her down to five fathoms and left the rocket port's harbor by an underwater exit. Here the conning tower's vidscreen showed only a dusky green obscurity.

"You'll find this hard to believe, and I'll not blame you," the Triton said. "But, briefly, the storm you said you saw, plus a computer malfunction, floated the hotel out of its moorings and drove it onto a submerged cliff. It went down like a stone—about a mile down, which isn't too bad considering that the hotel itself's thirty-five hundred feet in diameter, but bad enough. There were two million people aboard at the time— the worst marine disaster in history, unless we can get them out."

"Get them out!" Jothen said incredulously. "But the hull—the depth pressure—"

"The hull can take it," Storm said. "The hotel was built with a safety factor of five. It's mostly monocrystal iron fifty-six. The main problem is that the rescue area's at sixty fathoms. Needless to say, we're working around the clock. And it occurred to me, Mr. Kent, that since disasters are in a sense your profession, you might like a look at what's going on."

"I would indeed. . . . Kim?"

"Of course." She looked out at the murky water. "But will we be able to see anything?"

"Oh, the flyport—that's the work area—is illuminated. I can't take you down to see the repair crew at work on the damaged hull, though. That's beyond the safe limits for this boat."

The *Sea Dart* dived on a long slant, and the vidscreen darkened to a deep violet-blue. A nebulous, ghostly area of greenish luminescence appeared on the screen.

"There it is," Storm said. "We have lights moored all around the flyport."

"Those poor people," Kim said. "It gives me claustrophobia just to think of being in that thing."

"Me too," Jothen said. "Especially when I remember that you wanted to go there."

The luminous area slowly expanded as the *Sea Dart* approached. It emerged from the aqueous haze and became the circular yellow expanse of the flyport brightly lighted by a ring of buoyant shining globes, each reinforced with a cage-like gridwork of curved ribs. The globes were anchored around the rim of the airfield by mooring cables, which were delineated by the red dots of marker lights. The field had been divided by lines of phosphorescent violet paint into a huge checkerboard whose squares were identified by shining violet numerals. Many of the squares were occupied by a scapelock—a squat dome surmounted by a chimney-like airlock.

Two of the nearer airlocks were connected to what appeared to be either thick cables or flexible pipelines that rose at a steep angle into the deep blue darkness. They undulated lazily and were studded with equidistant, round, red marker lights. In reply to Jothen's inquiry, Storm explained:

"You might call them a pair of supersnorkel tubes. When the hull was ripped open the Barrier-hilthon lost a great volume of air, and every time we open a scapelock it loses some air. The people in the hotel consume oxygen. There is a reserve of compressed oxygen in the hotel but we want to conserve it. So air is pumped into the hotel's ventilating system through one pipeline and out of it through the other. The pipes are metal but long enough to have some flexibility. The pumps are mounted on motorized barges at the surface. They can maintain themselves in nearly constant positions against the wind and current."

The dark masses of five submersible ferries hovered at a low altitude above the flyport like giant sharks—sharks with red and green navigation lights instead of eyes. Scores of Tritons and dolphins were swimming in the space between scapelocks and ferries. Jothen was surprised at the true magnitude of the scene judged from the apparently diminutive size of the swimming shapes.

Periodically a scapelock opened and disgorged a flurry of bubbles in a glow of light, to be followed by an awkwardly swimming human figure wearing a mini-scuba mask. Immediately a Triton seized the swimmer and drew him rapidly upward toward a submersible. The lighted orifice of an airlock opened on the underside of the vessel's hull, the Triton thrust his passenger into the opening, waited until the airlock closed, and then swam down to his assigned scapelock.

A submersible freighter floated down from the upper darkness and came to rest at a level above the ferries. An oversize circular port gaped open in its belly, emitting a bluish light, and from it a scapelock descended at the end of a cable. A squad of Tritons converged on the scapelock, accompanied it during its descent to the airfield, and guided it to the center of a numbered square.

"We've been installing scapelocks since twenty-one hours last night," Storm said, not without pride. "There are fifty scapelocks in this load. We can install a scapelock and have it operating in twenty minutes and hope to cut it to fifteen. We have slightly less than one hundred operating, but the evacuation is still too slow. According to the latest report, fifteen thousand two hundred people have been taken out."

Jothen did some rapid mental arithmetic. "But—at that rate it will take over one hundred days to evacuate everyone."

"True," Storm said. "But the rate will increase as more scapelocks go into operation and as the teamwork improves. But we don't plan to rely on scapelocks alone. We're rushing construction of a larger model that a freighter can lock onto with its cargo airlock. Then we can deliver provisions directly into the Barrier-hilthon on a conveyor and take on a steady flow of passengers at the same time, through the same airlock, with a mobile escalator."

"Provisions. That would be a problem," Jothen said. "How much does the hotel have on hand?"

"Not enough. Routinely they carry a two days' supply. They're rationing what they have."

"I take it that the bulk food containers are too big to go through a scapelock?"

"Correct."

"Why not put the Barrier-hilthon on a ninety percent

liquid diet? Pump it in. Through a pipeline. Soups. Purees. Low viscosity pastes. It will be faster than unloading package goods. Then the other provisions will stretch further."

"Of course!" Storm exclaimed. "We have all the heavy-duty plastic pipe that we need, at Lizard Island. We were laying an underwater pipeline when the Barrier-hilthon sank."

"An underwater pipeline? For what?" asked Kim.

"It's a Deep Water Safari project. Its object is to pump oxygenated water to a pilot-scale slime culture at the five-hundred-fathom level. We transferred the Safari people down here as soon as we heard that the Barrier-hilthon had gone under."

Hastily explaining the Deep Water Safari and the slime culture project to Kim and Jothen, Storm called Lizard Island and gave orders for the food pipeline.

"We must move along," he added. "I have some inspections to make, and you've seen everything here that—no! You haven't! One more thing. See that flashing light?"

A blue-green light was blinking rapidly at the summit of one of the scapelocks.

"What does that mean?" Kim asked.

"It means that whatever comes out is to be given special care and attention," Storm said. "We'll cruise along until we're closer to it."

The scapelock was near the edge of the airfield. Storm halted the *Sea Dart* so that they were within fifty or sixty feet of the winking light. Three dolphins and a Triton were circling around it.

The hatch of the airlock swung open, releasing the usual cloud of bubbles. A transparent sphere, ribbed with a grid of reinforcing rods, began to float out of the airlock. A miniature blinking glow-panel illuminated the interior of the sphere.

"It looks like one of the airfield light globes," Kim said.

"It's one of the same type, but with most of the glow lining removed, and a heater and other modifications added."

The sphere was enclosed in a net bag with a line attached. A dolphin darted in, seized the line in its mouth, and soared toward the nearest submersible, the sphere floating above it like a balloon.

Inside the sphere, stirring restlessly in a nest of white silicose, was a small red, wrinkled baby.

"Well!" Kim said. "How did *that* happen to be in the Barrier-hilthon? It looks as if it were born yesterday."

"It may have been," agreed Storm. "Or an hour or two ago. I understand that the maternity ward had over fifty of them when the hotel sank."

"What *were* the parents thinking of? They must have known. . . . Why didn't they stay home?"

"When one makes a reservation at the Barrier-hilthon three or four years in advance, one doesn't stay home," Storm said. "One goes ahead with one's vacation and has the baby at the Barrier-hilthon. It gives the parents something to boast about. The child also, when it's older.

"Now who wants to go where? I'm about to make an inspection tour of the operation inside the Barrier-hilthon. Would either or both of you care to accompany me?"

Jothen spoke quickly. "I would."

Kim shuddered. "Not I. I've seen enough of this gloomy underwater world. I'd rather go to Seashore Reef and watch the surf."

A call via aquaphone to the Barrier-hilthon enabled Storm to locate another Triton who agreed to convey Kim to the reef in the *Sea Dart*. Jothen felt that he ought to go with her; but thus far he had no reason to suppose sticking by her would advance his cause any further than would parting from her for a while—and the opportunity before him now was one that would never be repeated.

Jothen experienced his first miniscuba transfer when he accompanied Storm into the Barrier-hilthon by way of the scapelock on the roof of the flyport control tower. Two recorded messages were awaiting Storm at his temporary office in the hotel. One was from Maintenance Supervision, with the information that repairs to the hull had reached a stage that permitted the opening of one of the flooded sectors, Number Seven in Level Ten. The other message, from the Council of Monitors, stated:

"All computer malfunctions have been traced. Total number, seven, four of them in the Master Computer. Examination of the effected modules show that the cause was the same in every case—a short circuit caused by a small insect lying across two or more segments of the printed circuits. All were either dead or moribund when found. A specimen is being forwarded to your message-receiving station. Still others have been found in the ventilation ducts. Presumably they were distributed through the hotel by this means. Their source is unknown."

The specimen was embedded in a square of clear plastic. It was a small, bristly, silvery-white creature less than half an inch long.

"Could things like *this* sink the Barrier-hilthon?" Jothen said incredulously.

"It would seem that they did," Storm replied. "How did they come here? I wonder if the Barrier-hilthon has an entomologist among its guests?"

The word "entomologist" rang a bell in Jothen's mind. He said, "There might be one by the name of Dr. Kemal Matouf. Ask the Guest Register Computer if he's still here."

Storm was informed by the computer that Dr. Matouf had been assigned to Room Ninety-Seven, Block Six, Zone Eight, Floor Five, Sector Seven, Level Ten; that this section of the hotel contained rooms provided with basic laboratory facilities for the convenience of guests on scientific missions; and that after the sinking of the hotel Dr. Matouf had ceased to answer his vidphone.

"Sector Seven, Level Ten," said Storm. "That's the one that's been reopened. I'll make a survey of the situation there and we can look in on Dr. Matouf at the same time. Let's hope he's alive."

Jothen followed Storm through a maze of halls and chambers directly beneath the airfield. Here a team of Tritons was preparing a throng of hotel guests for their transit through the scapelocks. The air rang with the clamor of many voices. The Tritons were adjusting miniscubas, repeating last-minute instructions, allaying the fears of the frightened. From this focus of activity an automatic elevator took Jothen and Storm to Level Ten— a two-thousand-foot plunge.

The halls in Sector Seven were wet and permeated by a dank, fishy odor. Clean-up crews were clearing the halls of assorted fish, crabs, streamers of seaweed, jellyfish blobs, sand, and other marine miscellany. Many rooms were untenanted, with doors ajar; their occupants had been moved to vacated rooms on higher levels.

Jothen stepped warily around a small octopus that lay upon the floor, squirming feebly, just as Storm halted before a closed door bearing the number 10-7-5-8-6-97.

"Here we are," said Storm. "This is the doctor's room." He pulled on the door handle but the door was immovable. "I'll have to violate his privacy by unlocking his door and walking in. It's possible he may not be alive to resent it. An imperfect weld, a ruptured service conduit, and the sea would have flooded his room in an instant."

This did not cheer Jothen much. Without any hesitation, however, Storm unlocked the watertight door and pulled it open, revealing a brightly lit and incredibly cluttered room. A swarthy, heavy-set man looked up from the trace on the ribbon of paper issuing from the infrared spectrophotometer clamped to a built-in worktable beside him. His face expressed angry astonishment.

"Is it your customary behavior to burst into the rooms of others, uninvited?" he demanded.

"By no means," Storm said. "Are you Dr. Matouf?"

"Of course I'm Dr. Matouf! Who are you?"

"My name is Storm. I'm supervising the Barrier-hilthon rescue operation under Dr. Sumter of Submarine Products. It's been impossible to get a response from you for many hours, although repeated calls were made by phone. It was suspected that you might be dead."

"You received no response because I disconnected the phone. Some prankster annoyed me with incessant calls about the hotel sinking. Obviously it can't sink when it's already on the bottom."

"It floated free and then sank," Storm said patiently. "It rolled badly a few times. Didn't you notice that?"

"There was an earthquake. I noticed that. They're not uncommon in this part of the world. The spectrophotometer is securely mounted and suffered no damage, so I saw no reason to be alarmed."

"If you doubt that the hotel sank, just look into the hall," Jothen suggested. "There's an octopus with arms a foot long just outside of your door."

The doctor's only response was a look of scornful disbelief.

Storm held out the plastic square containing the specimen. "Several of these creatures got into the computers and caused short circuits. Then all the trouble happened. Do you know anything about it?"

"Certainly I do. It's a silverfish, *Lepisma saccharina,*

one of the commonest species of *Thysanura*. I have two cultures of them here, as well as several other species. I'm making a study of the blood proteins of the entire order."

Further questioning revealed that three cultures of *saccharina* had been sent to Dr. Matouf by a North American collaborator; and during Dr. Matouf's recent absence the temporary custodian of the cultures had spilled the contents of a breeding jar. Since then the doctor's room had been inhabited by an indefinite number of roving silverfish.

Leaving Dr. Matouf's room, they discovered that the octopus had shifted its position and was now directly in the doorway. Storm bent over, picked it up by the tip of one tentacle, regarded the writhing mass thoughtfully, and tossed it into the hall. Jothen glanced back at Dr. Matouf. He was sitting in a state of complete immobility, wide-eyed, with his eyebrows at maximum elevation.

Farther on in Sector Seven they discovered an emergency clinic set up in a suite of connecting rooms. To Jothen's surprise it was staffed entirely by Tritons. It had not occurred to him that the Tritons would have their own physicians and surgeons. A steady stream of casualties flowed in for treatment. Another stream flowed out, to be transported to the Barrier-hilthon hospital in the upper levels.

"Does the hospital have room for all of them?" Jothen asked.

"No—by now it's jammed. Cases with minor injuries go out through the scapelocks like everyone else. Fortunately they're the majority. The cases who can't go through a scapelock with safety are kept here. They'll have to wait until we have our lock-on two-way cargo airlock in operation. Then they can be put aboard a freighter."

"What do you do with the dead?"

"The dead can wait," Storm said, shrugging. "They're in the morgue under refrigeration."

Storm's office computer had recorded two more messages for him when he and Jothen returned to Level Ten. One message was an Evacuation Progress Report:

"One hundred five scapelocks in operation. Rate of transfer of evacuees, six hundred thirty per hour, fifteen thousand one hundred twenty per day. With maximum number of five hundred scapelocks rate will be sixty thousand per day. The lock-on cargo-lock will add an estimated three thousand per day."

Storm rubbed his chin thoughtfully. "Still not enough. At that rate it will take about four weeks to get everyone out. We'll need more lock-on cargo-locks."

The second message was from the sewage processing plant:

"How soon will movement of outbound cargo be feasible? We are storing compressed blocks of processed sewage solids in vacated rooms and halls immediately above us. Storage problem not yet critical but suggest early removal to mainland fertilizer plant for esthetic reasons."

"How did they dispose of the processed solids under normal conditions?" Jothen said.

"A special freighter came every day and removed the accumulation."

"Isn't there some provision for discharging sewage into the sea in an emergency?"

"No. The designers of the Barrier-hilthon didn't foresee this kind of an emergency, any more than they foresaw that a day would come when the hotel would have to ration its food supply . . . and speaking of food, you must be famished. I'm keeping my promise that I would not be an ideal host. I can offer you two choices—eat here in the hotel, in which case you'll receive a variety but in small quantity, or I can get someone to take you to our home where you may help yourself to our autoserver and have both plenty and diversity."

"I'll wait a little longer and have the plenty and diversity," Jothen decided.

He made the short passage to Seahorse Reef on a hover-craft that was en route from the snorkel barges to Lizard Island. Darkness had fallen, the sky had cleared, and the brilliance of a full moon flooded sky and sea. The outer reef was a low, dark, irregular wall athwart their course. An endless succession of rollers marched out of the northeast, moonlight glistening on their rounded contours. The rollers struck the reef at an oblique angle, creating a parade of ghostly white spume geysers that traveled along the reef from north to south. Seaward, the flashes of rocket launchings on Osprey Reef, below the horizon, flared and died like heat lightning. Lizard Island, the Triton industrial center, lay westward, ablaze with lights on the horizon of the lagoon behind the barrier.

The hovercraft deposited Jothen on Seahorse Reef and churned away across the moonlight water, riding above a misty cloud of spray hurled into the air by the downblast of its rotors. The sound of its passage receded, became a pulsing hum, and ceased. Seahorse Reef was enveloped by a hushed, moonlit serenity—accented but not disturbed by the incessant march of spouting surf fountains that rushed along the coral ramparts of the barrier with a rhythmic soothing sound. Jothen felt that he had never seen such a luminous expanse of sea, such an immense arch of sky, such a host of brilliant stars, or such a radiant moon.

He spotted Storm's house about one hundred yards distant on the inner shore of the islet. It would have seemed no more than a rounded hummock of coral if it had not been for a lighted oval window and—on its summit—a rotating beacon that flashed alternately green and white. Sea shells crunched under his feet as he walked toward it over the sparkling coral sand. He became aware of a murmur of voices and an occasional burst of laughter.

As he drew near the house Jothen trod noiselessly on a dense, deep-piled, mossy growth that covered a broad area of sand and crept up the house walls. He wondered at its presence in this unpropitious environment of sand and salt air. A tectogenetic variant, perhaps? He rounded a moss-covered corner of the dwelling and discovered Kim and a Triton girl seated on a small flat-topped peninsula of coral that extended into the lagoon like a jetty. A dolphin's head was bobbing up and down in the water, uttering squeaks and chirps.

"Hello there!" Jothen called.

"Oh, there you are—finally!" Kim said. "Jothen, this is Storm's daughter, Ruvani. Ruvani, meet Jothen."

The dolphin whistled sharply.

"You forgot someone," Ruvani said. "Jothen, meet Molo."

"My pleasure," Jothen said. "That takes care of the formalities. I'm glad to see you've not been all alone, Kim."

"I've been here only a short time," said Ruvani, "but Kim has not been alone."

"Molo was here when I arrived and I've had visitors all afternoon," Kim explained. "Tritons from all up and down the nearer parts of the reef—mostly children—and I don't know how many dolphins. Everybody knew we were coming."

"I have two days' leave of absence from my work," Ruvani added. "We'll do some scuba exploring among the nearby reefs, if you like. I'll provide the gill-scuba rigs. Both of you can swim, I hope."

"I've never used scuba," said Kim, "but I never miss an opportunity to swim in the lakes in the Bio Preserve at Starved Rock."

Jothen said, "I think that I can qualify. I've used scuba when making inspections of dams and reservoirs and so on."

"Then we'll begin tomorrow," Ruvani said. "There's an old wreck just inside of Cormorant Pass that you might like to visit. It appears to have been a small cruiser for six people. You may find a few souvenirs on the bottom."

"Fine," Jothen said. "But I haven't eaten since we first hit Osprey Reef. Do you think maybe we could have lunch first?"

The sea sparkled under the midmorning sun as Kim, Ruvani, and Jothen stood at the water's edge on a beach of coral sand and pebbles. Each was provided with a belt pouch and a flattened bar of metal, curved at one end, for digging and probing. Kim and Jothen wore diving masks and were provided with a gill-scuba backpack. The gill-scuba consisted of artificial gills, the gill pump, the propulsion pump, and the necessary batteries. The twin propellent water-jet nozzles, mounted on the belt at either side, could swivel through 180 degrees in three planes. A control box attached to the front of the belt regulated gill flow, jet flow, and jet direction.

"When we first go in," Ruvani said, "we'll cruise around just below the surface for a while until you get the feel of the controls. Then we'll go deeper. Watch the depth gauge on your wrist. Don't go below six fathoms. We may go deeper tomorrow. Above all, we must stay close together. There are scores of reef-dwelling creatures with venomous spines or sharp teeth or sting cells and some of them blend almost invisibly with their surroundings. I'll point out the untouchables- with the thumbs-down signal. If I open and close my thumb and forefinger like a biting mouth it means barracuda. A big mouth made with both hands means shark. When we come to the wreck don't go inside. Several moray eels live there, and a moray eel has a nasty temper and a wicked set of teeth. If you want to speak to each other put your masks close together."

"Is there a signal for squid or octopus?" Kim inquired apprehensively.

"Yes. I'd hold up eight or ten fingers, as the case might be, but they're no cause for concern. They're retiring creatures, and there are nothing but small ones living around the reef. The big ones are far out and down in the Dark Water. Shall we go now?"

Jothen felt no sensation of wetness after he submerged. He was gliding through a pastel green atmosphere filled with the twinkling play of greenish sunbeams refracted through surface waves and ripples. He could not see the sky; the underside of the surface was an agitated silver-green mirror. In the distance the green atmosphere became a bluish-green mistiness. His exhalations escaped from the air vent with a twittering sound. He looked beneath him and felt that he was floating above a garden filled with the flowers of another planet. Whenever his shadow passed over the "flowers" many of them contracted into tight knobs or flicked into burrows in the sand. There were fan-shaped growths, varicolored domes of coral, sponges shaped like cups and vases, rippling meadows of algae, and everywhere multitudes of fishes as colorful as butterflies and hummingbirds.

Kim steered herself close to him, touched his arm, and pointed over her shoulder. He veered to one side, looked back, and saw that they were leading a long retinue of fish displaying all the colors of the spectrum. At a lower level, Molo and three other dolphins had added themselves to the convoy.

The bottom sloped gradually into deeper water and then dropped abruptly into the Dark Water. Just below the brink of the cliff lay a broad ledge covered by a forest of massive, branched coral. The branches were dappled dark green and maroon by lichen-like growths and studded with sea anemones and small clams; their tips were flattened like the tips of caribou antlers.

Ruvani signaled Jothen and Kim, in pantomime, to shut off their propellent jets and swim downward. A few strokes placed them on the same level as the coral grove and revealed a narrow avenue leading into it under the overarching stony branches. They swam slowly into this corridor, surrounded by the swarm of inquisitive fish. The dolphins remained behind, circling in the open water.

After a couple of turns the corridor came to a dead end blocked by the hull of the wreck—a sloping wall pierced by a porthole and encrusted with clams and barnacles. Ruvani probed the sandy bottom and brought to light a small, elongated mass of lime. She knocked off part of the crust and partially uncovered a blackened table fork.

Kim and Jothen began to probe the sand, occasionally waving their arms to disperse the fish that clustered about them. Kim had just uncovered a rectangular lime-coated object when, in an instant, the fish fled into the coral grove and vanished. The dolphins became audible, uttering a chorus of agitated clicks.

Kim brought her mask close to Jothen's and asked, "What happened?"

Jothen pointed at Ruvani, who was pointing upward with one hand and making the barracuda signal with the other. He looked up through the interstices of the rugged coral branches and beheld a long, lean fish shape gliding overhead. Then another, and another. Then several more in close formation. Actually they were five or six feet long, but Jothen's estimate—magnified by alarm—multiplied their length by two.

After a few moments the dolphins' clicking ceased. The bevy of fish returned one by one. Ruvani cautiously retraced their course through the corridor of coral, followed by Kim and Jothen. When they arrived at the exit they saw nothing but the twinkling green sunbeams, the four dolphins circling, and the cliff below them slanting down into a mystery of blue shadow.

Then Jothen detected a vague stir and shimmer in the blue depths. The escort of fishes vanished again. The dolphins withdrew a short distance and seemed to wait expectantly. The glimmering motion in the depths rose upward with an eddying motion and resolved itself into a school of barracudas. Jothen estimated their number at five hundred. Ruvani later maintained that there were not more than one hundred and fifty, but Kim forever after declared that she saw one thousand.

The barracudas arranged themselves in a compact school at the same level as the three watchers floating in the entrance to the coral arcade. Then they began an exhibition of precision swimming in formation. The barracudas patrolled back and forth, back and forth, perfectly maintaining their spacing in three dimensions. It seemed to Jothen that even their tails and fins moved in unison. They swam to the left, then each fish pivoted and did an about-face as if in response to a silent command, and swam to the right. Then about-face again and they passed in review to the left. At each pass they drew a little closer. It seemed to Jothen that the maneuver was purposeful and deadly, a deliberate and sadistic prolongation of trial by terror. He fancied that as the quasi-reptilian predatory shapes glided past, a host of cold, appraising eyes was cocked at Kim, Ruvani, and himself, and that each barracuda was thinking, "Will these three be enough for all of us?"

Then he became aware that Ruvani had left them and was swimming directly toward the barracudas. He heard Kim shriek inside her mask.

With a rapid movement, Ruvani plunged her right hand into her belt pouch and withdrew it, grasping a snub-nosed gun. She leveled it at the barracudas and ejected a stream of white fluid that dispersed into a milky cloud and enveloped part of the barracuda phalanx. Those that received the blast of toxicant began to quiver and writhe, and finally floated to the surface, belly upward. The remainder of the barracudas broke formation and fled in all directions.

After this encounter, both Kim and Jothen felt that they had had enough of exploration for one day and were guided by Ruvani via the shortest possible route to the house on Seahorse Reef.

Here they examined the rectangular object that Kim had found. After chipping away the incrustation of lime, a small, square slab of glass was exposed. From a shallow circular depression in the slab four channels extended to the corners of the square. Since none of them had the slightest idea of its intended use Kim dialed the library computer at the Canberra Historical Museum with a request for identification. The object was presented to the vidscanner at various angles. The library computer informed them that the artifact was an ashtray from the twentieth or twenty-first century. This was followed by a condensed discourse on the ancient ritual of smoking and the use of the ashtray.

"Imagine! An ashtray eight hundred years old!" Kim exclaimed delightedly. "What a conversation piece! Now I can show it to all my friends and overwhelm them with my erudition."

"Perhaps we may find something even better tomorrow," Ruvani said. "We won't go back to the same place. We'll explore along the inner side of Ribbon Reef. But after tomorrow I must go back to work and you'll be on your own part of the time. Probably you'll have visitors who will be happy to guide you."

"Triton children, I suspect," said Kim. "I talked to dozens of them yesterday. Mostly they wanted to know what it's like to live among wild Drylander animals in a Biological Preserve. Which reminds me—is it safe for children to be roaming around the reef by themselves?"

"They travel in schools, like fish," replied Ruvani. "Each one carries a toxigun and an electric shark-prod. The family dolphins always go with them and chase them home if they try to go into danger."

During the remainder of their vacation Kim and Jothen were the sole residents of Seahorse Reef most of the time. They had visitors, as Ruvani and Kim had predicted. Triton children and an occasional adult came every day. Storm twice visited them briefly. They saw Ruvani's mother once; she was supervising the task of reuniting dispersed families at the mainland receiving center for Barrier-hilthon evacuees. Ruvani came and went at irregular hours, dividing her time between classes in dolphin pathology and serving as an aide at a dolphin clinic.

One evening, while pondering the selections offered by the autoserver, Kim suddenly demanded, "Jo, how long have we been here?"

"About ten days, I'd say," Jothen said after some reflection.

"And how often have we listened to a newscast?"

"Good grief! Not once! We might as well be living on Pluto. It's time that we re-established contact with the world. Turn on the video."

Kim twisted the switch and a face appeared on the screen.

"Surprise!" said Kim. "A Triton newscaster."

"Don't you recognize him? It's Storm."

Storm's newscast had been picked up in mid-sentence:

". . . at the rate of eighty-five thousand per day. The latest tabulation shows that we have evacuated five hundred seventy-five thousand people or more than twenty-five percent of the total occupancy. If the present rate were continued about seventeen days would be needed to complete the operation. But the rate will increase from day to day and we estimate that only twelve more days will be needed for complete evacuation.

"Repairs to the hull are now complete and all previously flooded sectors are accessible. All casualties have been transferred to the mainland. Solid food is still being rationed, but Project Quickflow has alleviated the situation.

"Now comes a question for the future: What shall be done with the Barrier-hilthon? It could be refloated, but it would be difficult to return it to its former location. Submarine Products has suggested, and Transcorp has concurred, that it is inadvisable to build a new Barrier-hilthon identical with the old one. Few people would feel safe, in view of what has happened, in another hotel resting on a foundation of mud. The new Barrier-hilthon will be lens-shaped, partly above and parly under water, and supported on cylindrical columns that will penetrate the bottom ooze to bedrock. Construction of the columns will involve working at depths of more than three hundred fathoms, but will offer no insuperable difficulties, since we shall employ the Deep Water Safari technique.

"Much of the equipment in the old hotel could be transferred to the new one, but this is still under—"

Here the telecast was interrupted by telephone chimes.

Kim addressed the vidphone. "Kim Wernicke here. Proceed."

"This is Biond Smith. Is Jo Kent available?"

"Right here."

"Hello, Biond," Jothen said. "What's up?"

"Hello, Jo." Biond sounded distracted; indeed, almost desperate. "I've been chasing you for days. Listen, I'm sorry to interrupt your idyll, but—well, I'm afraid I'm going to have to order you home."

"What's the matter?"

"What's the matter?" Biond said with a bark of mirthless laughter. "What would be the matter when I need you? We're going to have a disaster, what else?"

"Listen," Jothen said. "Calm down a minute, Biond. If you mean the sinking of the Barrier-hilthon, we've already *had* that. I've been right here all the time."

"No, I don't mean that," Biond said. "Has somebody sunk the Barrier-hilthon? Oh—I see the report here. No, Jothen, this is a *big* one. Get back here fast. I don't know what earthly good you can do, or anybody can do—but get back anyhow."

"But what is it, Biond? Can't you say?"

"It's the end of the goddamn world. Will you kindly stop arguing and come home?"

The connection broke. Kim and Jothen looked at each other. There seemed to be nothing to say.

## BOOK TWO

### 6  Wreck Reef

By 2794 Dorthy Sumter had been head of Submarine
Products Corporation for nearly three years, but today
more than ever she was convinced that Prime Center was
either slighting her or ignoring her outright. Probably
it wasn't personal; it was simply that Prime Center still
thought of SPC as a mere junior partner in the job of
feeding the insatiable billions of the world.

Whatever the reasons, her attempts to reach Prime
Center heads by vidphone were being frustrated by
their office computers, which told her with mindless
politeness that the person called was not available
(which was probably sometimes true) but that a conference could be arranged for later. The time for one
of those conferences was now almost upon her; she
was waiting determinedly for it in her office at SPC's
Pacific regional headquarters.

The office was on the Great Barrier Reef in the Tritons' Lizard Island industrial complex. It was a circular
room at the summit of a tower, enclosed by a cylindrical wall of glastic—a wrap-around, panoramic picture
window commanding a magnificent view of part of the
Australian coast and the reef, whose labyrinth of shoals

and minor reefs lay exposed and glistening at low tide. Eastward, beyond the coral sea wall, lay the crinkled blue expanse of the Pacific, stippled with whitecaps.

On either side of Dorthy sat Storm and Tioru. Both were a head taller than Dorthy; their size and darkness contrasted strikingly with her slender blondness. Her skin was the type that resists the sun; it had tanned only to a light golden brown, but had brought forth innumerable small freckles. Her hair, upswept on either side into two massive rolls, made the Tritons look balder than ever. But they were not looking at each other, but at the clock.

"In a few minutes we should hear from Chen U," Tioru said.

"Or his office computer," Dorthy said grimly.

He touched her briefly, reassuringly. It was against office etiquette—to say the least of the matter—but Dorthy no longer cared. During the Barrier-hilthon rescue operation, their formal relation—corporation chief and deputy—had grown into a close, though unspoken, comradeship. To Dorthy's initial dismay, she knew that it wasn't going to stop there—and worse, that she didn't want it to stop.

Reason, as usual, was all against it. Of course there had been Triton-Drylander liaisons in the past; and, of course, usually they had been miserable. Many Drylanders still feared and despised Tritons, and their hybrids. As she watched the progress of the sweep second hand, Tioru's presence and touch were both comforting and disquieting, and her thoughts were a queer and chaotic mixture.

Can I stay with Tioru? How can we manage it? There are so many good reasons against it . . . I know them all. . . . Our worlds are different . . . love is a hazard to navigation. . . . But how can I tell him—and do they really matter. . . . I must think of something else for a minute. I'll never be any good at this job. . . . Why hasn't SPC been notified about this catastrophe of Biond's? All the other corporations have been told. . . . What was that about the new slime culture? Off Wreck Reef—Strain C-7. Something about bits of it separating and crawling away. What about the other cultures? . . . Please, Tioru, go away and help me think! . . . No, no, don't go . . . it doesn't matter . . .

The sweep hand pointed vertically up, the vidscreen glowed bluish-silver, and there was an outburst of electronic twittering. Chen U's delicately molded Mongolian features were suddenly before her.

"I regret that I couldn't talk to you before," he said gravely. "Nevertheless your message about the Deep Water Safari interested me greatly. But I hesitate to approve the experiment that you suggest, Dorthy. The hazards are too great."

"The sea is always hazardous."

"True. But as head of World Resources I have more to think about than the sea, and I have to be conservative. For instance, you yourself are a valuable resource which we wish to conserve. Otherwise we would never have named you to Prime Center."

Dorthy stared at Chen U's blank expression with renewed annoyance, but managed to swallow her frustration.

"I'm glad to hear I'm so highly regarded," she said. "But I'm not immortal. Sooner or later I'll have to be replaced, and even right now Storm and Tioru are both qualified to do it. So any threat to my personal safety is not critical."

"Nevertheless—"

"Besides, we're convinced that the hazards are minimal. We've checked the procedure from stem to stern and back again in the pressure tank, using chimpanzees that have been conditioned to tolerate gill-breathing gear. They came through it nicely."

"I am not conservative of chimpanzees," Chen U said. "But for a human being to go down five thousand feet in nothing but scuba gear—I know, the gill-rig will equalize the pressure in your body cells with that of the water, you'll take an enzyme injection against the oxygen-nitrogen toxicity, the Tritons will monitor you and have a decompression chamber handy—you see I really have read your memo. But it fails to answer one question. Why do *you* have to go, Dorthy?"

"I'll not ask another Drylander to do it before I do, that's all. Besides, if I'm able to go down a mile and stay there for a while—the enzyme effects last forty-eight hours—it will increase my usefulness to SPC tremendously, to say nothing of all the other Drylanders who are doing undersea work. Project Mile-Deep may be only the beginning!"

Chen U looked at the two Tritons. "Do you think it's safe?"

"Yes," Tioru said. "I had some misgivings at first, but we've been thorough. It's safe enough."

Storm nodded. Chen U sighed and tapped his fingertips together judiciously. Probably he'd heard rumors about Tioru and Dorthy. It could not have been kept a secret. And she knew that he regarded the Tritons as essentially human—which they were—and did not share the revulsion that many Drylanders would feel toward such a match. She had an impulse, quickly repressed, to add: *Besides, I'll feel that I'm a little nearer to being like a Triton.*

"You make it difficult for me to refuse," Chen U said at last. "But I'll have to talk to the rest of the Center. In the meantime, Dorthy, I beg of you, don't do any more diving of this kind—not even tank tests."

His image vanished from the screen, which glowed blankly for an instant, then went dark.

"Blast!" Dorthy said. "Delays, timidity, obstacles! How much longer do we have to wait?"

"Until," Storm said mildly, "we hear again from Chen U, no doubt."

The Barrier-hilthon, even sunk, was still Transcorp's property, but it was a white elephant on their hands, and Dorthy and SPC had a major plan for disposing of it. Dorthy had nevertheless been putting off calling Transcorp about it, because it would involve talking to Transcorp's chief, Marg't Splain, of whom she stood somewhat in awe. Dorthy had met Marg't only once, when she and Storm had attended the conference of Prime Center's officers just after her appointment as head of SPC. Marg't had impressed her as cold and aloof, and full of the condescension—in her case tinged with contempt—that Dorthy sensed in all of Prime Center's dealing with SPC.

And now, perhaps, Marg't would regard SPC with jealously as well, since the Tritons and SPC—not Transcorp—had engineered the rescue of the two million guests, plus hotel staff, from Transcorp's own foundered resort.

All the same, Marg't would welcome constructive suggestions on what to do with the hulk—and it might be a month, or even two, before a decision came through on Project Mile-Deep. At worst, Marg't could only hem and haw. Dorthy put the call through.

The whirling vortex with the pulsating red core on a pale green ground that was Prime Center's insignia faded at last, to be replaced by the statuesquely impassive visage of Marg't Splain, crowned with a towering coiffure whose contours seemed frozen under an icily glinting transparent sheath. Dorthy stilled a tiny quiver of panic, tilted her chin slightly, and said:

"Storm you have met before. This is Tioru, my second deputy."

"My pleasure," said Marg't. As she looked at Tioru, a corner of her mouth seemed to lift slightly, but she said only, "Is there something we can do for you?"

"Yes. I'd be pleased to have the ownership of the Barrier-hilthon transferred to SPC."

"That could be arranged. We've decided to salvage the fixtures and have the hull broken up for scrap. Your people should be just the ones to do it. Do you think you could handle the job?"

"Certainly," Dorthy said, with some sharpness. "But that isn't why we want it. We can use it as it is, with alterations."

"As a hotel? Come now."

"No, of course not. We could use it as a new home for our Pacific HQ, as a pilot plant for separating amino acids from our sea-bottom slime cultures, and as an oceanographic research station. We'll anchor the hull to bedrock with vitrolith columns sunk through the bottom ooze.

"Do you think you'll need that much space?"

"If not now, then later. We're expanding rapidly."

Marg't was silent for a moment. Then she said, "I can't give you an answer now. Biond Smith of Disaster Plans Board says he may want the place as a shelter for some of the evacuees from the asteroid impact zone."

"That would mean repairing it completely and pumping it out completely. There isn't that much time."

"Hmm. You're probably right. Well, I'll let you know how the Board votes."

"How soon will that be?"

"Not until this asteroid business is over. We're too busy hauling people out of the danger zone, or preparing to, to think of anything else right now. Sorry."

The screen darkened. Dorthy said grimly, "Blocked by an asteroid! Much more of this and I'll begin believing in astrology."

"That's not our only problem with the Barrier-hilthon," Storm added. "As usual, they seem to come in batches."

"For instance?" Tioru said.

"For one thing, about thirty-five hundred people who've decided they want to stay on at the hotel."

"What on Earth for?"

"They're originally from the asteroid impact zone," Dorthy said. "They feel that they might as well stay where they are as go home and then be transferred to a Disaster City. Transcorp and Disaster Plans are no happier about that than we are. When the asteroid strikes, there may be an underwater shock wave that may crack the hotel's hull. But the holdouts called a meeting and decided to take the risk. Only seventeen people got scared and left."

"And they're making a carnival of it," Storm added. "Down there at six hundred and fifty fathoms they can be as noisy as they please. We have to keep them fed and entertained, and out of the way of our people who are still trying to clean up and repair things. And of course the situation isn't static."

"In what way?" Dorthy said, her mind only half on what he was saying.

"They're having babies." She felt a sharp interior shock. "In the time since we rescued everybody who wanted to be taken off, eleven children have been born. When the holdouts leave the hotel, more of them will go out than went in."

By the time Dorthy had recovered her self-control, Storm was gone. It seemed to her that all his arrivals and departures were made when she wasn't looking. She could not recall a time when she had actually seen him enter or leave a room.

She rose from the console and walked slowly to the seaward part of the transparent wall. The tide was coming in and all the lagoons and channels among the ridges, boulders, and coral archipelagos of the reef were alive with swirling foam-flecked currents, white-crested rollers, and leaping jets of spume. Far away across this flashing, foaming turmoil she could see the small dark figures of a band of Triton children running along a sandbar, diving into the rollers, and reappearing on a little beach at the base of a jagged pinnacle of rock that the waves had sculptured into a natural Gothic arch. She regarded them pensively.

Tioru came up behind her and gently laid his arm across her shoulders.

"What are you thinking?" he said.

"About us."

"About children?"

"Yes."

There was a catch in her voice that was almost a sob. Then she burst out, "Oh, Tioru! What's the use of marriage if we can't have children? I think and I worry and I can't decide!"

"But we *can* have children. There have been Triton-Drylander marriages before and most of them had children."

"That isn't what I meant. I mean—we can't know what they'll be like!"

"One can form a rough idea of the probabilities. I've been investigating. During all the time since the beginning of the Tritons, there have been something more than two thousand Triton-Drylander children. Three of them were short-lived abnormalities, ten were stillborn. The rest were either normal Drylanders or Tritons, or intermediates. Mostly intermediates."

"Intermediates! Yes. They worry me as much as the monsters, I think. They're the In-Betweeners—between two worlds and part of neither. They live in a third world."

"That's only half true. The Drylanders frequently don't accept the In-Betweeners very well, but you can't bring that charge against the Tritons. To many a Drylander we're a weird, abnormal sort of folk ourselves, so we can be sympathetic toward the In-Betweeners. You should know a few. There are several right here on the reef."

"That's true."

"Do they look, talk, or act as if they were unhappy?"

"Well, no more than anyone else does occasionally— I guess."

"Then what's the problem?"

"You're driving me into a corner with logic, but I don't know! I don't know! What is it really like to be an In-Betweener? What do they think and feel when they wake up in the middle of the night?"

"I've known several In-Betweeners intimately enough to ask them how they felt about themselves," said Tioru. "All maintained that they'd rather remain half Triton and live on the reef than to be a Drylander, if they had the choice. I doubt that there's anything that would persuade them to live in a Drylander city. You grew up in Great London. You know what it's like."

Dorthy shuddered. "It spreads over half of England and has pushed out to sea on pillars and arches. It's a people reef. They're almost as sedentary as coral polyps. Most of them are unemployed and *like* it. Everybody sits in apartments watching 3-V, talking to friends on the vidphone, making love, eating Food Corporation meals out of the autoservers, and doing the prescribed daily exercises. If they fancy themselves as intellectuals they watch 3-V fiction from Bibtek Central. If they venture out into the city beyond their immediate neighborhood to visit friends in person it's a great adventure.

It takes them a week to make preparations and to work up courage to do it, and they talk about it for months afterward. The local customs vary from city to city, but the pattern's the same everywhere. The human race is slowly dying of dry rot."

"Then they're being surprisingly prolific while dying," said Tioru. "Those who have jobs are not dying of dry rot. You're not. The Tritons are not."

"*That* I'll have to admit. The Tritons are the only ones who know what it is to live freely and joyfully. They've escaped into the sea and they have it all to themselves—except for Drylanders like me who work for SPC."

Tioru looked at Dorthy quizzically. "You're a Drylander only by accident of birth," he said. "You've associated with Tritons for so long and lived in and around the sea for so long that you've become a sort of In-Betweener yourself. So why should you shrink from becoming the mother of In-Betweeners?"

"Because in spite of all that you've said, and in spite of everything that I tell myself, I still can't feel sure of anything. How could I be sure our children were really normal and happy? They could be haunted by all sorts of dark, inexpressible fears and sorrows. How could we know? And what right have we to sentence them to a lifetime in the sort of world that we're in?"

"Did you have secret fears when you were a child?"

"Yes."

"Why didn't you tell someone?"

"I couldn't. My fears were too elusive, and I was afraid of being laughed at. One of my fears was—how shall I start? Well, we lived deep down inside Great London, not in an Outside Wall apartment. Until I was six years old I had never seen the sky, or sunrise or sunset. I never went farther from home than the precinct school, three corridors away. Then one day they took my entire class to a children's hostel on the roof, where we could see the outside. I saw the daytime sky, clouds, the Forest, sunrise and sunset, the night sky, the stars, the moon, the Milky Way. There was a thunderstorm while we were there. I had seen it all before, on 3-V, but I thought that it was just a sort of make-believe. I could scarcely believe it. I kept thinking to myself, this is *real!* This is *real!* Then we had to go down inside Great London again and I felt that I might as well die. None of the other children seemed to care. Most of them were glad to go back.

"From then on I was afraid that I'd never see the outside again. I dreamed about it constantly, and I was sure that I'd live and die in the same apartment, a human blob, another polyp in the people reef.

"I was about fifteen years old when I was sent away to a Bio School in the Cornwall District of Great London, in the Land's End precinct. There was a promenade deck on the roof that ran along the rim of the city wall for miles, where the wall stands out into the sea like the prow of a ship. I went there whenever I could and watched the Atlantic in fog and sunshine, storm and calm, summer and winter. I knew, the first time that I saw it, that the ocean was my home, I never went back to the old apartment again.

"But if we have children, what can they do about their fears and sorrows? They'll be In-Betweeners. Where can they go? What can they do?"

Tioru turned Dorthy so that she faced him, placed a hand under her chin and lifted it so that she was looking directly into his eyes and said, "They can be a bridge."

The screen came alive again with the insignia of Prime Center. But this time the vortex of scarlet lines was spinning at dizzy speed, the central disk was blinking rapidly, and the display was accompanied by a clamor of chimes. The chimes ceased, and a deep bass synthetic voice, resoundingly authoritative, issued from the console. It was not unduly loud, but it conveyed the impression of tremendous size, as if a giant were speaking from the depths of a cavern.

It said, "This is the World Communications Coordinating Computer at Prime Center transmitting via the Restricted Beam Satellite Circuit. Urgent and Absolute Priority, to Dorthy Sumter, Head, Submarine Products Corporation. We are informed that the asteroid Flavia is on a collision course with the Earth. Efforts to alter Flavia's orbit have produced a slight deflection but not enough to prevent collision. Attempts to fragment the asteroid have been only partly successful. Therefore you are ordered to report at Prime Center for a Full Council conference within forty-eight hours after the date and hour appearing on the printed confirmatory message, which is now being transmitted by Restricted Beam Facsimile. The conference will determine what measures should be taken to prepare for the collision and to handle the disaster conditions that will prevail afterward. We have three weeks to prepare. Repeat—three weeks. End of message. Please acknowledge."

"Message acknowledged and recorded," said the voice of Dorthy's office computer, and the screen became dark.

"Well, thanks for nothing, Prime Center!" exclaimed Dorthy. "After everyone but SPC had been officially notified and after we've alerted Great Barrier and all the other Triton colonies around the world, we get a formal, official notice that a disaster's brewing!"

Tioru said, "Forty-eight hours. That's rather short notice."

"Regardless of the short notice there are two things that I'm going to take care of first," said Dorthy. "Number one, I'm going to fly out to Wreck Reef and find out about the trouble with that new strain of slime culture firsthand. Number two, in the same operation I'll go ahead with Project Mile-Deep and try to make it all the way in one dive."

"But you were going to do it gradually, and Chen U said—"

"He said no more tank tests. Very well, I'll stay out of the tank and use the Pacific Ocean instead."

"That's a quibble."

"So I'm a quibbler. But if and when I go to their Full Council conference, I want to confront them with an accomplished fact."

Wreck Reef is a lonely little outpost of Great Barrier Reef, about 170 miles east of its southern extremity. It is the summit of a precipitous, submerged mountain peak, a small, drowned plateau, elliptical in shape, with a tiny islet near either end—like the foci of the ellipse. On the easternmost of the two, Bird Islet, stood a cluster of low, domed, hurricaneproof structures anchored deep in the coral by reinforced vitrolith roots. They provided docks, living quarters, and laboratories for the employees of Submarine Products who tended the slime culture one mile offshore and a thousand feet down.

The training barge bearing Dorthy, Tioru, and a crew of Tritons was not built for speed, either horizontal or vertical. Basically it was a forty-foot-square self-propelled submersible raft. Mounted amidships was a spherical steel decompression chamber with multiple gill flanges flaring out from it. Under water the barge could rise, sink, or float suspended at almost constant depth. It had emerged from the atoll encircling Bird Islet and was plowing deliberately toward the rim of the sunken plateau where the bottom dropped off steeply into the depths.

"We've aroused the curiosity of a pair of dolphins," said Tioru, pointing. "Over there to starboard. They seem to be racing each other toward us."

"I think they're convoying something," said Dorthy. "Whatever it is, it's leaving a trail of bubbles between the dolphins. I don't know of anything that moves that fast, judging by its bubbles, except a water scooter."

Dorthy's surmise was quickly verified. The scooter surfaced and sped toward the barge, bouncing over the choppy waves and throwing sheets of spray on either side. Two people could be seen lying prone on the deck behind its transparent deflector. The little craft slowed, then was obscured as it glided alongside the barge, whose sides rose above it.

A young voice called, "We want to talk to you. Would you mind if we came aboard?"

Dorthy and Tioru exchanged questioning glances, and Dorthy said, "Come aboard, and welcome."

There was a murmur of voices, the rattle of a mooring ring, and a young boy scrambled on to the deck of the barge, reached down, and hauled up a Triton girl. Both were reddish-bronze in color and the boy was obviously a hybrid. He had ears as well as antennas, and the latter were slender unbranched tentacles about two feet long and in constant motion. They coiled, uncoiled, and quested quiveringly this way and that like the antennas of an insect. His pate was smooth and glistening, devoid of either hair or tubercles.

The Triton girl, like all her sex, appeared to have hair, but it was not hair in fact. It was a mass of sentient blue-black filaments that rippled and stirred with semi-independent life. Each filament was tipped with a bead-like organ, which, seen by daylight, resembled a minute pearl.

Both boy and girl wore utility clothing—as did Dorthy and her companions—of tough, fluorescent orange-yellow plastic as a protection against abrasive coral reefs and the spines and stings of the reef denizens. The Tritons wore shin guards, short boots, and armless, legless swimsuits. Dorthy wore insulated coveralls, since she did not have the Triton's immunity to the lower chilly waters. None of them wore flippers, since they did not intend to make exploratory trips away from the barge.

"Who are you? And aren't you a long way from home?" asked Dorthy.

The boy said, "I'm Mokimoki, but I'd rather you'd call me Squid. Squid has a special sound to it and Mokimoki doesn't. And it fits better. On account of my antennas. Everybody says that they're like squid arms. She's Limpet."

He pointed at the girl.

"Really I'm Numu," said the girl. "Squid calls me Limpet." Then with a touch of pride she added, "Squid has longer antennas than anybody on Great Barrier. You're Dorthy Sumter, aren't you? And you're Tioru."

"Yes, for both of us," said Dorthy. "Why do you want to talk to us?"

"We want to know if you and Tioru are going to get married," said Limpet eagerly.

For a moment Dorthy became rigid, then she glanced at Tioru, who rubbed his chin and shook his head in bafflement. Dorthy made a helpless gesture and said, "It hasn't been decided."

"Well, you *should* decide," said Limpet firmly. "You really should. You worry me."

"Oh, let's talk about something else!" said Squid. "That isn't what *I* came to ask."

Dorthy felt a wave of apprehension. She drew a deep breath and said faintly, "What *did* you come to ask?"

"I want to work for SPC. Can I?"

"What would you do?"

"I'd be an ocean-bottom explorer and lead a big Deep Water Safari."

"What would you look for?"

"Prehistoric Tritons."

"Prehistoric Tritons!"

"Yes," said Squid. "I think that millions of years ago there was another race of Drylanders and they all got civilized like now and invented Tritons. Then there was a big war and all the Drylanders were killed except one man and one woman and all the Tritons went down to the bottom of the ocean to get away from the radioactivity and they've been there ever since. So I'd like to go down and see if they're really there."

"Well!" said Dorthy. She paused, collected her thoughts, and continued, "I could never have imagined that so much brashness and imagination could be concentrated in only two people. Certainly both you and SPC can do something for each other. First ask your parents about working for SPC. Then go to Storm's office on Lizard Island. Anyone there can tell you where it is. Someone will talk to you. Tell them I sent you. I'll leave word."

Squid and Limpet uttered simultaneous whoops and dived over the side of the barge. Squid's face reappeared briefly. He said, "Thank you!" and disappeared again. Limpet could be heard saying, "Hurry! Let's go and tell the others!"

Then the water scooter, convoyed by the two dolphins, was rushing away from the barge, leaving a widening V-shaped wake of foam. It sank lower and lower until scooter and dolphins submerged in a foamy swirl.

For a few moments there was silence on the barge, broken only by the steady drone of its motors. Then Dorthy said, "After that shattering experience I can face Project Mile-Deep without a tremor. Let's get on with it."

But she was thinking, "How would I feel if Squid were my son? He's horribly tactless, but so was Limpet. I suppose they'll outgrow that. He's an attractive child nevertheless, and certainly not cowed or neurotic. I wonder if he's ever been away from Great Barrier and met an ordinary Drylander? Probably not, he doesn't seem a bit cautious of me."

The Triton helmsman brought the craft about so that it nosed into the current and adjusted speed until it compensated for the drift.

"Where are we now?" said Dorthy.

"About one hundred yards out from the drop-off at the rim of the reef," said the helmsman. "The center of the slime carpet should be straight down under us. The aquaphone operator in the dome says that his sonar indicates that we're almost vertically over him."

"I'm feeling the side effects of my detoxymoid shot," said Dorthy. "The sunlight's unnaturally brilliant—a white glare. The barge looks as if it were blanketed with snow. Help me with my gear."

The gill components of the deep-dive gear were larger than in the ordinary rig. They projected from her back like semi-circular wings. A dome-shaped helmet was placed over her head and connected to the gills. Molded in one piece with it was the face mask, which fitted snugly under her chin and included a built-in nosepiece containing the inhalator tubes that fitted into her nostrils. Telemetry sensors were attached, which would enable a Triton medical team on Bird Islet to monitor Dorthy's physical state during the dive.

She said, "As they say on 3-V, the moment of truth is here. Submerge."

Air began to escape slowly from the flotation tanks with a soft rumbling sound. Dorthy grasped the handrail in front of her as the deck sank under her feet. Water surged across the deck, rose to her knees, to her waist, to her neck, closed over her head. Now she was afloat in a greenly luminous world, gripping the hand-rail.

A gurgling curtain of bubbles like pulsating quick-silver spheres and ellipsoids rose all around the barge, then ceased. The barge was now slightly heavier than water and continued to sink slowly. The water was faintly cloudy and the escarpment of the reef, a shadowy dark green wall, was only dimly visible. Minute living specks and sparks swirled and darted in the turbulence above the sinking barge. A school of little fish flashed over the bow, a cloud of ruby-red tinsel flakes. Quivering wave-shadow lines swept across the deck. The green luminosity grew dimmer and dimmer, became bluish. The barge continued its descent with its lights out, keeping its distance from the reef by sonar.

Through the aquaphone contact transmitters behind her ears Dorthy heard a burst of beeps, whistles and chirps. This was the sea voice of the helmsman, originating in the electrical impulses from the nerves and muscles of his vocal apparatus as they went through the motions of silent speech and were picked up by sensors attached to his throat and neck. With training, these sounds could be understood as readily as normal speech. Over the centuries this means of communication had developed into a language of considerable scope and versatility. It was necessary because the vocal organs of a submerged Triton are full of water and so cannot function as they do in air. The helmsman had announced the depth: "Two hundred feet."

"Hold it," said Dorthy, and her aquaphone throat mike transmitted her voice to the contact transmitters attached to the helmsman's antennas.

The hover screws began to whir softly and the barge hung suspended.

Another voice—a normal voice this time, not a sea voice—sounded in Dorthy's transmitters:

"This is Bird Islet. How do you feel? Your blood pressure is up a bit."

Dorthy said, "Excited. Wondering what it will be like deeper down. Not nervous, if that's what you're wondering."

The descent was resumed after a five-minute wait. Down two hundred feet, wait five minutes. Down another two hundred feet.

At eight hundred feet they were sinking through a wonderful, superlative, dark blue twilight. Dorthy had seen this before, from a bathyscaphe, but never like this. She felt that her eyeballs and her very brain were saturated by an overwhelming blueness that could never fade. Tioru and his fellow Tritons were surrealistic, faceless, limbless figures painted on a field of blue, their invisible heads crowned with domes of luminous silver tubercles and their swimsuits, boots, and shin guards revealed as shapes of orange-yellow phosphorescence.

An enormous form glowing with a flickering green light drifted into Dorthy's field of vision.

"Tioru!" she exclaimed. "Look! Dead ahead of us! The grandfather of all squids! It must be over a hundred feet long!"

"I don't see any squid," Tioru said. "You're not beginning to hallucinate, I hope."

"You're not looking in the right direction! It's right in front of us!"

She pointed, forgetting that in this dark blue realm, with all lights off, Tioru could not see her finger. Then she jerked back her hand with a startled cry. She had touched the squid. It was a tiny thing that had been floating at less than arm's length. Alarmed by her touch, the squidlet went rocketing off into the all-enveloping blue.

"There, I saw it," Tioru said. "It passed within a foot of me. I was looking for something big."

"How do you know it *wasn't* big?"

"I recognized the species. If I hadn't, I might have been fooled myself."

Dorthy felt a moment of humiliation. She wondered what he was thinking. Would little things like this keep happening all the time if they stayed together?"

A diffused glow lit up the water below the barge, revealing the rugged, almost vertical face of Wreck Reef's understructure astern of the craft.

"They've turned on the floodlights in the culture area," said the helmsman. "In about four minutes we'll be down to the shelf, one thousand and ten feet. . . . Someone's calling from the dome. Sounds excited. . . . What's that? You've *what*? . . . He says they've lost part of the culture!"

"How does one lose part of a four-acre slime culture?" Dorthy demanded of no one in particular.

She released her grip on the handrail and swam a few strokes beyond the barge, trailing the telemetry cable. Looking down, she saw the slime culture shelf— a natural terrace on the side of Wreck Reef Mountain, brightly lit by a circle of floodlights. The culture was a glistening dark gray carpet, with the dome (actually it was a four-legged sphere) standing on an elevation at the center of it. Two Tritons were swimming hastily toward the dome; one of them veered upward toward the barge. Dorthy could see that there was something wrong with the culture; it did look smaller than she remembered it.

The upward-swimming Triton spotted Dorthy and swam toward her, maintaining himself at her level when he was near her. He was wearing a sea-voice communicator—standard practice for Tritons underwater. As he was approaching, silhouetted against the diffuse glare of the floodlights, Dorthy recognized his swimming mannerisms and remembered his name.

"What's this about losing part of the culture, Neratino?" said Dorthy.

"It's true," Neratino said. "Little pieces of it have been breaking off around the edges and crawling away. But only a few minutes ago a huge piece—about forty thousand square feet, nearly a fourth of the whole culture—came loose, lifted up, and took off. It just went rippling away like a flying carpet. We tried to hold it, but we were left with lumps of slime in our hands."

"What have you been doing about it?"

"We managed to catch most of the little bits that crawled away and sent them up to the lab on Bird Islet. Some of them have been sent to Lizard Island and the Tecto Lab people there are doing a gene analysis to see what went wrong. We're keeping some specimens in aquariums down here and feeding them. They don't hunt food. They just collide with it. If they make contact with a fish they stick like glue and envelop the fish. The slime contracts into a ball for a while. When it crawls away there's nothing left but fishbones and the glob of slime is a little bigger. They'll take crabs, clams, sea anemones, sea jellies—anything. One of the lab men said that we have a Frankenslime to deal with."

"I guess we do," said Dorthy. "We'll have to kill the whole culture. The sea is full of enough hazards as it is. We don't want to add another."

"Check," said Neratino. "Kill slime culture strain C-7."

"But keep all the specimens that you have," said Dorthy. "And take another one—say one hundred pounds—from what still remains. This might be a clue to something useful. We'll have to hunt down the piece that got away. Send out a general warning. Do you know of a good slime killer?"

"Yes. Copper oxyquinolate is deadly to it. We have some in the dome. You'd better charge some of your jet guns with it in case you see the detached piece later in your dive."

"How can we get close enough to shoot it if we do?"

"It can't travel very fast. The barge can out-maneuver it. It won't attack. Just get above it and lower a piece of shark meat into it. We have some for our aquarium pets. When the slime forms a ball around the meat and starts to sink, that's your chance. Follow it and start shooting."

The barge hovered near the dome until the crew had received the promised shark meat and copper oxyquinolate. Then it glided above the slime culture to the edge of the shelf and continued its descent, paralleling the slope of Wreck Reef Mountain but standing off from it. The barge floodlights were turned on and Dorthy watched the crags and gullies of the declivity as they rose out of the blackness below and vanished into the blackness above, revealing a sparse population of dark red and brown and maroon sea growths, small scurrying crabs, and somberly colored fish.

Down two hundred feet and pause. Down another two hundred feet and pause, over and over. No sound save the humming drone of the barge motors.

Somewhere between the one thousand foot and the two thousand foot levels another broad shelf appeared. Dorthy said, "Lay to here for a while. Douse the lights and stop the motors. I want to look and listen."

The darkness closed in with almost the effect of a physical impact. After her eyes had adjusted themselves she saw that the blue had vanished and become violet, but it was a violet so deep and intense that it was almost black. Or was the violet an illusion? Was the depth pressure affecting her perceptions in some subtle manner? The luminous bodies of swimming creatures were like stars moving in a black-violet sky.

For a time she heard no sound save occasional clicks and snaps—crabs, perhaps, or shrimp. Then came a new sound. It was like the dying vibrations of a great bell after it has been struck, a faint deep-toned humming that swelled slowly, died away, then swelled again in a regular cycle.

The voice of the telemetry monitor cut in:

"Bird Islet here. Is something disturbing you? Your blood pressure and respiration indicate it."

"Probably because of a sound that I hear. A faint bell-like sound. Do you hear it?"

"No. We're not linked to your hydrophone circuit."

Tioru spoke. "I hear it but I can't tell you what it is. It's a minor mystery and there have been all sorts of speculations about it. One of them is that it's an amplified earth sound. The earth's always stirring and vibrating internally. Right now we're between the boundary surfaces of two salinity layers and they may form an enormous resonating chamber. Why does it bother you, Dorthy?"

"It . . . well, it makes me think of Big Ben."

"Big Ben? What's that?"

"A huge ancient bell back in Great London. It must be a thousand years old. Strictly speaking it isn't the original bell. It cracked several times during the centuries and was melted down and recast each time. It strikes the hours and the sound is piped all over Great London. Everybody has an almost religious feeling toward it. When I was a little girl, I thought Big Ben was a magic giant who had created the bell, and that he was still lurking in a wizard's cave under the city. And when I was worried because I believed I'd never see the outside, I thought that if I tried to run away and escape, Big Ben would know it, come after me and catch me, and take me back."

"Well, you'll hardly meet Big Ben down here."

"I can almost doubt that. I'm beginning to have an eerie, anything-can-happen feeling."

"This total darkness brings strange fancies sometimes, even to Tritons. Better turn the lights on again."

The barge continued its downward progress with the lights on. At thirty-three hundred feet a small, grayish-white object zigzagged down out of the upper darkness into the glare of the floodlights and was swallowed up by the lower darkness. Then two more twinkled down and vanished. Something grazed Dorthy's cheek and struck the metal deck of the barge with a sharp clink. She swam down to it, picked it up. It was a shark's tooth. Its size indicated that it had belonged to a good-sized shark. Then there was a rapid tattoo of clinks all over the barge, and sea-voice exclamation from the crew.

Someone cried, "It's raining sharks' teeth!"

Then came a hailstorm of small fish bones.

A frightening realization dawned upon Dorthy. She looked upward and saw, poised about thirty feet above, a circular, gently undulating canopy of dark gray material. It sagged in the center. At the moment its diameter was about twice the width of the barge, but it was gradually expanding horizontally in all directions.

"There's our flying carpet culture right over our heads," she called loudly with a quiver of repugnance in her voice. "It must have just finished digesting a shark. And a school of fish. Now it's flattening out again."

The helmsman said agitatedly, "It's following us down at the same rate that we're sinking. It keeps a constant distance. Neratino said that it doesn't hunt food."

"I don't think it's following us," Tioru said. "More likely it's being sucked down by the turbulence in the wake of our sinking. But we'd better move out and get over it. If it caught up with us, we might become its second course."

By the time this maneuver was completed the slime carpet had expanded into a disk almost three hundred feet in diameter and was leisurely rippling on an erratic course. The barge cautiously descended to within forty feet of the disk and the slab of shark meat was lowered on the end of a line. The slime disk adhered to the slab on contact, ceased its rippling motion, began to stream inward toward the meat, enveloped it, and finally concentrated itself into a roughly spherical mass about twenty feet in diameter. The mass began to sink slowly, agitated by slow, slow internal heavings and writhings that threw its surface into ever-changing convolutions and furrows.

The barge crew opened fire with their jet guns at a distance of ten feet. The guns expelled rapid bursts of long pencil-thin slugs of blue-green liquid. The slugs were ejected under such high pressure that they traversed the water with very little diffusion and penetrated the slime globe.

The globe convulsed. Short pseudopods as thick as a human torso were extruded and retracted. Fissures opened and closed like gasping mouths, emitting bubbles of gas. Pallid white blotches appeared, spread, and coalesced until the entire mass was a greenish, fish-belly white. Then disintegration began. Ropes and tattered white films separated from the sinking mass and themselves disintegrated into dissolving white strings. The partly digested chunk of shark meat fell out and dropped into the nether darkness. Soon only a tangle of white shreds remained, which in turn dissolved and vanished.

Dorthy covered her face mask with her hands and floated shuddering, anchored to the barge by the telemetry cable. She could still see the dying agonies of the slime ball, like the death of a brain.

"Are you all right?" the Bird Islet liaison monitor asked anxiously. "Do you wish to end the dive? What's going on?"

"I'll be all right in a moment. This is what happened," said Dorthy, and described the killing of the runaway culture.

The barge resumed its methodical descent. Thirty-eight hundred feet. Four thousand. Forty-two hundred. Forty-three . . .

"Five thousand!" cried the helmsman. "We did it!"

"Does the sonar show a level place where we can put down, not too far below?" asked Dorthy.

"There seems to be a ledge at about fifty-three hundred," said the helmsman. "I don't know how big it is."

"Let's go down and have a look. That will be just a bit more than a mile. I want to leave the barge and actually stand on the bottom, one mile down."

The words kept repeating themselves in her mind: "One mile. One mile down. One mile. One mile down."

The ledge that the helmsman had mentioned proved to be a triangular promontory jutting from the flank of Wreck Reef Mountain. Dorthy watched it as it emerged into the illumination of the floodlights.

The barge drifted down upon the promontory, bounced lightly, and came to rest. Dorthy swam over the edge of the barge, then downward, with her hands extended. When they contacted the promontory's surface she found it covered with a compact silt. She withdrew her hands and contemplated the two hand prints that she had made; then reversed her position and made two foot prints. She floated above the prints and gazed at them. Tioru swam down and floated beside her.

"In all the billions of years since the seas were formed," said Dorthy softly, "there never have been human hand or foot prints in the ooze this far down. This isn't at all like making a dive in a bathyscaphe. In a scaphe one's in a little world of one's own, a detached observer. Here I'm exposed, naked—the coveralls don't count—with tons upon tons of depth pressure bearing down upon me. But I don't actually feel it. It's as if I were a phantom. It's frightening. I hadn't expected this."

"Strange," Tioru said. "To me, the deeps are places of peace, serenity, beauty. Places for meditation."

"Another difference. How many other differences are there?" she thought. It's almost as if they really were another race. She said, "Douse the lights again. I want to see this as it looks to . . . to the fishes."

Again there was the sense of near physical impact as the blackness engulfed her; then the gradual emergence of the black-violet texture. Then she could see that the silt layer that covered the promontory, as well as the face of the cliff from which it projected, was clothed with the pastel blue glow of a bacterial film. As her vision grew more discriminating it became a dim tapestry of many tints—indigo, sapphire, violet, aquamarine. A swarm of yellow-green luminous dots drifted across it like languid fireflies. She had seen this bacterial glow before, during bathyscaphe dives, and had admired the delicate colors. But now she saw no beauty in it. It was alien and ghostly.

A small, mad-goblin thought whispered in her brain. "You're going to pieces. You're going to panic." "No," she told herself, "*no*. This is something I have to conquer. I'm scared because it's a totally new experience. I'll be all right. Go away."

But the goblin thought did not go away. The feeling of panic was like a quivering mass in the pit of her stomach. It was rising up into her throat.

She heard a sound, a sound as of ponderous footfalls far away . . . thud . . . thud . . . thud . . . thud . . .

"Tioru," she cried, and her voice was high and thin, quite unlike her own. "Do you hear that? Something walking! Something walking on the bottom of the sea! Listen, listen!"

"I do hear something," he said, with controlled gentleness. "The sound of my own pulse. Just as you hear yours. There's no other sound to distract you—that's why you notice it."

"It can't be that! It's too loud! It's something huge—coming toward us!"

She was horrified to find herself screaming inside her face mask. But she could not stop.

The mad-goblin thought whispered again. But the footfalls were louder. They were the steps of the terror of the deeps—the black behemoth that walks the ocean floor.

Thud-thud . . . thud-thud . . . the footfalls were more rapid now. In a whirl of terror she tried to remember something, something about a bell and a malevolent giant. She was trapped. There were thousands of feet and millions of tons of water over her head, a whole world of blackness that was pressing down to enfold and crush her.

That other voice was still screaming, "We'll never get back to the surface! We'll die down here! We'll never see the sky again! Never, never!"

She heard Tioru's sea voice. "Lights here! Give me a hand!" And then that was all.

Dorthy lay with her eyes closed. She no longer cared where she was. She was aware of a padded surface beneath her, the throbbing of a motor somewhere, two voices conversing quietly. Her diving gear had been removed, but she could feel the telemetry sensors still attached to her. Someone was firmly clasping her left hand.

She opened her eyes and looked up at a sea-green, domed ceiling with a luminous disk at the apex of the vault. Only then did she realize that she was in the decompression chamber on the barge.

Tioru's face bent over her, filled with tenderness and concern.

"What's the matter? Why am I here?"

"We thought it'd be better to revive you in here, rather than outside. We're on our way up. Another five hundred feet or so and we'll be at the surface."

To her amazement, she began to weep.

"Look at me, Tioru!" she sobbed. "I'm hopeless! I'm no good at anything! I can't even control my emotions. I was going to do so much—for us, for everybody— and I flubbed it!"

"No, love. You set out to make a one-mile dive, and you did. As far as we can tell, you're none the worse for it, except for a flash of panic. Naturally it overwhelmed you. Later on, we can start again and do it the way you first planned it, step by step."

"No! It won't work! Nothing will work! Oh, Tioru, don't you understand? Nothing at all!"

He only waited. After a while she said, more quietly, "I have to go to Prime Center and tell them. And I— I'm not coming back. I'm finished. Everything's finished."

"No, it's not," Tioru said. "I'm going with you."

"No, no!"

"Why not? I'm your deputy—and I love you."

And so it had at last been said. Sighing, Dorthy gave in. It was surprisingly easy.

## 7 A Torrent of Joneses

Biond Smith was nervous and distracted, and small wonder. As the story came out of him, by small fits and starts, it began to appear to Jothen that he did indeed have a real blockbuster on his hands.

"Or a planetbuster," Biond agreed. "This is going to be a fearful business, Jothen. I assure you I didn't call you back for nothing. Damn, I'd better tell you what I'm talking about."

"It wouldn't hurt," Jothen said, watching Biond worriedly.

"Well, it's like this. We are going to be hit by a meteor. One *hell* of a meteor—effective diameter about a mile."

"Is that big?"

"My God, Jothen! There's been nothing like it since the Little Moon hit northern Argentina, nearly seven millennia ago. Really we've been very lucky to have gotten away without a major hit for so long. It's going to fall in the Hudson's Bay area, and there will be nothing left of the Northwest after that. Nothing!"

"From a bolide only a mile across? Biond, I don't have any expertise in this area. What *do* we know about this thing?"

Biond picked up a stylus and began doodling nervously. "A fair question. The critter's name is Flavia, named after the wife of the astronomer who discovered it. It's not any ordinary rock, but an asteroid—one of those erratic little bodies like Eros that used to scare people green by coming within a few million miles of the Earth, and then vanishing again before anybody could work out its orbit. It's a granite tetrahedron, roughly, about eight miles in diameter along the short axis, about twelve miles measuring the other way. We guess that it may have been a crustal fragment of one of the asteroidal protoplanets—perhaps the one of which Ceres was probably a moon."

Biond threw the stylus down and stared belligerently at Jothen. "But not one word of this stuff does us any good. We might as well not know it at all."

"I'm not sure," Jothen said, with careful calmness. "You said that it's a mile across—and then, you said it's eight miles across, the short way. Which is it? Are you trying to break it up, Biond?"

"God knows we're trying to break it up," Biond said, with bitter energy. "We thought we might bomb it, but when we thought about what might happen when a radioactive cloud *three hundred* miles in diameter hit us, we gave up that idea. Instead, we have men drilling the rock and planting explosive charges in the holes, for a start—three of them killed already—in the hope of fragmenting it, spreading it out. And I think we can use lasers on one side of it, to boil off some of it and deflect it a little by vapor pressure.

"But when it hits, Jothen, when it hits, it's going to be about a mile in diameter all the same. And do you know what that means, Jothen? Do you *know* what's going to become of our history-long effort to accommodate all our people? It will all come to nothing, Jothen. Nothing."

"It'll be bad, I don't doubt that. But why that bad?"

"I have to exaggerate," Biond admitted, "otherwise I can't hope not to be surprised. Physically, only central Canada and the Great Lakes area are likely to suffer direct shock. But that means the destruction of about fifty moderate-sized cities and maybe ten large ones. I can see very little hope of saving the Twin Cities complex, for instance. Even though a lot of it will probably be left standing, communications and supplies are going to be knocked out for a long time. Sheer structural damage is only the beginning of the story. That's why I'm going to need your city right away, and all the other stand-by cities in the Middle West."

"Obviously," Jothen said. "You'll have to evacuate the Twin Cities, and so on."

"Oh yes, but that's only the beginning. We are also going to have to evacuate Chicago."

"Impossible!"

"My sentiments exactly," Biond said, "but there it is. So, what shape is your town in?"

"Ready and waiting." Then Jothen remembered. "No, wait a minute. The Jones Convention is still going on there—or should be, if nothing disbanded it ahead of schedule while I was in the Pacific."

"A relatively small family convention, I seem to recall your telling me," Biond said. "That is to our advantage."

"Yes, I think I can get them all out of there in no more than three weeks."

"One week," Biond said.

"Biond, that's impossible. Sure it's a small family— but there must be a million of them in Gitler for this convention."

"Get 'em out," Biond said stonily. "In one week. By the end of three weeks, I'll be started moving refugees from Chicago in. But I don't want any of the Joneses trampled in the rush, either. Let's go, Jothen. Our friend Flavia is on her way—and she won't wait!"


A torrent of faces poured down the penstock of Goring Boulevard, distorted with roars of almost religious joy, and capped with funny hats. From a glastic-clad overlook just under the roof of the street, Jothen tried to keep his mind on his flow meters, and failed miserably; he had never before seen so many people in his life, and he did not know whether to be fascinated or terrified.

The Jones Convention went by him regardless, like an avalanche. Plump boys plunking two-stringed kithera, wild-eyed old men charging through the air on super-charged autocrutches, fat, sterile women parading squeakily talking animal dolls with heads like babies, and twitchingly animated grotesque family totems of all kinds—many so tall that their idiot heads bumped along the roof of the boulevard—went by singing old synthetic songs in old forgotten keys, or clinging to clang-orous floats blazoned UP YOUR JONES! or MCDOBIE BRANCH FOREVER! and followed by complicated self-blowing kites and pennons in the shapes of crucifixes, germs, ances-tors, birds, insects, hobbits, appendixes, directives, auto-mobiles, clotheslines, codas, guardian angels, reprints, ice cubes, genealogies, horses, taxes, and other mytho-logical monsters.

"Funny, aren't they?" Alva McGee said, behind Jo-then's back.

"They scare me, Alva. How are we going to get rid of them? I've just been through something like this when the Barrier-hilthon was shipwrecked, but those people were sane. What are we going to do with all these mad-men?"

McGee looked shrewdly at Jothen, but had nothing more to say for the moment; and Jothen realized sud-denly that McGee was as big a puzzle to him as the Joneses. Finding the man assigned to him as an "ad-ministrative assistant" for the evacuation of the Joneses had been a surprise, and not entirely a welcome one, particularly after Jothen discovered that McGee's quali-fications for the job included the title of mayor but did *not* include any special knowledge of the water sys-tem or any of the rest of the fine structure of Gitler.

Apparently, the presence of McGee represented only some last-minute notion of Biond Smith's that the stand-by city's technical crew would need help with their paper work.

Even his title was baffling; no city had had a mayor, or been otherwise independent of the overriding ecology of the overridden world, for almost as many centuries as Jothen had fingers.

Whatever the answer to this puzzle, Jothen did not judge McGee capable of much help, and his specific technical ignorances simply added pedagogy to the press of Jothen's other duties. It would almost have been better to have been assigned a Triton.

"They're not as mad as all that," McGee said equably. "They're noisy, but why not? They're having a good time. These family conventions are the citizens' one big chance in a lifetime to cut loose and behave almost as antisocially as they could have every day, back in the Age of Waste."

Jothen groaned inwardly. McGee's occasional fits of history were already a cross to him.

"It amazes me that Prime Center allows them at all—the conventions, I mean."

"Therapy, my boy—therapy. Besides, they give Transcorp a golden opportunity to process vacationers in blocs of a million or more at once, instead of one at a time. All perfectly rational."

Jothen pointed to the dolls and banners. "*Those* are rational?"

"No, but they're helpful," McGee said. "If you know what to look for. All those things are just rags and tags of quasi-religious traditions—a kind of Jungian-Gravesian substrate, decorated with vague memories of lesser cults. They imply all sorts of beliefs, not all of them quite extinct—reincarnation, racial memory, ancestor worship, telepathy, historical fatalism, traditional supernaturalism, momism—"

"Whoa!" Jothen said desperately, quite unaware of the totem he was himself calling upon.

"But the Joneses don't know any of that. Lucky for us. If worse comes to worst, those things give us handles to manipulate them by."

"Good. Go manipulate them, Alva. I've got to check the water, the food, the power supplies from top to bottom, and help the rest of the city's operating crew make Gitler ready for occupancy. In the meantime, I want the Joneses gotten out, by any form of transportation you think convenient—the tubes would probably be best, but check Transcorp for advice. If you need any help, you can always call me. I'll be aloft. All clear?"

"As you command, effendi." McGee made an exaggerated bow and started to leave. Then he thought the better of it. He said:

"Jothen—have you ever heard of a ward heeler?"

"No. What is it? Another Jones totem?"

"Not precisely. See you later. I won't call unless I have to."

He slipped away, quietly for so tubby and talkative a man. Below, the torrent of faces poured along as noisily as ever. Jothen was relieved to be able to get away from them both.

Nevertheless, maybe McGee was going to have his uses after all. To do him justice, he had already eased Jothen's worries a little, by reminding the harried engineer that some moderately large proportion of the Joneses—perhaps as many as twenty-five percent—probably did not need to be sent home at all. As members of a chiefly North American clan, that many probably lived within the areas due to be affected by the arrival of Flavia; and there would be no sense in shipping them back there, because since their specialties (those of them who were employed) would no longer be needed at home, a lot of them would simply be exported right back to Gitler. It would take a little paper and computer work to identify this subgroup, but that was precisely the kind of thing that McGee was supposed to be good at. The idea simply hadn't occurred to Jothen.

It had occurred, however, to one Fongaváro Jones.

It was, in fact, the main reason why Fongaváro was at the moment hiding in one of the deepest service tunnels of Gitler, feeling like a hunted man. He was not exactly hunted, yet, though he was looking forward to it. Instead, he was stalking a Rest Stop, just for the practice, since again he did not expect that there would be anyone in it, yet.

Fongaváro was classified by UNOC as a communications system specialist, and hence, like Jothen, was one of those most fortunate of all citizens, a man with a job. But there the resemblance ended. He looked rather more like an orang-utan, a stocky, muscular man with long arms and large hands. In his native city—Tananarive, in Madagascar—he probably would have attracted no attention; but in these dim, empty corridors he was a startling, perhaps even a fearsome, figure.

Of this he was well aware. More—he was counting upon it.

If the usual Jones was as crazy as Jothen took them all to be—which was doubtful—then in this, too, Fongaváro was a specialist. A great part of his life had been spent in the labyrinthine service tunnels between the walls and under the floors of Tananarive, and he was thoroughly suited for it; in an earlier age he might have been a spelunker. Beyond the average UNOC citizen's natural mild case of agoraphobia, he actively enjoyed living at the bottom of a hole. The pleasure had been completely unconscious, simply because until very recently nothing had ever suggested any other way of living to him; he had been as adjusted as a mole.

Then had come the journey to the Jones Convention—his first venture outside his own city, his first sight of the whole blue void of the sky, his first projection into nothingness on a jet plane, his first direct encounter with the boundless expanses of the sea and of the World Forest. Until it happened he had thought of the trip only as a sort of longer, duller version of a tubeways jaunt from one Madagascan village to another. He had, of course, known that he would have to fly part of the way to Gitler, but he had never dreamed that it would be like *that*.

He spent the whole air trip falling, falling helplessly out of his chair, desperately nauseated, struggling not to look out the window, feeling stifled and trapped by his harness, fighting against the pills and injections they tried (successfully once or twice) to give him—and, above all, raging at how his own body, his own ignorance, his own gullibility, his own manhood had betrayed him.

The ordeal had been terrifying beyond belief—but worse than that, it had been humiliating . . . *totally* humiliating. He had no intention of ever facing it again.

The early recall of the Joneses startled him a little, but did not dismay him. He had already known precisely what he was going to do, as soon as he had found that there was no official place in Gitler for him (which he had also expected). It was simplicity itself to hole up in the service tunnels of Gitler, in a sector that had never been occupied by the Joneses or anyone else. The system was not identical with that of Tananarive, but the similarities were close enough for this purpose.

The Rest Stops, here as at home, were located at strategic points throughout the network, for the convenience of the maintenance staff when they were on tours of inspection. Except that they had no windows, the Stops differed little from the average man's apartment: eight rooms with complete living facilities, including autoservers, so that staffmen could remain on tour for days at a time without having to return to the home technie village under the flyport. In a mostly empty stand-by city, no keys to the Stops were needed.

As long as Fongaváro could stay clear of Gitler's own crew, in short, he had it made. He could go underground and stay there.

With the second general announcement, however—that Gitler was soon to be occupied by a still greater horde than the Joneses, this time of refugees—he was less pleased. As was usual procedure every day and around the clock in any working, occupied city, two- and three-man teams would now be fanning out through the tunnels to check the utilities, and the Rest Stops would be needed. From now on, Fongaváro knew, he would have a tough time remaining undiscovered.

All the same, he was never going to go back to Tananarive—not for Jothen Kent, not for UNOC, not for White Mother Jones herself. To prevent that, *any* alternative was thinkable.

The next Rest Stop was before him at the end of the corridor, its closed iris door looking as cozy as the entrance to a burrow. He stopped just around the bend and listened. No, there was nobody inside—the little green telltales showed that—but nevertheless he thought he had heard a movement.

There it was again. Footsteps—one set of them.

Somebody was behind him. The steps were confident, unhurried, and not at all furtive. Fongaváro did not think that he was being stalked. It was probably just a service man. But from here on, the corridor was a blind alley.

All right, let him come on. Fongaváro glided silently through the Rest Stop door, which irised shut as silently behind him. The telltale, of course, turned yellow, but that couldn't be prevented—and besides, the newcomer would probably welcome the idea of company. He was going to get it.

Any alternative was thinkable.

## 8   The Wooing of Flavia

Not much more than three million miles away, Biond Smith's spoilage crew toiled clumsily in their vacuum suits, chewing steadily into Flavia's vitals with prolapse drills. They had less than two weeks left to break up the asteroid before the lasers would focus on her remaining mass and turn her into a lopsided sunlet; but thus far, even with the loss of three lives, they had not succeeded in doing much more to her than spoiling her shape.

An alarm sounded in their helmets and the drilling stopped. It was time for another blast on the earthward side of the planetoid. Inevitably, some of the resulting pieces would take off for Earth a good deal faster than Flavia herself was already traveling, but that would just have to be borne, since it would slow as well as lighten the main mass.

There was a thudding jar deep in the rock, a soundless flash of yellow light, a slowly spreading cloud of dust in the eternal sunlight. The men went back to work. Somehow, Flavia did not look a single inch smaller to them than she had before.

153

### 9 People Reef

Tioru's decision did not produce anything like the emotional upheaval in Dorthy that he had expected. She only said, after a long silence, "If you come with me, where would you live?"

"Ashore for a while, of course. In a Dryland city."

"Away from the sea? You couldn't endure it!"

"How can I be sure of that?" he said. "I'll never know if I don't try. I know the Triton way of living. I think I ought to know something, firsthand, about the Dryland way."

"What would that solve? We'd still have the same old argument."

"If there's a solution, we won't find it half a world apart."

"I suppose that's true," she said dubiously. "Where would you live, then?"

"Philadelphia, I suppose. It's only fifteen minutes from Prime Center by local jet."

"Philadelphia! That's another people reef, like London! More than half a billion. You'd feel smothered!"

"Maybe not, I'll ask for an outside apartment. And a pool-bath."

"Not a chance, dear. You could wait for years before you got one. Just make a reservation for an apartment, period, and take whatever they offer. You'll be lucky if they have a vacancy. Your job status may help a little—but don't count on it."

"Whatever you say. You're the Drylander."

Dorthy winced slightly, but she said only, "I'll stop off with you in the city . . . and steer you around till you're settled."

Aboard the jet, Tioru sat in the auto-conforming seat beside Dorthy, but the deep-cushioned upholstery gave him no comfort. All his muscles were taut, and there was a persistent ache between his shoulder blades. He was acutely conscious of the void beneath the plane. Every nerve and muscle in his body was conditioned to the all-encompassing buoyancy of water. He did not even believe in the air.

Over Hawaii, he ventured a quick look below, and saw a dazzling white fleece of stratus cloud at the bottom of a blue abyss. It made him dizzy.

He leaned back into his seat, but that wasn't much better. The pressurized air in the plane had a faint taste of deodorant, acrid and medicinal, which left residues of bitterness in both his mouth and his gill chamber. He had a curious feeling that, even up here in the stratosphere, he was about to be buried alive.

Dorthy touched him. It did not seem to help much. "Are you all right?"

"I guess so."

"We're coming in to Philadelphia," said Dorthy. "You can see only part of it. The rest of it's under a cloud deck."

Tioru took another quick look. The visible part of the city rose out of the green sea of the World Forest. At several points its forested roof-terraces thrust up into pyramidal terraced mesas, each with a flyport on its flat summit. Part of the city's outer wall formed a dam along one end of a huge, elongated, meandering body of water.

Tioru exclaimed, "A lake! I can swim there!"

"Don't be optimistic," said Dorthy. "That's the reservoir. The city fathers may consider it unsanitary for anyone to swim in it. I can't see a beach anywhere."

After landing at one of the city's flyports Dorthy and Tioru were carried by a moving ramp from their plane to an elevator provided with oddly shaped seats. Tioru welcomed escape from the plane, but his muscles remained stiff and his back ached. A voice issued from a grill in the ceiling of the elevator.

"This is a high-speed elevator. It will not start until all passengers are seated."

As soon as Tioru sat down he was gently but firmly embraced by components of the seat that pressed his head against a headrest and immobilized his arms and legs. The elevator then seemed to go into a free fall. Tioru felt that he had left his viscera several levels above. The other passengers chatted unconcernedly. The downward plunge came to an end, the doors opened, and the voice from the grill said, "Municipal Services."

From the elevator a sequence of computer voices, flashing signs, luminous arrows, and moving floors took them to their destination—the Apartments Applications Bureau, a series of parallel corridors, each with two-way moving floors between two rows of soundproof cubicles with transparent sliding doors.

They came to an unoccupied cubicle.

Dorthy said to Tioru, "You go in here. A seat will come out of the wall. Sit on it and put your chin on the chin-rest that you'll see in front of you. Then wait."

Tioru entered, seated himself, and placed his chin on the chin-rest. He found himself staring into a pair of round dark lenses, like expressionless eyes, in a rectangular box on the wall.

"Please insert your ident compact into the slot indicated by the flashing lights," said the impersonal voice of a computer. Two luminous dots twinkled briefly.

Tioru inserted his compact—a palm-size, square, flat case containing a recording of his personal statistics, which turned on automatically and played into the computer. The dark lenses lighted up, peered into his eyes, scanned the patterns of his retinal capillaries, went dark again.

"Your ident data coincides with the information in your reservation request," said the computer. "The lock on your apartment is now keyed to open whenever you insert your ident compact into the lock. Here are the directions for arriving at your apartment."

A plastic card slid into a tray underneath the box on the wall.

"Any information or services that you may need can be obtained by calling Tenants' Services," said the computer. "Your Certificate of Occupancy and your travel cases have been delivered to your apartment. That is all."

The door slid open soundlessly. Tioru picked up his card of directions and read:

"Go to lobby of Applications Bureau. Take Express Elevator Number 17 to tube-train station on Level 133. Tube-train B-14 to Corridor Station 29. Take eastbound corridor strip to your apartment, Number 203."

Tioru came out of the cubicle.

"After I get into my apartment," he said, "how do I get out of it and find my way through this labyrinth, in case I want to go somewhere else?"

"Call Tenants' Services and ask," said Dorthy.

The experience of being immobilized in a conforming seat was repeated in both the elevator and the tube-train.

While they were riding the eastbound strip of Corridor 29 the stream of people on the westbound strip stared at Tioru with wide-eyed curiosity, some even a little fearfully. A transparent wall, inlaid with a pattern of flowering vines in colored enamel, separated the two strips. He became increasingly aware of a taste-smell quality in the air that he had noticed as soon as they had entered Philadelphia from the flyport. It was the aroma of people. It was not nauseating or disgusting, but it was unpleasant—a humid, sickly, oily odor—the odor of oils present on even well-bathed skins—plus a whiff of perfumed antiseptic. Out in the open, in the presence of small numbers of people, it was negligible. Here it was concentrated. The total effect was oppressive, as if the multimillions above, below, and around him were tangibly present.

When they opened the door of Apartment 203 they were confronted by a picture window on the opposite side of the living room, giving a view into the foliage of a forest of giant tectogenetic poplars. The leaves were stirring in a light breeze. The window was about twenty-five feet above ground level; that is to say, above the level of the soil on the roof of the next lower set-back of the city-structure.

"An outside apartment!" said Dorthy. "You're in luck."

The voice of the apartment computer spoke from a grill in the ceiling:

"Welcome to Apartment 203. Everything is in order. Is there anything you wish?"

"No," Tioru said, walking toward the window. His back ached, and he needed a swim. He was beginning to feel dehydrated.

Then he saw a sparkle of water between the moving poplar leaves. Suddenly he felt much better.

"Water! There's a stream out there! Can't we open the window and get out for a minute?"

"No. That stream is a rain sluice," Dorthy said indulgently. "There must have been a shower just before we arrived."

"Oh. Do you think there's a pool-bath here?"

"Not likely, I'm afraid. Maybe a shower stall."

This proved to be true; there was nothing but a small, windowless bedroom and a multiple-jet stall about the size of a closet. Tioru said nothing, but in his heart he was appalled. He had once tried a shower stall in the Barrier-hilthon. The needle sprays had forced water into his gill slits, the spray had reeked of detergent, the rinse had been choking with antiseptic. The bed did not look much more inviting; he had been accustomed all his life to sleeping afloat, and the flat white object before him now made him ache prospectively in muscles that he hadn't realized he had.

Dorthy watched him with a mixture of indulgence and anxiety. He tried to smile. He loved her, but . . . but this was a sad place for a honeymoon. He said cautiously, "Could I exchange this apartment for one with a pool—or have one installed?"

"Maybe, since you have a job," she said dubiously. "I'll ask, anyhow. . . . Query to computer: Do any of the apartments in this city have pool-baths?"

The computer said promptly, "I have no information regarding pool-baths or the furnishings of other apartments. For further information, call Tenants' Services."

Dorthy said something ungentle under her breath and passed the vidphone handset to Tioru. He, too, was answered by a computer, of course; but this one was a little more polite, since his voice pattern had been recorded and filed by the Apartments Application Bureau. He said tentatively:

"This apartment doesn't have a pool-bath. May I exchange it for one that does, or have one installed?"

"No, sir," the computer said, in a voice like a motherly oboe.

"Why not?"

"Pool-baths have been obsolete for generations. They

waste water and space, and are prohibited under the Revised Building Code. Your shower is controlled by the Apartment Computer, which has a directive from the Master Municipal Computer to supply you with a metered quantity of water daily. You may schedule the number and duration of showers to suit your convenience with the manual controls. If you avail yourself of less than the metered amount per day the unused ration will not be carried over to any succeeding day."

"Who is the person in charge of Tenants' Services?"

"Thaniel Brewster."

"May I speak to Thaniel Brewster?"

"Why do you wish to speak to him?"

"To ask about a pool-bath."

"Nothing else?"

"No."

"Then you may not speak to him. I have already answered your questions. I have a strict directive not to refer any inquiries to Brewster that I am capable of answering. That is all."

There was a *ping* as Thaniel Brewster's computer broke the connection.

"It seems that we can't break through Brewster's electronic curtain," Tioru said.

"I think I can break it," said Dorthy. "Any writing materials here?"

A search of the apartment turned up two sheets of sketch paper and a drawing pencil.

"Now," said Dorthy, "I'll write Thaniel Brewster a note, sign it with my official title, and send it to him as a parcel."

Puzzled, Tioru said, "What good will that do?"

"I'm not quite sure," said Dorthy, "but I think he'll make a person-to-person call."

After dispatching the note addressed to Thaniel Brewster in a cylinder coded to Tenants' Services through the parcel conveyor tube, Dorthy said, "Now we'll see what's to be had from the autoserver, and wait."

About one hour later, while they were sipping kaffina, the vidphone chimed, the screen lit up, and disclosed a man's face—gaunt and deeply lined and topped by a close-clipped fuzz of bristly hair. He was obviously flustered. He looked at Dorthy and said, "I'm Brewster. I take it that you're Dorthy Sumter. Why did you send me this blasted handwritten letter?"

"Because we couldn't get through to you any other way."

"Well, you've gotten through. Also you've thrown my entire office into an uproar. Don't you realize that we have no equipment for processing or filing a communication of this nature without resorting to unconventional routines? Our operations are geared exclusively to sound recordings and Universal Phonetic Print on standard message tape. I've been working here for thirty-seven years and not a soul in this office, including myself, has ever seen a handwritten letter in script. Only two people on my staff can read script. What are you? Some kind of antiquarian? Now what's this nonsense about a pool-bath?"

"It's for me," said Tioru. "I'm a Triton, as you can see."

"But I don't see. Tritons have scales and fins, don't they?"

Dorthy said, "I've been associated with Submarine Products Corporation and with the Tritons for many years. I can assure you that they have neither scales nor fins. Tioru *is* a Triton. Did you ever see a Drylander with antennas?"

"No. So I was mistaken. I'm sorry about the pool-bath, but it's out of the question. It's illegal to begin with, and if we start making exceptions we'll be stuck with an endless round of remodeling apartments."

"Well then," said Tioru, "how about giving me a permit to swim an hour or two every day in your reservoir?"

Brewster looked shocked. "Swim in the reservoir? Certainly not! There's an ordinance against it!"

Tioru said, "I'm not making this request just because I enjoy swimming. To me, periodic total immersion is a physiological necessity. If I'm denied it for too long a time the results could be serious."

Tioru could almost see Brewster's mind shifting gears. He said, "I'll see what I can do. I'll let you know."

After Brewster had switched off, Tioru said, "At least there's a glimmer of hope. Dorthy, that letter was a great idea. Perhaps tomorrow I can swim again. In the meantime I'll have to settle for a shower, like it or not."

Then he paused, sniffed several times, and said, "The air in here's changing. There's a different odor."

"I can't smell anything," said Dorthy. "What's it like?"

"Like the wind that blows off the land after a rain. A wet earth smell."

He prowled about the room, sniffing, and stopped before the door to the bedroom.

He said, "It comes from in here," and walked through the door. Dorthy followed him.

"Now I can smell it," she said. "If we weren't in a closed apartment I'd swear that it was drifting in from the Forest."

Tioru circled the bedroom part way, stopped at the door to the bathroom, and declared, "It's strongest here."

Dorthy came and stood beside him. Tioru slid back the green glastic panel that served as a door to the shower stall.

"There you are! The back panel!" said Tioru.

The metal panel that formed the back of the stall was also a sliding door, and stood ajar a few inches. There was a glow of light in the chamber beyond.

"I know what that is," said Dorthy. "The apartments in Great London are built the same way. It's the emergency exit. But it's supposed to open only by computer command."

The sliding panel yielded easily. They stepped through it and found a service compartment, the ceiling panel alight. Nearby, a narrow escalator came down from above, another continued to the level below. Neither one was in motion. The compartment was silent except for a muted surging sound that was borne in on a slow current of humid air.

"What's that?" said Tioru. "It sounds like surf."

"Or the wind in the trees," said Dorthy. "Incidentally, over there may be the explanation of why the panel was open."

She pointed at the floor. An open tool box stood near the wall with electrician's tools scattered near it. A square panel in the wall was open, revealing a recessed cavity containing a maze of electronic components. One of them had been removed, exposing the holes where it had been plugged in.

"Usually these technicians work in teams," Dorthy said. "They must be somewhere around."

"Then let's get moving before they come back. They'd probably order us inside," Tioru said. "We can walk down the escalator to the next level. This draft must be coming from an open door down there."

"Probably. But why bother?"

"I want to see if I can find that stream we saw from the window. It may be deep enough for me to swim in."

Near the foot of the escalator there was indeed an open sliding door. Outside was the green shade under the giant poplars. Here the wind in the leaves was like the seething of rollers on a reef.

There was no underbrush. The Forest floor was carpeted with a turf so dense and short-bladed that it resembled moss. It was wet, and occasional water drops fell from the trees. Dorthy and Tioru picked their way over it gingerly. Their feet sank into it as into a deep-piled rug. The air was warm.

Abruptly the wind subsided and the surging of the leaves was stilled. A leisurely *pat, pat, pat* marked the drip of water.

The stillness was unnerving. Tioru felt as if he had gone backward in time to some period before there had been humans, or even pre-humans. The trees were overwhelming; it seemed impossible that any plant could grow so big. They seemed to be watching.

Yet it was better than being indoors. There, the air was heavy with the scent of people. Out here, he could at least see patches of sky. All the same, the Forest was far from natural. The trees grew in ranks, with aisles between them, as regular as the arrangement of atoms in a crystal. And it was completely silent: no birds, no insects, no animals. They were all shut up in the Bio Preserves.

No, not completely silent. Tioru stopped. "I hear water running—somewhere ahead of us."

A few steps more brought them to a semicircular sluice about five feet wide, lined with vitrolith. The water was less than a foot deep.

"I can't swim in that," Tioru said regretfully. "But at least I can splash it over me."

He let himself down the curved side of the sluice and knelt in the water. It was rather warm. Forming a cup with his hands, he filled them with water, inhaled it, and ejected it from his gill slits. Dorthy knelt on the bank and watched him, laughing.

"Ever been in a Bio Preserve?" she said. "You look just like a bird bathing in a puddle."

"Then I'm the world's only bird with gills." He climbed

out of the sluice. "This fresh water has a flat taste. But it's better than water flavored with detergent."

He took a step. At the same instant, a sledge hammer seemed to slam into his left calf. He fell like a stone, clutching at his leg.

"Tioru! What is it? What's the matter?"

"Cramp," he said between his teeth. "Not used to all this walking."

"Drylanders have them too," Dorthy said, kneeling beside him. "Roll over. I'll massage it."

"A fine fiasco this is," he said disgustedly. But he felt the knotted muscles slowly relaxing under her hands. "Thanks."

"Feel better? Good. Now . . . do you think we can find our way back to the door we came out by? No matter which way I look, all I can see is trees. Frankly, I think I'm lost."

Tioru raised himself on his elbows and looked at her over his shoulder. It had never occurred to him that a Drylander could get lost in his own environment.

"Let me think," he said. "When we saw the stream through the window, it seemed to be flowing straight across our line of sight, not very far away. So if we just go off at ninety degrees to the sluice—"

"In which direction? Besides, this might not be the same stream. All we really saw of it was a glimmer through the leaves."

"True enough," Tioru said gloomily. "All the same, we ought to get moving—the sun is setting."

"Can you manage?"

"I'd damn well better. Just go slowly at first."

He found that he had to lean on Dorthy and slide one foot at a time, slowly and tediously, two or three inches per slide. It was humiliating.

Darkness fell with almost tropical suddenness. They groped their way cautiously. Tioru tripped over a small hummock and the muscle knotted again. This time, at least, he managed to fall in a sitting position.

"A Triton has no business on dry land," he muttered.

"You'll be all right. We just tried to do too much at once."

"It must be catching." He got up slowly.

A light breeze began to rustle the leaves, and a wan flickering of moonlight filtered down into the Forest. The tree boles became dimly visible. Then they saw fitful beacons shining through the moving leaves.

"Lighted windows!" said Tioru. "At last, something to steer by."

When they came to the setback wall they searched along its base and found many exit doors, all closed and immovable. The glow from the multitude of windows above was diffused back from the nearer trees and provided an illumination of sorts.

The window sills of the lowest story were six feet above the ground. Dorthy was not tall enough to see over them even when standing on tiptoe. Tioru's eyes were just above the sills when he stood flatfooted. He did not attempt to stand on tiptoe for fear of causing another cramp. He rapped on several windows but could not attract the attention of the occupants of the apartments. All were watching 3-V, with their backs to the windows.

"This is stupid," said Tioru. "Rapping on double-pane windows while a noisy 3-V drama is going on. Everybody's watching it. They can't hear me."

"You can see what they're watching?"

"More or less. Seems to be some historical battle thing. Flashes of blue fire, purple smoke, a big ponderous machine lumbering about and knocking down buildings."

They moved on to another window.

"Perhaps I can attract some attention here," Tioru said. "Everybody's back is toward us except for one girl. She's sitting on the floor, sideways to the window. Maybe she'll turn this way for a moment, if we wait."

They waited.

"Now the girl's getting up," Tioru said. "She's walking this way, speaking over her shoulder. There! She's turning her head toward us!"

Tioru raised his arms above his head and waved them. The girl saw Tioru—to be exact, two eyes peering over the edge of the sill, the phosphorescent dome of his cranium, a pair of fern-like antennas, two wildly waving arms. Her hands flew to her mouth, which opened in an inaudible scream. The group before the 3-V screen turned toward her, wide-eyed. The girl leaped toward the window, and the panes turned a smoky blue, then opaque black.

"I gave her a shock," Tioru said. "I should have realized . . ."

"No matter. She'll almost surely report it," Dorthy said. "Now all we have to do is wait for a search party."

They sat down on the wet turf with their backs to the wall, which still retained a little of the warmth of the day. The air grew cooler. Dorthy shivered, and Tioru put his arm around her.

They waited. And waited. And fell asleep.

Tioru was awakened by a bright light shining in his face. From behind the light, a harsh voice said, "What are you doing out here? Tenants are not allowed in the Forest."

Dorthy said sleepily, "Take me inside. I'm cold."

They were taken back home, with another warning. After the rangers had left, Dorthy paced nervously around the living room.

"First I want some hot kaffina," she said. "I'm still shivering. We ought to eat, too. And then I'm going to catch the next plane to Prime Center."

"In the middle of the night? Must you? Surely the morning—"

"It isn't a case of 'must.' I have the jitters. I don't know just when the meeting will be called, but I want to be there when it is. I'm sure that it will be an ordeal—for me—and the sooner I get it over with the better."

The following morning Tioru received, via facsimile transcriber, a permit to swim in the reservoir for one hour daily. But there was a condition attached: he would be accompanied to and from the lake by an escort of six uniformed bodyguards. The reason for this was not to protect him from possible physical violence, it was explained, but because he would be an object of great curiosity, and since he was a transient visitor, the citizens would not regard him as protected by the usual rules of etiquette regarding invasion of privacy. He might easily become the center of a throng of inquisitive people eager to bombard him with annoying personal questions.

The arrival of his escort of six Precinct Guards was announced by the apartment computer, which was connected to a watchful electric eye in the corridor. After asking Tioru's permission, it opened the door. The guards were uniformed in berets, tunics, flaring knee breeches, and half-length boots of silvery material that flashed and glittered like metal. For a moment Tioru thought that they were clad in armor. They fell into two triangular formations of three—one ahead of Tioru, the other behind. As they were borne along on the moving floorstrip in the corridor Tioru felt uncomfortably self-conscious.

"This is silly," he thought. "I feel like a parade."

There were people ahead of him on the same strip who kept turning their heads to look. Others turned around and rode the strip backward, staring openly. Tioru heard a steadily increasing murmur of voices behind him and looked over his shoulder. He had acquired a close-packed following of, he estimated, one hundred people, and the number was steadily augmented by others emerging from apartments along the way.

He overheard snatches of conversation: "He doesn't look like a Triton. . . . What did you expect? Don't you watch 3-V? . . . What are those things on his head? . . . I didn't know they could live out of water. . . . Does he speak our language or does he squeak like dolphins? . . . They eat seaweed, don't they?"

The transparent partition that separated him from the people on the oppositely moving strip prevented him from hearing what they were saying, but he could see their lips moving and their heads all turning in unison as they passed him. At the intersections with the cross corridors, where the moving floors were interrupted to permit interchanging, there were small crowds, all agog, waiting on the stationary squares.

"How did they know we were coming?" Tioru asked one of the guards.

The guard shrugged. "Friends down the corridor behind us phoned ahead and told them," he said. "You'd be surprised how fast word gets around. Next to watching 3-V, talking on the vidphone is probably the world's favorite pastime."

They arrived at an elevator lobby. Two more guards stood before the open doors of one of the elevators. They stood aside while Tioru and his escort entered, then came in behind them.

"Now it's eight guards," thought Tioru. "The permit said six. Oh well . . ."

After a long plunge—too long for Tioru—the doors opened and revealed two more guards.

"Ten!" exclaimed Tioru involuntarily.

"You spoke?" said one of the guards.

"It's nothing," said Tioru. "Never mind."

But he was thinking, "What goes on here? If I accumulate any more guards it *will* be a parade."

From the elevator they stepped into an arcade two hundred feet wide and high, with a luminous vaulted ceiling. Here was the Precinct center for distribution of commodities, the Precinct medical center, the crematorium receiving station, the air-conditioning plant, Guard headquarters, cosmeticians' salons, fortunetelling robots, electronic games. The moving floors were twenty feet wide and crowded with people. Between the moving floors lay a wide strip of greensward. At intervals down its middle were huge blue ceramic bowls containing flower beds from whose center rose lattice-work columns of black metal, forked at the top like a letter Y. Giant philodendrons with leaves as big as elephants' ears climbed the columns. But in all this greenery there was not a single living plant. They were plastic flowers, plastic grass, plastic philodendrons.

The oily, faintly perfumed aroma of people hampered Tioru's breathing; it was like the light, steady pressure of a rubber bandage around his chest. He was grateful when they left the arcade and came into the open air on a promenade along the top of the city's outer wall where it formed a dam across the reservoir. The towering figures of great tawny lions molded in vitrolith sat stiffly erect at regular intervals along the parapet of the promenade. A helicopter was standing on the promenade, its rotors idling. A crowd of spectators had gathered.

"We're going to fly you part way up the reservoir and put you off," said the Guard captain. "It's dangerous at this end on account of the intakes for the hydroelectric plant. The copter will cruise around in your vicinity until your hour is up. If you want to be picked up before then, surface and wave. The copilot will be watching for you with binoculars."

When the helicopter had flown several miles the pilot brought it down to within a few feet of the water, near the shore. Tioru slipped on a headband bearing a forehead spotlight, diving in, submerged, and inhaled deeply. At last he was water-borne again. The water tasted flat, like the water in the rain sluice, but with an additional bitter flavor.

He was curious to see what kinds of life he might find and set out on a tour of exploration. The side of the reservoir was a wall of smooth gray material; he presumed it was vitrolith. Nothing was growing on it; not even a patch of green algae. He found a few spots that were slimy to the touch, like bacterial film.

He followed the wall down until he reached bottom. He judged it to be about two hundred feet below the surface. It was covered by a layer of gray silt that showed no signs of life—no burrows, no worm tracks, no algae.

It was dim and green on the bottom, but his headlamp allowed him to see clearly for about twenty feet. It dawned upon him that he had seen no fishes. Where were the fishes? He swam up and down, back and forth. No fishes.

This fishless condition did not indicate that the World State disapproved of fresh-water fishes. It was simply the inevitable condition that had resulted when the World State confined all of the world's wildlife in the Biological Preserves and substituted the highly artificial ecology of the World Forest, devoid of all fauna other than soil organisms.

"If there's anything living in this water," thought Tioru, "it must be microscopic. The place is sterile. It's a place of death."

He sculled along near the bottom, shining his light on the smooth gray silt, occasionally flashing it ahead. It was depressing. He was accustomed to the teeming vitality of the reefs. Then he saw a wavering movement ahead.

As he drew nearer he saw what appeared to be a clump of dark-colored algae, swaying gently. It was attached to one end of an elongated dark object lying on the bottom.

He started to swim closer, then recoiled. There was a new taste in the water. It was not unknown to him; he had encountered it before when he had killed sharks or scraped himself on sharp coral. It was the taste of blood.

Shuddering, he resumed swimming toward the dark object, directing his light toward it. Now he could see what it was—the prostrate body of a young woman in the green uniform of a Forest ranger.

Her feet were tied together and attached to a cube of some dark material. The front of her uniform was all one great dark stain and there were slashes in the fabric over her breasts. Her face was white and calm, with a marble immobility; her eyes were open, and her dark hair floated in the water like black seaweed.

Tioru kicked against the bottom, launched himself upward, and surfaced. He looked about, spotted the circling helicopter, and waved until he saw an arm wave in acknowledgment. The helicopter veered toward him.

While he was clambering aboard the helicopter he said, "Get a fix on this spot! There's a dead woman down there with a weight tied to her feet!"

Tioru stared moodily and unseeingly at the 3-V screen in his apartment, oblivious to the news program then in progress. He was still shaken by his experience in the reservoir and could not turn his thoughts away from it. He had been minutely questioned about the body of the girl. A squad of Precinct Guards with scuba gear had been sent to recover it, and both he and the helicopter pilots had been ordered to talk to no one about the discovery until the killer was in custody.

The news commentator's words caught his attention; ". . . distinguished visitors from Great Barrier Reef."

"That must mean Dorthy and me!" thought Tioru, becoming alert and leaning forward to watch, and in that instant the scene changed. He was looking at the promenade and its parapet with the vitrolith lions overlooking the reservoir. He saw himself with his escorts of guards emerging from the arcade and marching toward the helicopter. He was marching in step with the guards; he hadn't been aware of it at the time. He watched himself enter the helicopter and take off.

The commentator explained that Tioru had been granted permission to swim in the reservoir "for reasons of health." Flick! The scene changed again, showing the returning of helicopter, then Tioru climbing out and re-entering the arcade with the two pilots. All three of them were surrounded by an augmented bodyguard.

"I wasn't marching in step then," thought Tioru as he saw himself stumble twice.

The commentator passed on to other matters. No mention of the body in the reservoir. Evidently the hunt for the killer was still on.

Tioru turned off the screen and stood up. "No use in staying up all night," he said aloud. It relieved his solitude somewhat.

Tioru prepared for a shower by inhaling water from the drinking fountain in the bathroom until he had filled his gill cavity. Then he entered the shower stall, turned on the cleansing shower, and ejected water from his gill slits while the shower was running. This prevented the detergent-laden needle jets from injecting themselves into the slits. He repeated the operation during the antiseptic rinse, then waited for the drying whirl-blast of warm air. Then he stepped out of the shower, stretched himself on the bed, and said, "Lights out."

The computer obediently plunged the apartment into total darkness.

"Correction!" said Tioru hastily. "Turn on two percent of full."

A faint glow filled the apartment and Tioru closed his eyes.

But sleep did not come quickly. He kept seeing the dead girl in the dim greenness of the reservoir, the pallid mask of her face, the gently waving cloud of dark hair, the great stain on her uniform.

When he did fall asleep he was bedeviled by a nightmare. He was swimming madly through an endless green twilight of water, without top, without bottom, pursued by a bodiless, expressionless white face with a trailing streamer of black hair like the tail of a comet. Then two faces, three, four, five, ten, a hundred, a veritable swarm of hounding white-faced Furies. He had some sort of gun in his hand, which he fired at them. It discharged with a strange staccato noise like the slamming impact of metal on metal. He awoke and sat up with a start, sweating, his heart pounding violently. He had an odd feeling that the noise had been in the apartment. Had something fallen? Or broken? It seemed unlikely.

He said, "Lights on full."

The lights came on and he prowled the apartment looking for the source of the noise. Then it occurred to him that the computer would have recorded it if there had actually been a noise.

Tioru said, "Query to computer: Was there a loud noise just now?"

"Yes."

"What caused it?"

"A man in the corridor stepped off the moving strip

at your door, struck the door with a metal bar, and continued on his way."

"Are you sure it was not a child?"

"It appeared to be an adult."

"Were there other people about?"

"Yes."

"Did they try to stop him?"

"No."

"It's senseless!" said Tioru. The computer offered no comment.

He returned to bed, ordered the lights turned down, and tried to sleep again. But now he was wide awake, his thoughts circling futilely around the puzzle of the blow on his door.

Then the vidphone chimed. Tioru groaned, ordered the lights on again, got up, and walked back to the living room. When he ordered the screen on it displayed the frowning face of a young girl.

She cried shrilly, "I know who you are, you window snooper! You're Tioru the Triton! Snooper! Snooper! Snooper!"

"Wait!" cried Tioru as the screen went dark. He had recognized the face. It was the face of the girl whom he had frightened when he had appeared at her window. How had she traced him? The 3-V news broadcast! That had identified him. But his vidphone code? How could she know that? Then another memory came to him. One of his bodyguards had said, "You'd be surprised how fast word gets around. . . ."

Tioru thought, "Scores of people must have seen me come out of Apartment 203. With six bodyguards how could they fail to notice? Then the vidphones must have started to ring up and down Corridor 29. Within minutes most of the people along the corridor must have known about the peculiar stranger in Apartment 203. It spread from there."

He sighed and returned to bed, ordered the lights turned down. He had scarcely settled himself when the vidphone chimed again. He rose wearily, ordered on the lights, and walked to the vidphone muttering, "Enough of this!"

This time it was a bearded man who merely shouted "Snooper!" and vanished. At the same time something whacked twice against his door.

Tioru switched the vidphone to Incoming Recording, then called Tenants' Services and reported what had happened. He was surprised to find himself talking to a man, not a computer.

"We've been expecting to hear from you," the man said. "We know the facts in the case and are sorry that you're being bothered. We've received several complaints about the window snooper. We were hoping that no one would ferret out your vidphone code. I'll have a screening and tracing computer put on your line and no more nuisance calls will be allowed to come through. The Precinct Guard will station two men outside of your door."

After this Tioru was not disturbed again, but he awoke once during the night and thought that he heard the remote, hollow sound of many shouting voices coming out of the bedroom ventilator.

Corridor 29 was deserted when his bodyguard arrived the next day to escort him to the helicopter. All tenants of the corridor had been ordered to stay inside and to keep their doors closed. Ther were no crowds at the cross corridors, or in the elevator lobby.

On his way down in the elevator Tioru almost decided to tell the guards that he did not wish to swim in the reservoir. It had lost its charm after his grisly discovery of the day before.

When the elevator doors opened on the arcade of the Precinct Center they revealed a milling crowd of thousands of people. Phalanxes of the silver-uniformed Precinct Guard were maintaining an open lane between the elevator and the doors at the end of the arcade. As soon as the crowd saw Tioru he was greeted by an angry roar punctuated by shouts and screams. They began to throw things. A pulpy mass with a fruity aroma splattered against Tioru's forehead and its juice trickled down over his face. He began to distinguish individual voices in the midst of the uproar.

"Kill the slimy Triton!"

"Smash his ugly face!"

"Murderer!"

"Bash his head in!"

A woman's voice rose piercingly above all the others: "Kill 'im! Kill 'im! Kill 'im!"

The arcade became filled with a flickering play of blinding white flashes. They were so intense that they erased all color and temporarily reduced the scene to a study in garish black and white. They seemed to emanate from slender cylindrical weapons wielded by the guards. The ranks of the guards began to give way before the pressure of the mob. Several people broke through but were thrown back.

Tioru closed his eyes against the coruscating brilliance and saw a pattern of green afterimages. He had an impression that the guards were wearing gas masks and dark goggles. Someone entered the elevator, the door closed, and the tumult became inaudible.

Tioru opened his eyes. The newcomer was a captain of the Precinct Guard. He said to Tioru's escort:

"Stay in the elevator and go down to the next level. Go through the service tunnel and come up the escalator near the copter. We've stopped the floors. We're going to use knockout gas as soon as the airflow is shut off. We don't want to gas the whole Precinct. We can't hold this mob much longer with shockprods and blinderflashes."

"What's going on?" asked Tioru. "They were shouting murderer!"

"You'll be told after you're in the copter. And you can't go back to your apartment. There's another riot up there now. Get moving!"

The escalator from the service tunnel delivered Tioru and his guards to an exit in the hollow pedestal of one of the lions on the parapet of the promenade. The helicopter was only a few steps away. People were staggering out of the exit from the arcade and collapsing on the pavement. A few had escaped the knockout gas and were fleeing down the promenade, but were being pursued and rounded up by guards on miniscooters who were coming out of the pedestals of the lions.

After he had boarded the helicopter and was in the air, Tioru said to the pilot, "Now, please tell me what all that uproar was about."

The pilot said, "Last night we traced the killer of the girl—the one you discovered in the reservoir. He was easy to find—a Forest ranger who shared a patrol area with the girl. The motive was jealousy. The stabbing was a clumsy job. He never touched a vital organ. The girl bled to death. It happened about the same time that you and Chairwoman Sumter were locked out of your apartment, but miles away from where you were. The next day, when the girl's lover heard that you were diving in the reservoir he panicked and committed suicide. But he taped a confession first. The whole thing went on the air."

Tioru said, "But where do I fit in?"

"First there was the hooraw about the window snooper and you became a sort of public enemy. Communications put on a short every-hour-on-the-hour broadcast explaining how you got lost in the Forest and were locked out, and that you really weren't snooping."

"I missed the broadcasts. I didn't do much 3-V watching last night."

"The broadcasts didn't do much good anyway. Some people want to believe the worst no matter what. Then last night came the murder story, and a lot of people put two and two together and made six."

"I don't follow you."

"It's like this. You and the chairwoman were in the Forest when the girl was killed. At one o'clock in the morning Chairwoman Sumter caught a plane to Prime Center, leaving you the scapegoat."

"They think that Dorthy and I—"

"In a city this size, with most of half a billion people on the dole and with nothing in their heads, they invent things to get stirred up about. That 'lost in the Forest' story, for instance, they say is just a cover-up. The taped confession is a fake. You got a special permit to swim in the reservoir, and the rumor factory has it that the reason for *that* was to allow you to pretend to find the body."

"It's crazy."

"Sure it is. But we were charging around all night breaking up demonstrations after the murder story went on the air. First it was just marching and shouting, but it got worse. The riot you saw didn't begin until after you left your apartment this morning."

"Great," Tioru said. "Just great. Where do I go now?"

"Well, I doubt that you want to go swimming."

"No," Tioru said. "I don't even want to go near the reservoir, after finding . . . I just want to go somewhere to rest and think. . . . But where would that be?"

"We have a safe place all ready for you. There's a new five-mega-unit addition almost completed and you'll have it all to yourself except for the technicians.

They're still checking and testing everything. One unit has been turned on for you, complete, and you can stay there until the facts catch up with the rumors."

"I'll be isolated, in the middle of five million vacant apartments?"

"Right. How much safer can you get?"

Tioru was guided to his new apartment by the guardsman-pilot of the helicopter. Technicians were still at work on the corridor floor-strips and Tioru and his guide were forced to walk part of the way.

Although all the electrical equipment in Tioru's apartment had been turned on, electricians kept coming and going, checking circuits and making final adjustments. They warned him that some of the equipment might not operate normally for several days to come.

The apartment was high in the uppermost tier of the city and its window commanded a view across the forested roof, studded with square pyramidal terraced mesas, each one crowned by a flyport. Tioru glanced listlessly at this panorama. He felt drained of emotion.

After showering perfunctorily he lay on the bed in a state of apathetic gloom, not bothering to order on the lights when the twilight gathered and deepened. He was dully aware of scrapings, clinks, and tappings between the walls, overhead, under the floor. He reflected that the technicians probably worked night and day, in shifts. The city grew; that was its first law.

He became alert when he heard the corridor door slide open, squeaking. That squeak would have to be fixed. When he ordered the lights on full they responded with only a dim glow. Another adjustment to be made!

He groped his way into the living room. Here the window admitted considerable illumination from the distant flyports, now sparkling with lights. The door into the corridor was visible as a black rectangle. He went to it, looked into the yawning dark cavern of the corridor, and called, "Hello! Anybody there?"

Tioru shivered and hopefully ordered the computer to close the door. There was a brief hum. The door squeaked, trembled for a moment, but remained open. He returned to the bedroom, stretched himself on the bed, sighed, and closed his eyes.

The thought of the black rectangle of the open door kept nagging him. It made him uneasy. Long-dormant childhood fantasies rose from the depths of his memory, trailing after them vestiges of the deeper primordial fear of prowling nocturnal carnivores. He felt that there were ambiguous presences lurking in the blackness of the corridor, waiting to steal in on noiseless feet. Not people, but *things*: shadowy gray, long-bodied, four-legged, squint-eyed *things that bite*. Was that a stealthy rustling in the living room? He became rigid, held his breath.

The multiple sprays in the shower stall came on of their own accord with explosive force. Tioru sprang from the bed with a cry of terror, then stood in the center of the room quivering with nervous shock while the shower completed its cycle. When he had recovered his composure he sat on the edge of the bed with his head in his hands.

This jumpiness was insane. People lived safely all their lives in apartments like this.

From somewhere came a subdued, velvet-smooth, mechanical whir. Then he realized that the corridor floor-strips were moving.

He returned to the open door and looked into the corridor. Far away on the left he could see a light. The lights were on in a cross corridor. Then the corridor in front of him lit up for as far as he could see—two brightly lit, empty perspectives of identical doors facing each other, divided by the central transparent partition with enamel inlay, converging to a vanishing point in either direction.

There was a distant murmur of voices. Two people emerged from a remote cross corridor and were carried toward him on the floor-strip. They were merely two minute figures; he could make out no details.

The lights in the corridor went out again, but came on full in Tioru's apartment.

"Blast this circuit testing!" he thought. "When will they be done with it?"

It had seemed to him that when the corridor lights went out he had heard a startled cry, diminished by distance. It had a feminine quality, he thought, but he wasn't sure. He listened intently. He could still hear the murmur of voices, closer now. Then a few words floated down the corridor, blurred by echoes; "I see a lighted door. That must be Tioru's apartment."

Dorthy!

"I'm here!" he shouted. "It's me, Tioru! Where you see the light!"

She called something in reply, but the echoes turned it into nonsense. He heard the sound of running. Moments later Dorthy burst through the door and was in his arms.

After a bit she said, "What have they been doing to you? The guard—he's back there somewhere—said they had to snatch you away from a mob!"

"I've been living from shock to shock. I'm as out of place here as a dolphin on top of Mount Everest. You were right. Triton and Drylander can't mix."

"Tioru! That isn't the way you talked to me on Great Barrier!"

"I was ignorant. I was wrong."

"Then you don't love me after all," she said dully.

"I—can't say that. I didn't mean that. Unfortunately,

for both of us, I do still love you. But there's nothing we can do about it. We're licked, Dorthy."

Someone coughed discreetly. A guardsman was standing in the doorway.

He said, "Is there anything further I can do for you?"

"No—or anybody," Tioru said. "Good-bye, Dorthy. I'm sorry, but . . . we've got to face up to it. I'm taking the next plane out."

There was a long pause.

"Perhaps that is the best thing," Dorthy said at last. "Things may look different when you're back on the reefs. Listen, I have an idea. I'm going to Great Inagua in the Bahamas. Why don't you come too? The sea is there . . . and I still need you, Tioru. Unless you want to quit—"

"No—no, of course not," Tioru said, fighting against hope. "All right. How do we get a plane to Great Inagua?"

For the first time in the new apartment, the computer spoke. It said, "For plane schedules call Tenants' Services."

## 10   The Piper of Dis

His honeycomb helmet unaccustomedly heavy on his head and shoulders, Jothen rode up a secondary utility stack toward Gitler's main distribution center. The Joneses, once out of his sight, were also almost out of his mind except en masse, as an abstract complex of technical problems—but those were quite complex enough to suit him. He would let McGee deal with the Joneses as people, as long as possible.

As he ascended, he thought again of Kim. For a while he had been sorely tempted to press his suit with her by asking her just *who* had sunk the Barrier-hilthon; but reluctantly he had decided that blackmail was not his style.

Besides, with the new and greater disaster impending, she now had much the more difficult task to undertake—he had only to make ready living space that was supposed to be virtually ready anyhow, whereas she had been charged with the utter destruction of untold thousands of living creatures, all of them so rare as to be priceless, and all of them creatures she had devoted her life to cherishing and protecting lest they escape and alter the ecology of the World Forest. For her, the slaughter of the Preserve would be like the murder of a child, multiplied manifold.

It was better, he decided, not to think about that.

He stopped at the next way station and phoned Piscetti, his chief of operations.

"Everything's normal on the lines," Piscetti reported. "But Jothen, we've had a killing. One of us—Guivrec Krantz."

"My God. Who—where—"

"I don't know who. Where, in Rest Stop BB-596, way down in the bottom levels, strictly nonresidential and always was. He was strangled. It looks like he was taken by surprise, because there's no sign of a struggle."

"All the rest of our people accounted for, I hope?"

"Yes," Piscetti said. "I checked that right away— none of them has been anywhere near that area in at least a year. It has to have been one of those crazy Joneses, somehow or other."

"Crazy is the word for it. See what else the computer

can give you. The man may have given himself away in some way—a minor arrest, a lost ration card, some other such bit of business. Anybody who's got a special report of any sort."

"I'll try it," Piscetti's voice said dubiously.

"All right. I'd like to stop him fast if we can. We've got enough trouble as it is. I'm going on up to Distribution and I'll call you from there."

Nearly in shock—for though Guivrec had not been a close friend, he had known the man casually, and the maintenance crew was jealous of its own—Jothen resumed his ride up the stack. It discharged him at last into the throbbing darkness of the distribution center, its gloom relieved only here and there by the little stars of telltales and safelights.

It was not a reassuring place to be, under the circumstances, familiar though it was. He felt distinctly uneasy, and his eyes kept darting off into corners. Knotted across the far-away ceiling were the complexes of pipes that tapped shunts from the main overhead supply line. That colossal feeder—so large in diameter that it could accommodate a six-man personnel capsule, and now and then actually did—served chiefly to bring in Gitler's water supply direct from the water table up north, but that was far from all that it carried. It also bore food, fuels, rock slurries, and almost every other kind of supplies or semiprocessed materials that could be moved in the form of self-contained peristaltic packages. Most of this material either originated with or had been routed through the Municipal Services Center in the Kansas City complex. The pipeline was Gitler's jugular vein.

At the moment, there seemed to be something wrong with the sound that it was making.

Jothen doubted that he ought to be alarmed . . . at least as yet. Though he knew most of its moods as well as a creche mother knows the noises of a nursery, it seemed logical to him that the master conduit might make a sound new to him when it was approaching peak load, as in preparation for the refugee influx it was now doing for the first time in its history. After all, until the Joneses had arrived, it had effectively just been sitting there since Gitler was built, seventy years ago; the burden the technie village alone put on it was miniscule.

Still, it was second nature in him, just as it would have been with a creche mother, to check such matters. Climbing through the dimness to a catwalk where there was a slave meter board for the Traffic computer, he called for a read-out on pressures, rates of flow, and what kinds of loads Kansas City said it was sending.

For an eternal fifteen seconds, he found it impossible to believe what he saw. Maybe it was not after all as bad as it had seemed. As a last precaution, he asked for a Chicago manifest for the day.

Then he pushed every red button in sight.

The Joneses—all but one of them—heard nothing but the continued bawling of the public address system, directing them to the tubeways; and then, Jothen's voice, calling for McGee. But the work areas, the machinery decks, the utility stacks, the technicians' village and homes all jangled and squalled with leather-lunged alarm. After a while, lights on the slave board showed that Jothen's emergency staffmen were coming onto their posts; but it was several minutes more before the phone rang to bring in McGee's voice.

"What's the matter, Jothen? Everything's going swimmingly down here—or at least it was until now."

"You may have to swim for it in earnest," Jothen said grimly. "Where are you concentrating your people?"

"At the tubeway stations, just as you suggested."

"Yes, but which ones? The main outgoing depots,

in the subbasement? . . . That's what I was afraid of. The thing is, there's a very good chance that our prime feeder line up here is going to show a major break in about ninety minutes."

"How come? It's hardly ever been used!"

"That's probably the trouble," Jothen said. "Evidently there was a small flaw to begin with, or else it crystallized out during disuse—and I suppose the first strains, after the Joneses came in, made it worse. Anyhow there's a weak patch where a shunt goes off toward the flyport fuel tanks. I still think it's nothing we couldn't handle normally, but Chicago is shipping us a big bolus of premelted gallium as a moderator to start our main nuclear pile with, and when that hits the bend—"

"Why didn't your computer show that shipment long ago?" McGee broke in irritably.

"It hasn't come onto the Kansas City block yet. I just picked it up off the dispatcher's waybill from Chicago. Anyhow we'll get nowhere arguing about it, it's on the way."

"All right, but it still seems like a sloppy way to run a pipeline. What do you want me to do?"

"Get everybody up to the roof," Jothen said. "We'll have to evacuate them from the flyport, and from the terraces, too. Luckily there's plenty of roof space, and no air traffic to speak of."

"Everybody? A million Joneses—in *ninety minutes?* Miracles aren't my specialty, Jothen."

"We won't have to evacuate them in that time, just get them aloft. You may have ten extra minutes, even after the main breaks. It'll probably be that long before the liquid parts of the load cascade down to you. I'm hoping some of the gallium will solidify fast enough to block off some of the semihard junk in the pipe, but I can't count on it—its melting point is around eight-five, and the temperature up here is only fifteen degrees below that right now. Better move fast—and good luck."

"Thanks," McGee said, with more than a hint of irony.

Jothen cut over to another line. "Piscetti, Jothen here. Any chance of our moving a nugget-grade coal hopper into the shunt room in time to catch—? . . . Too bad. Okay, in that event the first thing I want is a fluted baffle over the shunt-room drain, so the gallium won't plug it. Check storage for something light enough to truck in here fast. Set it up so that it slants the stuff off into the utility stack. . . . Yes, but I'd rather have to chip spray out of the stack than try to free metal chunks from a roomful of frozen valves. . . . Damn it, I know we ought to drain the aero fuel, but we'll need it up here for the incoming evacuation ferries—and besides, where'd you suggest draining it to? Do you want it stored *under* a jet of hot gallium? . . . Right. Now, I'm closing the living areas in ten minutes, and putting all public stairs and walkways off limits to the crew, to give McGee queue space—we'll use the stacks only. Also there'll be a gas alarm in thirty minutes for the work areas. Whatever that stew from the pipes generates when it mixes, we won't want to breathe it. Got all that? Timing starts in fifteen seconds . . . *mark*."

"Mark," Piscetti said unemotionally, and his light went out. Overhead, the great pipeline gave a premonitory groan. Jothen yanked the power jack out of the slave board, resettled the honeycomb helmet, and ran for cover, hoping that the master computer had eavesdropped and understood his timing instructions.

It took him four minutes plus to make the main gallery overlooking the pump hall. Fronted with polarized, laminated plastic, the gallery was theoretically immune to heat shock, and to most mechanical insults. If it wasn't, Jothen would be allowed only a few seconds of life to regret it; he had to stay here until the accident arrived,

since the gallery held the only gang board he could
have hoped to have reached beforehand.

Pulling down his gas mask, he checked the timing—
yes, the computer was clocking both deadlines. The hot
line from Kansas City was producing a silent red scream.
He snapped it open.

"Gitler, are you aware that a capsule of molten gallium—"

"Yes," Jothen said grimly. "Why didn't you stop it,
KC?"

"It had crash priority. What's the matter, can't you
handle it?"

"No—but now we've got to try. Get off the line, we've
got troubles enough."

"Very well, Gitler. However, please record that we're
shunting the river around you as of now."

"What!" Jothen shouted. "Listen, get me a senior monitor up there—this is no time for computer handling.
We can't do without the river—"

"This is Monitor Control."

"But—how do we drain off this mess you sent us, then?"

"You'll have to store it," KC said primly.

"Store it in what?"

"Your problem, Gitler. We can't allow you to contami-
nate the water table downstream. Good luck. Out."

"Out upon you, you—"

The KC line went dead.

"Piscetti . . . Piscetti! . . . Oh, damn . . . master computer! Give me a radioactives storage deadhead!"

"Radio storage tanks are sealed," Gitler's computer said.

"Open them, and reroute all drainage channels for re-
ceipt of sewage."

"No access," the computer said. "Radio storage is under UNOC seal except for emergency dumping of nuclear wastes."

Jothen shut the mike off for a moment and swore.

Obviously he could not dump the city's two working power piles; that would leave the whole of Gitler without electricity. But on the other hand, what choice did he have? He had to get rid of the incoming garbage somehow, and the river was now closed to him.

"Dump the technie village pile in—let me see—twelve minutes after the mark. Dump the city's stand-by pile three minutes thereafter, barring a countermanding order from me, and nobody else. At eighteen minutes, shunt all city effluent into the radio storage tanks. And give me a rate-of-fill estimate for the tanks, keyed to radiation hazard for personnel in the subbasements."

"Minirads for personnel will be reached in fourteen minutes after the mark," the computer said, with perfect indifference. "Radio storage capacity will fill and reseal at two hours aught two minutes. Subbasements will be uninhabitable for personnel thereafter for approximately twenty-eight thousand, five hundred and thirty-nine years, give or take four years."

"That's no good. Advise Kansas City River Control that we will overflow hot onto the water table after *one* hour unless they let us spill into the river instead, and give them a complete rundown on what isotopes to expect, halflives and all. Don't tell me, tell them. Also, tell Radio Census Washingtongrad we're going to have a long-term hot spot underground here, same data. Mark and move on all orders when I switch out."

"Ready to mark," the computer said, almost as disinterestedly as Piscetti.

"All right. Out."

Another call light lit. It was Piscetti back again.

"Hello, Jothen, glad I located you. I've been picking up your program. But I've got something else, too. I think we've identified the murderer."

Jothen was astonished to discover that he had forgotten all about the death of Guivrec. "Who is it?"

"A Madagascan technie named Fongaváro Jones. He tried to join our maintenance staff a day or so after he got here, but Tananarive—that's his home town—wouldn't release him. Then he disappeared, and there have been unexplained small drains on the Rest Stops in the murder area ever since."

"Sounds convincing."

"There's more. The news leaked out somehow, and the rest of the Joneses have been blowing up the rumors in the usual way. The last version I heard was that a homicidal maniac is on the loose with a laser metal cutter. They say he's already killed and dismembered fifteen people, all ages, both sexes."

"I'm not surprised," Jothen said grimly.

"No, but it's still feeding back. Fongaváro evidently has been listening in from one Rest Stop or another, because he now seems to have the idea that he can frighten everybody away—maintenance staff included—and have the city all to himself. He just tried to broadcast a general warning, something very grisly about 'The Stalker Who Strikes Unseen'—wonder what he's been reading lately? Anyhow, the computer intercepted it, compared the voice with the one recorded on the transfer application, and there we were. It's Fongaváro, all right."

"And psychotic for sure. Put a squad after him, but don't risk them unnecessarily—that area's due to be flooded. I'd rather have him just kept below than captured, if there's no other alternative."

"Will do. Be sure to get out yourself."

"Right. Out."

A sharp hiss from the shunt-room floor made him jump, but it was only the discharge lock, splitting lengthwise to emit a capsule whose green cocarde said it contained pine nut flour. It lay quiescent on its receiving truck for a moment like a fat white worm, its flexible sides still glistening with the water that had pushed it into Gitler. Then the truck hummed away with it along the tracks toward the community kitchens.

The groan he had heard earlier must have been in response to the arrival of that load; evidently the crystallized spot in the main line was in even worse shape than he had feared. The discharge lock had already closed, and at the moment the usual torrent of water was rushing along the line in its usual silence—but that wouldn't last.

He glanced at the clocks: only three minutes to go! It seemed impossible that so much time had already passed; yet now that he was watching the tumblers and sweep hands, they seemed to freeze into immobility. The last sixty seconds were the longest in his life. Was it *never* going to happen . . . ?

The line groaned once more. Then, with a crack like the snapping of a tree bole, the main line split. Water jetted out of it. Under the intense pressure behind it, the jet was as smooth and hard as a sheet of glass; and it shattered like glass when it hit the baffle over the drain. The air in the hall became one solid, terrible shriek. Were it not for the glastic barriers, the sound alone would have killed him.

He looked quickly over his shoulder to make sure that the one-man lift to the flyport control tower was still standing open and ready. At that instant, the noise stopped. In the aching, intolerable silence, the crack in the main lengthened, and something came swelling out of it like an obscene balloon—the gallium capsule or a pseudopod of it.

Jothen did not wait for the sequel. He was into the little drum-shaped lift and shooting skyward in six seconds flat.

Beneath him, the computer stolidly continued to watch, filming a miscalculation it could have prevented, had anybody had time to ask it esoteric and unlikely questions about rare-earth chemistry. As the hot spray of silvery metal hit the moist air of the shunt-room, most of the trivalent stuff converted to the sesquioxide. The air seethed. Spitting like dragon's poison, the oxide flakes struck the baffle, which was magnesium only slightly alloyed to prevent burning. As it splashed over the baffle, the dragon's spittle reduced to metallic gallium again, promptly and violently.

The explosion shook the top levels of Gitler like a temblor. Jothen's car, the compressed air on which it was riding snatched out from under it, slammed to a stop halfway to the flyport control tower. Trembling and swearing, Jothen began to climb the rest of the way.

*Anyhow,* he thought, *so much for Fongaváro Jones.*

He had never before had so prompt an answer. From somewhere behind him, a shot pierced his temporary deafness, and ricocheted squealing away from the riser three inches from his left foot, leaving a bright weal in the metal.

It had been easy enough for Fongaváro to come by the gun. Except for the very small and inexperienced police squad—half of which was already hunting for him—nobody in Gitler went armed, of course; but here, as in Tananarive and in every other city, there was a small cache of sidearms in every fifth Rest Stop, stored there for the technies' use against the possibility of a really major riot. Though he had never fired a gun and expected to continue to prefer strangulation, Fongaváro had appropriated a pistol early on, just in case.

It would probably have been rather more difficult for him to say exactly when he had come to believe that Jothen Kent was the principal agent of all his troubles. In one sense, the realization had swept over him when he had listened in on the Gitler official's directions for hunting him down—or allowing him to drown. At least, it was then that he had realized that killing Jothen Kent would now be only self-defense.

But in another sense, it seemed to him that he had always known it. After all, it must have been Kent who had turned down his original petition to be transferred to Gitler's working crew; surely no computer would have been entrusted with an application so important. It was on Kent's orders that the Joneses were being evacuated, obviously a transparent maneuver to ship Fongaváro home by force under cover of a fake emergency—what sane man would believe that story about a giant meteor?—no matter how many other people's civil rights were violated in the process. And surely it must have been Kent who had cunningly alerted the computer to any possible further message from the fugitive; Fongaváro knew something about computers, and had carefully and cleverly worded his warning to get it past any mechanical intelligence that lacked the guidance of a human enemy. But for Kent, it couldn't have failed.

In any event, it was now perfectly clear that Fongaváro could not hope to have Gitler to himself while Jothen Kent was alive. Without Kent, the evacuation of the Joneses would fall apart—this McGee with whom Kent was trying to confuse him was obviously only some sort of minor politician or other flunky—and the milling hordes would then be easy to panic. In addition, the hounding of Fongaváro himself would stop, deprived of the leadership of the one man who was really out to get him. It all made perfect sense.

Avoiding the patrols, and getting out of the subbasements, was simple. After all, he could hear every order that Kent issued, even those that didn't seem to bear directly on hunting him down. For the same reason, finding where Kent was working, and was planning to go next, had been equally easy. Fongaváro worked his way cautiously up the utility stack, stalking the stalker.

The explosion threw him, and enraged him. He had not expected Kent to be ready to destroy a part of the city to get him. He was almost as surprised to see his prey erupt from the lift-shaft in midair, so to speak, and go on up toward the flyport on foot. But he was determined to let nothing that Kent could do rattle him—nothing!

Regaining his footing, he pointed the gun and jerked the trigger.

Of course, he missed, and nearly lost hold of the little automatic, to boot. But it did not look like he had missed by much. He took aim again, this time using both hands.

"Fongaváro!"

That was Kent's voice, echoing down the stack. It was bound to be a trick.

"*Fongaváro!* Cut it out, man! Don't you *want* to get out of this alive?"

"I'm not getting out," Fongaváro said—to his own surprise, for he had not meant to answer at all. "You can't scare me away—"

"Then you're being a damn fool. The main feeder line's broken and the city's flooding. Throw away the gun and come on aloft with me. I'll help you if I can. There are planes up there, waiting to take you all home."

At the word "planes," the whole of the stack washed out into a red blur, and Fongaváro's ears roared with the pulsing of his own blood. Through the pounding confusion, he heard the gun go off . . . but when he could see again, Jothen Kent had vanished.

The provisional emergency exit debouched Jothen into a section of the city with which he was unfamiliar—and worse, it was empty. It appeared to be a residential area, perhaps the topmost one under the technie village.

The air of the street was full of settling dust, which confused him further, since he had never seen such a thing before. He could only guess that it was some aftermath of the explosion, and was glad his gas mask was in place.

There was, of course, no way to lock the emergency exit and he wasted no time seeking ways to jam or block it. His only impulse was to run. He did not like being shot at.

But run to where? In the distance, he heard a compound rumble of many voices, some of them shouting. That might just be the sound of a column of Joneses, being led up motorstairs toward the roof. If so, there might be one or two of his own men there who would be armed; or, at worst, he ought to be able to lose himself in the crowd. Panting, he took off.

There was a blurred yell, hardly human, behind him, and then another shot. How many rounds did that gun have in it, anyhow? He remembered, not too certainly, that the standard automatic was a high-velocity weapon that bit tiny splinters of lead azide off the end of a roll of plastic-fill tape; if Fongaváro had one of those, it was good for at least a hundred tries at Jothen before even a dub at guns would have to try to reload it or throw it away. Jothen promptly tried to run faster, but short of free flight, he was already making better time than he would before have thought possible.

He careened around a circle of silently watching coupon shops, all as empty of merchandise as they were of people, and slowed down at the main entrance to another utility stack. It was sealed—by his own order. But the crowd noise now seemed quite close. Cutting down a deserted avenue, he found himself charging now into an exchange plaza.

His heart gave a bound of hope. The plaza was full of pushing, flushed, scared figures in torn costumes, some carrying or tugging at quarreling or squalling children, others dragging baggage they had never had to carry before, still others finding it difficult to shuffle their own two feet. From the midst of the mob, two broad spiral escalators, twined around each other like twinned genes, wound upward through the remote roof, packed with restive Joneses.

He tried to work his way through them, and was indignantly shoved back at, until the people around him took second looks at him and saw the honeycomb helmet. Then they gave way, but slowly and sullenly. The Gitler crew was not, it was painfully clear, very popular around here at the moment.

Slow though his progress was, Jothen should have been pleased with it, for he was surely quite buried in this mass of flesh now. But instead he felt stifled, and himself on the verge of panic. Sweating, he went on shouldering his way forward, trying to pull through the gas mask thick, wet air that completely refused to move into his lungs.

The helmet jolted suddenly on his head and shoulders as he jammed himself onto the nearest escalator—somebody had tried to punch him where it usually counted. Then he was on the stairs and being swung up and up, around and around, and the plaza was fading into a lake of bent heads and angry upturned faces. Breathing a long sigh of relief, he looked back at the boulevard by which he had come galloping into this press of people.

Fongaváro was standing there, the street empty behind him, his monkey body and ragged filth marking him off from the other costumes almost as readily as the neat, vicious little gun in his hand. Jothen felt an impulse to thumb his nose; but at the same moment the foreshortened Madagascan raised the pistol at the end of both long arms and fired it squarely at Jothen's head. How could he tell which of all these stair-riders—

The helmet! Even among all these unintelligibly costumed people, there could be no mistaking that bulging, functional carapace; it said *Gitler* to all the Joneses, and *Jothen* to Fongaváro, like a scarlet tattoo. And Jothen did not dare take it off, even if the spiral swath of bodies around him had left him any cranny in which to hide it; it was now his only contact with Piscetti, with McGee, with the crew, with the world at large.

Where the hell was the armed squad? How long was this damned go-around motorstair ride going to take? How far up—

*Splat!*

The sound of the automatic was only a stitch in the fabric of the crowd's noise, but Jothen—and probably Jothen alone—could hear it all too well. He flinched helplessly inside the honeycomb, feeling as though the whole front of his helmeted head was one enormous target.

But Fongaváro, amazingly, did not seem to think he was getting anywhere at all. Jamming the still potent gun somewhere inside his rags, he scuttled almost on his knuckles along the fringes of the mob until he came upon a fat and fussy old Jones in a Pierrot suit who seemed to be trying to load his life's possessions onto a battered but still floating autocrutch. Dumping the oldster and the luggage with a single brutal sweep of his forearms, Fongaváro straddled the machine and scooted in a long, wobbly parabola toward the top of the motorstair tree.

The hole in the ceiling swallowed Jothen before he saw the end of that crazy ride. He was just as glad, but he knew better now than to draw any deep breaths; he was still on the run.

The next level was the floor of the technie village, quiet and bucolic and familiar ordinarily. Now it was a shambles. The overflow Joneses—out of sight and hence out of mind of Gitler's few and tentative police—were making up for the loss of their totems and baggages by looting the technies' homes. There was nobody around to prevent them, or even to herd them back toward the roof; they were spreading out all through the level, giggling, singing, and throwing bottles at each other. Fuming with indignation, Jothen threw a leg over the stairs to get back down to the floor; somebody had to break up this orgy—

*Splat!*

Another poisonous, explosive little bullet flew by his helmet and drove him back to his main interest—flight. Casting frantically about for the shot's source, Jothen saw Fongaváro roweling his autocrutch, riding tail up and sidewise, out of the mouth of a ventilator shaft about half a mile away. The Madagascan's expression was unreadable at this distance, but his whole posture telegraphed black murder in any language.

There had to be some way out of this cul-de-sac. It was ridiculous that Fongaváro should be able to make better time through the pores and doors of Gitler than Jothen himself could. The technies' access shaft to the flyport control tower had to be on this level, if only he could bull his way off these damn *stairs.*

Like a scuba diver, Jothen rolled over the moving handrail of the stairs and dropped to the floor of the village. Fongaváro banked around the stairs and swooped down over the heads of his scampering cousins, but he was having a hard time with the lurching autocrutch, which had not been designed for aerobatics. He overshot Jothen so fast that he nearly rammed into the far side of the square.

While he was still fighting to regain control of his clumsy metal broomstick, more than half of the lights dimmed and went out, to a groan of dismay from the

Joneses. The computer, restricted now to battery power, was economizing.

The sudden gloom was just what Jothen needed. By the time Fongaváro was in condition to look for his quarry again, Jothen was already in the lift.

"Has anybody got a gun?"

In the control tower, heads turned blindly toward Jothen, with the tense impatience of men distracted from serious work by nonsense. Then one of the crew recognized him.

"I think there are some signal pistols up here, Mr. Kent. If they're still operative. We don't expect to need them."

"Won't do. I mean a gun I can kill somebody with."

"Kill somebody? No, sir, nothing of that sort," the towerman said stiffly, and went back to work. Only one other operator had been listening to the brief exchange, and that with less than half of his attention. His expression clearly showed that he thought he had probably missed a key word somewhere.

Jothen sighed and looked out over the flyport. From here he could see no trace of the explosion, unless he counted a small but rapidly rising column of white smoke from a ventilator head about a mile away. The rest was silence. Beginning right at the edge of the flyport, the Monterey pines, hybrid poplars, bamboo, and giant sugar cane—the food of the world—covered the whole of Gitler, marching solemnly down the terraces and Chinese walls, and joining the rest of the World Forest so smoothly that the city's edges were impossible to define from the air. From here, the world was in a pastoral sleep.

Overhead, the autumn dusk was deepening, soft and clear. There was no moon, but already the night gave promise of a blaze of stars, with, of course, no sky glare to mock them. Among one constellation's scatter of suns—he could not tell which—Jothen could make out several distant moving lights, probably the first planes of the ferry fleet. Transcorp had moved fast, as usual.

Evidently McGee had also moved fast. A growing murmur of many voices, like a distant sea, told Jothen that a surf of Joneses was already out on the roof of the city. He could see several amoeboid batches of them, dim and sad in their drooping finery, clumping together like slime molds on the flyport's staging apron; but most of them were invisible, masked by the trees. That accounted in part for the uneasy edge to the susurrus. Ordinarily, nobody was allowed in the World Forest but rangers, and repairmen of the Pipeline Corps, and the Joneses doubtless were finding the open air and the towering silent woods disquieting.

"Let's stick together, friends and clansmen!" McGee's voice bellowed suddenly. He was using a bull horn, but even so his voice was tinny with distance. "Don't wander, don't wander! There's grandfathers in them trees! Stay by the flyport—don't get left behind!"

"Up your Jones!" a much tinier voice shouted. A ragged chorus returned the cheer.

"That's it! Up Joneses! Stay close!"

McGee seemed to be managing; so far, so good. But what had happened to Fongaváro? And why was it so dark? The Joneses should find it easier to stick close to the flyport if they could see its lights, but those were steadily going out. Even the beacons were mostly dead. Jothen pulled his cheek mike into place to reassume direction of his city, and found that that, too, was dead.

The computer's economy measures were becoming drastic. It could not be faulted for that; battery power does not last very long. But the power failure was damn dangerous, and would complicate the evacuation; even if the motorstairs continued to work, for instance, the ferries would have to land blind, by PPI radar.

And no wonder McGee was using a bull horn instead of the public address system. The man was resourceful, that had to be granted.

It got slowly darker, despite the emerging stars. The Forest whispered, as if remembering the ghosts of long extinct animals. Underfoot, something thumped—a secondary explosion?—and the murmuring of the Joneses grew louder. They were already confused by the conflicting orders, angry at having had their fun cut off, and probably still making everything worse with the undertow of rumor. And now, also, they were becoming afraid of the strange noises and the deepening night.

Something like a bat—or what Jothen imagined might be like a bat—swooped suddenly in front of his face. It took him a moment to realize that the thing was actually some distance away; and then, that it was Fongaváro on his autocrutch. He was flying very badly. That was not surprising, for the fan-driven prosthetic machines had never been designed for the open air; but the wild way he was lurching around the sky could not be entirely the fault of the crutch. He was fighting not only the machine, but himself—*terror fugatis.*

Jothen looked away. There was nothing he could do now; he had gone as far as he could go. He switched his headset to the emergency channel. It responded with a gratifying hum.

"McGee?"

It would not have surprised him had the putative mayor never heard of the emergency channel; but McGee responded at once.

"Hello, Jothen—where the hell have you been? Never mind, noisy down here. Have to talk to you later."

"Hold on—"

"Sorry. Got my hands full of Joneses. Are the ferries coming?"

"Yes, on the way. Are you—?"

"Good. Hold fast, and be of good cheer. Out."

While Jothen spluttered, the bull horn began to sound again. Torches began to light, too, some of them among the trees. *Fire in the Forest?* Jothen bawled into his cheek mike, but there was no answer.

More Joneses poured out into the flyport and into the woods. The tower deck rumbled under Jothen's feet.

Then, there was light.

First the tops of the trees turned silvery. Then, on the roofs, the blackness became stippled with tiler's dots, as hundreds of thousands of white faces turned skyward. A long moan rolled through the Joneses like a comber. Jothen, too, looked up.

A falling star, so immense that it might almost have been a falling sun, was streaking with preternatural slowness over the city, lighting the whole landscape with a garish blue-white glare. The side of a nearby ferry, just settling in for a landing, gleamed in the glow as though a searchlight was playing upon it.

The light seemed to be what Fongaváro had been waiting for. Either he had dropped the gun, or had forgotten it in his fear of the open sky and the mechanical besom of which he was astride. Instead, he swerved toward the immobile giant of the control tower and came bulleting directly at the broad windows.

The noise of the meteor's passage had already reached the ground, a loud rumbling like the thunder of distant artillery. Cries of awe and fright rose from the Forest to meet it. For a wild instant, Jothen wondered if this were the monster Flavia herself, ahead of schedule and far too far to the south; but in the same second he realized that it was probably only one of the fragments

Biond Smith's crew had chipped off the asteroid—a small one, probably no more than a hundred tons.

Two thirds of the way across the sky, the meteor exploded, blindingly. Fiery streaks rayed away, nearly to the horizon. Fongaváro, almost close enough now for Jothen to see his features, jerked his craft upward, half rolled, and ran side-on into a descending ferry.

The ferry, only dented, lurched and righted itself, but the autocrutch disintegrated. Its bright fragments and the sprawling black figure of Fongaváro Jones rained down from Heaven together toward Chaos and Dis, in a blast of sound from the exploded bolide that made the explosion in the shunt-room seem like it had been only a warning slap.

Fongaváro's long nightmare of falling had come true, and now was ended.

The cries of the Joneses grew louder, edged with hysteria. On the flyport apron, a woman's voice was screaming "The end of the world! Grandfather is fallen! The end of the world!"

Jothen, shaking, tried again to call McGee, and then Piscetti, but if either replied their voices were drowned out in an enormous waterfall that seemed to have gotten started inside his earphones. When he got his sight back, he saw why—the passage of the meteor had left a broad trail of glowing white vapor stretched across the sky like an infernal rainbow. The ionized wake had completely wiped out radio reception, probably all across the spectrum.

Below, the torches began to swirl. The crowd noise was rising to a roar. The dented ferry, rocking on its fans, was settling to the apron, and another was coming in.

"Too late," Jothen thought numbly. "They're going to panic."

And there was exactly nothing that he could do about

it, even had he had any idea of how to proceed. The shadowy figures of the tower stand-by crew, mustered to replace the out-of-action computer, were already bustling in the gloom around him, ready to assist the ferry landings the moment radio contact could be established —or perhaps they were using FM and had never lost contact in the first place. He would have to give them whatever helping hand he could—

Another meteor bloomed in the night sky, rumbling like a thunderhead. It was not as big as the first, but the Joneses were by now in no mood to be discriminating. The crowd roar grew still louder.

Then Jothen heard McGee's voice cutting across the din, his bull horn turned up to full amplification—a gargantuan bellow that must have been audible even in the still airborne ferries. Astonishingly, the mayor was singing. Had he gone mad too?

> Raise the totems, Gott soll hueten,
> Fa-la-la-de-rol and cordon bleu!
> Jericho immune to tootin',
> Mighty Mother, we love you!

Or so Jothen heard it—surely those couldn't really be the words. But the Joneses seemed to recognize them; a family hymn? Scattered voices took up the song, and then, many more.

"That's it, Joneses! All together now!"

The second meteor blew up. Under the light and noise, and that of the ferries' fans, the singing became defiantly louder.

> Hubbard's husband, Hubba's wife,
> Smith's disaster, Brown's dismay,
> Guard of Uncle unoc's life,
> Faithful shepherd, a-ok!

205

Jothen heard himself emit a nervous giggle and suppressed it angrily. Dammit, that surely wasn't how the words went! He tried to pay attention to something that mattered. Six or seven ferries were on the ground now, and Joneses were pouring out of the Forest toward them, led by a tiny, frenetically waving figure. McGee seemed to be leading some kind of a snake dance onto the tarmac.

A third and a fourth meteor arched across the sky together, roaring. The crowd howled back its challenge. The first ferry was loaded and taking off. By several of the others, Joneses about to board were ceremoniously snuffing out torches in upended metal drums that seemed to have materialized by magic for just this purpose.

Another ferry buzzed off; then another.

"All right, neighbors! Everybody now! Hit it!"

The piper's charges raised their voices in a deafening chorus. Nothing else in the world could have been heard above such a choir, not even a major earthquake—by now there must have been nearly half a million people involved, spread out all over the roofs; it was as though hell itself were singing. Distance muddled the hymn into a shapeless, tuneless thunder, but Jothen could still hear McGee:

> ConEd cons us, UNOC bombs us,
> Devils hearstle at our bones—
> Still the jolly heartside chorus:
> Love us all, and up your Jones!

The sky was full of planes. And then, suddenly, the flyport lights went on; whether or not Piscetti had gotten the floods under control, the master computer had reached the end of its allotted clock time and had restored power to the city.

The evacuation of the Jones Convention would keep right on going, for many days—but the crisis was over. Useless, tubby McGee had piped his rats aboard.

Jothen had stopped shaking by the time he got back to his office, but he could not honestly have described himself as unshaken. He was glad—God knew—that it was all essentially over, but there were still major questions that he could not begin to answer for himself. He sat down at his disordered console and thought about them conscientiously, but not to much purpose.

He still had no notion of how he was going to cope—both practically and emotionally—with the Chicago influx after having spent most of his adult life virtually alone in so heavily populated a world. He had not done very well this time; indeed, he had damn near gotten himself killed, and the city was in terrible shape. He felt both incompetent and oppressed.

It seemed that there was no such thing as a single crisis. Every one was a fall of dominoes. It took a lot of footwork just to stay abreast of them.

He noticed with a start that the line to Prime Center was blinking at him. Numbly, he opened it.

"Jothen?" Biond Smith's voice said.

"Here. Hullo, Biond."

"How did it go? KC tells me you're having a terrible scramble. Did you get the Joneses moving?"

"They're on their way," Jothen said. He was surprised to hear that Biond, too, sounded oppressed. Evidently world directors also had their troubles.

"Good. Have you heard anything from Kim?"

"No—haven't you?" Jothen said in alarm.

"Not yet, but I assume she's plenty busy seeing to it that the contents of the Preserve are all killed. Was McGee of any use? He's fairly good with paper, I've found."

"He was invaluable," Jothen said. "Especially during the meteor shower."

"Meteor shower?" Biond said, his voice cracking slightly. "Did those fragments come down as far south as Gitler? Obviously they did. Damn, somebody's miscalculated. I'll have to get on that. And now we get to the meat of the matter—Flavia, and the *real* evacuations. You'd better keep McGee there, as long as he was helpful. He doesn't know a dyne from a dinosaur, of course, but all the same these ward heeler types have their uses. I'm one myself. Glad you're all right, Jothen. 'Bye."

The line went dead.

Taking a deep breath, Jothen set his face and his soul in order and went out to meet his world, or his doom. Maybe by now there was no longer any difference.

But somehow he felt that he would be more on top of things if only he could figure out what a "ward heeler" was.

## 11    Hybrid Vigor

The Atlantic Regional Headquarters of SPC on Great Inagua strongly suggested a fortress, as, in a way, it was. Squat and massive, it had withstood every assault of tempest and wave that the Atlantic Ocean had hurled against it for over two hundred years. Built chiefly of reinforced vitrolith, its few outer windows and doors could be closed by massive, watertight storm shields so that its outer surface offered no edges or angles to the elements. Hurricane winds had blasted at it, thundering tons of water had battered it, but it had never so much as sprung a leak.

From Dorthy's office on the topmost level she could see Little Inagua Island northward, and beyond that, the open sea; but the view failed to move her now. Nothing had been going right. First her panic during Project Mile-Deep; then the aborted trip to Prime Center; then Tioru's abrupt turnabout; and now, Operation Safeguard was dying before it had properly gotten off the ground.

But it was Tioru that she could not stop thinking about. She could not imagine why it was that she was so dismayed; yet she felt hurt and lost. Maybe, she thought grayly, I was just kidding myself—pretending to be undecided, waiting for him to make up my mind for me . . . a fine act for the head of SPC to have to put on for herself!

But why had he, too, changed so suddenly, in only a few days? Had he been hoping for some convenient excuse to call it all quits? No, damn it, that was unfair; he never dreamed that Dryland would be so . . . and yet he's being so impersonal and efficient, as if . . .

Love, love!

Dorthy squeezed the tears out of her eyes and turned away from the blinding sea-borne horizon. She had to show a little efficiency of her own. To begin with, to think of some way to persuade her skeptical, impersonal, efficient Tritons to make Operation Safeguard work.

Safeguard was a disaster plan, Dorthy's share in the preparations for the imminent collision with Flavia. It provided for the evacuation of all the Triton communities in the world, bar none. Those who were able would swim, warded by their dolphins. Those who could not— the young, the old, the ill—would be taken out on submersibles or barges. All would rendezvous five miles offshore of their homes, and ride out the crisis in the cradle of the waters, afloat or submerged.

But it wasn't going to work. It absolutely demanded a preliminary, world-wide test evacuation, so that the operation itself should have no holes left in it. And the Tritons—almost all of them—were quietly, silently, politely having none of it. Half of them had already disappeared from their reefs into the deep waters; more were vanishing by the hour. They simply did not believe in Flavia; no mass that fell in the subarctic zone of Unistam could hurt their tropical and isolated settlements, let alone disturb the eternal sea. The whole thing smacked suspiciously of a Dryland scheme. . . .

"Dorthy?"

Dorthy started. "Tioru! I didn't hear you. Did you come out of thin air, like Storm?"

"No, not like Storm. You were just brooding, Dorthy. But about Safeguard—I've got a couple of reports."

"Good, I hope."

"Not very. They're from the seismic monitoring network. For one thing, there've been only three major quakes in the past five years—a long quiet period. The stresses around four of the main quake centers have been building up. One good shock could set off a chain of them—and Flavia could well pull the trigger. I don't think even the reefs will be immune."

"That's what I've been saying all along," Dorthy said. "What else?"

"A minor clue. Mount Pelee is showing signs of life—for the first time in ninety-three years. Nothing much—just a small plume of smoke and steam rising from the crater. But in context, it's a bad sign."

"Well," she said, "it's bad. But maybe if we relay the news to the reefs, it'll help the skeptics to change their minds. Try it, anyhow."

"I already have," he said quietly. He made no move

to go. There was a long, awkward silence. At last, Tioru cleared his throat.

"Dorthy . . ."

She nodded, looking off at the horizon, not trusting herself to speak.

"Dorthy, I could have phoned you. The reports could have waited, or come up on the vidphone—anything. But I had to talk to you."

"All right." She tried to sound casual, but she nearly choked on the second word. "Talk."

"Listen to me, Dorthy. We haven't begun to talk yet. On Wreck Reef, you were in despair because you thought you'd fumbled Mile-Deep. In Philadelphia, I was in a panic because I thought people hated me— and because I found a dead girl. We can't make any sense to each other under conditions like those—and neither of those things has anything to do with us."

With her fingertip, Dorthy traced loops and zigzags among the buttons and switches of her communications console.

"What's on your mind?" she whispered.

"A start. A second start. It's ridiculous for both of us to try to be so damn impersonal. If we could start again —well, we might find something new to think about. Something that would help."

Filled suddenly with frustration and self-hatred, Dorthy swung to him, weeping helplessly. He seized her hands.

"I can't believe it—I can't!" she sobbed, her fingers clenching around his. "You know what would happen. We'd talk, and we'd talk, and in the end—we'd have talked ourselves into the same old impasse. Do we have to go through all that again? I couldn't bear it, Tioru."

"I can't guarantee that we won't talk ourselves into an impasse, but I'm sure that if we do it will be a new one, not the same old one."

"A new one! How mysterious you sound. What do you mean?"

"There are some facts about Tritons that you don't know, and they will almost certainly change your outlook when you do."

"Well, for goodness sake, tell me!"

"It's not for me to tell you. Storm will have to do it."

"Storm! When?"

"He'll be here tonight. He's on his way now from Great Barrier. He wants to meet both of us on Little Inagua."

"Tioru, what are you up to?"

"You have a suspicious nature. I'm not up to anything, except trying to iron out our difficulties. Whatever it is that Storm has planned, I had nothing to do with it. He phoned me several days ago and said that he wants both of us on Little Inagua at twenty hours today. He also asked me to find a beach there, somewhat removed from everything, as our meeting place. I found a beach that seems to meet the requirements."

"A beach, removed from everything, for three people? It sounds like a meeting of conspirators."

"It isn't a conspiracy. It's—well, you'll just have to wait."


A twilight calm lay upon the channel between the two Inaguas. Along the western horizon the sunset had dwindled to a band of jade-green, which blended upward into a broad zone of dusky blue. This in turn merged into a violet arch of the zenith, finally deepening into the fathomless violet-black of night where the first stars shone.

Dorthy and Tioru, prone on the deck of a water-scooter, skimmed smoothly across a sea that had become a deep green mirror striped with shining, limpid, pale green ribbons of the afterglow reflected on its gently undulating swells. Northward, ahead of them, lay the long flat profile of Little Inagua. Over the sea beyond Little Inagua a colossal thunderhead reached for the zenith—a cumulo-nimbus tower with a flat top drawn out at one side into a point like the beak of an anvil. It was in somber blue shadow save for the westward side of its summit, which caught the last coral-pink sunset glow. Internal lightning flares flickered through it.

"How are you going to find the beach where we're to meet Storm?" said Dorthy. "I don't see a beacon anywhere."

Tioru said, "You can't see it from here. It's on the other side."

He steered a course around the easternmost point of the island, then northwest. An orange glow in the sky ahead of them, its source hidden behind another promontory, threw into black relief a skyline like a crenelated wall. Tioru veered around this enigmatic headland and entered a circular lagoon that had been cut back into the island.

The lagoon was bordered by a beach, and behind the beach was the curving mass of a huge ruin—a façade of shattered walls, broken arches, and standing isolated pillars rising from a jumble of fallen blocks of structural glass, chunks of reinforced concrete bristling with protruding metal rods, and warped sheets of corroded bronze. Its middle portion was ruddied by the light of a bonfire blazing at the center of the beach, but the more distant portions of the crescent were only vague masses looming in the darkness.

The figure of a man was silhouetted against the fire. He raised an arm and waved.

"That's Storm," said Tioru.

Dorthy said, "I've seen this old ruin before, by daylight. One of the people with me said that it dates back to the twenty-second century, but that was all they knew. Why did you pick such a strange, wild place as this?"

"It's what Storm wanted," Tioru said.

The scooter slowed, grated on a coral dome, and stopped. Dorthy and Tioru lowered themselves into the waist-deep water, freed the scooter, and, with Storm's help, beached it.

Dorthy said, "Now, please tell me the meaning of these mysterious goings-on before I explode."

Storm smiled and said, "Please don't do that. You'll know everything before long."

She was astonished by that smile. Heretofore all of Storm's smiles had been mere ghosts of smiles, gone before they were fully formed. This time he had smiled a full-blown, indubitable smile.

Between the fire and the water's edge, but nearer the fire, lay a great flat-topped chunk of some bone-white material partially embedded in the sand. It could have been a massive inverted block from an ornamental cornice; traces of geometrical designs were still dimly visible upon it and one side was formed like a flight of steps. Its flat top was almost level, rough-surfaced, and provided a natural podium. The lower, intertidal portion of its sides was encrusted with barnacles, clams, skeins of sea wrack, and other marine growths. Storm motioned toward it.

He said, "Now if you please, Dorthy, we'll go up these steps to the top of the rock. You stand in the center and face the fire."

"This seems silly. What happens now? I feel as if I were expected to deliver a speech. Where's the audience?"

Storm and Tioru seated themselves on the front edge of the platform, one on either side of her.

"You don't have to make a speech," said Storm, "but you do have an audience. Look."

Dorthy looked across the leaping flames, surveyed the beach from end to end, and at first saw nothing unusual—only the sweeping concave curve of the beach with the giant ruin as a backdrop and above it all the night sky, now filled with stars.

Then, with a sudden shock, her perceptions came to a focus and she really saw what was before her. She gasped and covered her mouth with her hands.

There were hundreds of Tritons facing her, men and women, old and young. They were spread out along the central portion of the beach, back among the rubble where the firelight was dim—standing, sitting, reclining on and among the tumbled blocks and shattered pillars, silent and motionless as statues. At Dorthy's gasp and gesture of amazement the tableau dissolved in a wave of laughter and applause.

"We have a presentation to make to you," said Storm. "You're about to meet the two people who were the instigators of it all. Look straight ahead of you across the fire, and watch."

Directly opposite her, between two mounds of tumbled masonry, Dorthy discovered a narrow open lane that led to a triple archway in an intact section of wall. Through the arches she could see nothing but darkness. No—something was moving in the shadows under the central arch. Two people became dimly visible, slowly advancing into the firelight.

Dorthy peered and tried to identify them. As they came farther into the light she felt that there was something familiar in the two figures, side by side. She had seen them before—somewhere, sometime. One was taller than the other.

They came slowly down the open land and into the full light of the fire.

Involuntarily Dorthy cried out, "Limpet and Squid!" Both children had their eyes fixed on Dorthy with expressions of intent solemnity. Limpet was carrying with both hands a circular casket of carved ivory.

They separated, walked around the fire, approached the platform of rock, mounted the steps, and stood on either side of Dorthy, facing each other. All the other Tritons had become silent and motionless again.

Limpet began to speak in a clear little voice that trembled at first, then steadied as she went on.

"There's people here tonight from all over the world," said Limpet. "At least one from every reef. It was Squid's idea at first, but Storm got it all organized. The box and what's in it is my idea and they're from everywhere too. The box is pieces of narwhal ivory all put together. Here, Squid, you hold it."

Squid took the box and held it. Limpet pressed the edge of the lid, it flew open, and Dorthy saw that it was lined with satiny white material. Resting in this lustrous setting was a golden bandeau spanning about two thirds of a circle; it was formed of intertwined golden dolphins, each one with a small pearl for an eye. Projecting from the bandeau were two curving fern-like golden fronds simulating the antennas of a Triton.

Limpet continued, "This is from everywhere too. The white stuff is sea silk. The gold's from coins that someone found in an old wreck off the Florida Keys. The pearls are all from different places all over the world, one from each place."

Removing the golden bandeau from the casket, Limpet adjusted it on Dorthy's head and positioned the antennas so that they appeared to be sprouting from her forehead.

"This stands for the love of all the Tritons in the world," said Limpet, "because you're the one Dryland person who cares the most about Tritons, and it means— it means . . ."

Here Limpet became unable to speak, compressed her lips, and pressed her clenched fists against her bosom.

"It means that now you're a Triton!" said Squid in a voice that was heard by every Triton on the beach and that reverberated in the recesses of the ruins.

"I—oh—I . . ." Dorthy began. Then both she and Limpet were overwhelmed by their emotions, embraced each other, and burst into tears.

"I *knew* this would happen," muttered Squid. "I *said* it would happen!"

Storm stood up, raised his voice, and said, "Dorthy has been declared a Triton. Do we all agree?"

"*Yes!*" shouted the Tritons in unison, then converged on the platform. Limpet and Squid escorted Dorthy down the steps, followed by Tioru and Storm. Everyone wanted to clasp her hand. She had never seen so many outstretched hands and had never been so deluged with affection. She could think of no response other than variations on the theme of "I'll never, *never* forget this!"

After the turmoil had subsided the Tritons congregated near the fire, where they sat or reclined on the sand. A cobalt-blue beach rug patterned with white sea horses was provided for Dorthy.

"You haven't heard everything yet," said Storm. "There's more to come."

"More!" said Dorthy. "What could that be?"

Tioru said, "Don't you remember? There are some facts about Tritons that you've never been told."

"Why have you waited until now?"

Storm said, "Because by general agreement among Tritons we've never told any Drylander and we don't intend to—not for a while. There are still billions of people who disapprove of tectogenetics and who feel that the Tritons shouldn't have been created in the first place. If they knew what I'm about to tell you, their hostility would increase and the results might be very unpleasant for us. We can tell you because you've been taken into the family. By the same token we're trusting you to keep the information secret."

"I promise not to repeat it—whatever it is. But go on! I'm bursting to know!"

Storm meditated and said, "Did you ever hear someone refer to hitting the jackpot?"

"No. It doesn't mean a thing to me. What is it?"

"It's an archaic Dryland expression. It means risking something in the hope of realizing a gain and then to reap one far in excess of one's expectations. Well, when the Drylander tectogeneticists created the Tritons they hit the jackpot, in a way. But they didn't know it."

"A reward in excess of their expectations? What was it?"

"The hybrids."

Dorthy sat bolt upright and exclaimed, "What!"

"The hybrids. Or, as I think you've called them, the In-Betweeners."

"I don't understand."

Storm reflected again, and then said, "Did you ever visualize something so clearly that it was almost as if you were looking at the thing itself?"

"Yes. I suppose that everyone has done that sometimes."

"Did you ever visualize something so strongly that you could actually see it as if it were an external, material object?"

"No. And if I did I'd call it a hallucination."

"Exactly. People *do* have hallucinations. They're an inherent capability of the human mind. But ordinary hallucinations are unpredictable, and don't happen because you will them to happen."

"There are drugs that will do it."

"Yes, but the results are beyond control. You have to

take your drug hallucinations as they come. Wouldn't it be useful if you could hallucinate at will according to your own specifications?"

"That's a weird idea. Why would it be useful?"

"Suppose you were an artist, a designer, architect, engineer, or writer. Or an executive of any kind. You could hallucinate your ideas and they would be externalized, right before your eyes. The architect, say, could hallucinate his plans, and the completed building. He could change, modify, revise in an instant. Think of the time, sketches, and false starts it would save."

"I suppose it would. But how did we get off on this wild tangent? It isn't possible."

"Oh yes, it is. Some of the hybrids can do it."

"I don't believe it. It's too fantastic!"

Storm dropped on one knee in front of Dorthy, cupped his hands together, and said, "Look at my hands."

And as Dorthy looked at his cupped hands, suddenly they were full of fire. Little yellow flames leaped and danced. Then they were gone.

For a few moments there was a great stillness. The bonfire crackled loudly and a swarm of sparks swirled up toward the stars.

"It's a trick," said Dorthy. "And *I* saw it. If it was a hallucination, it was mine."

"We both saw it. It was my voluntary hallucination, but I made you see it also. We call it a transfer hallucination."

"We? You said the hybrids—! Storm! You!"

"Yes. My father was a Dryland Maori. The fact is buried in my personnel file somewhere. I happen to be a hybrid who looks like a normal Triton, just as some of us appear to be normal Drylanders."

Dorthy swallowed and said, "I'll believe that you used hypnosis to make me see a handful of fire. I don't know how you managed it. But I just can't accept that it was a hallucination controlled by you and transferred to me."

Storm said, "Dorthy, what do you think of first when you think of me?"

"Well—for one thing, you always arrive and depart unseen."

Storm said, "Like this?" and vanished.

Dorthy cried, "Storm! Where are you?"

"Right here. I haven't moved," said Storm, reappearing. "Your perception of me was blocked. That was a negative hallucination—also one of the most elementary. It's the best that I'm capable of. I'm not a very gifted hallucinator, but the talent develops with use. I practice the simpler exercises and hope that I'll go on to the more difficult ones. I can't hallucinate a rigid object. The outlines waver like smoke in a breeze."

Dorthy felt a rising tide of weakness. A curtain of shadow seemed to be forming before her eyes and gradually becoming darker. She said, "All this is too much. I think I'm going to pass out."

She heard Tioru's voice say, "Here, drink this."

The brim of a cup was pressed to her lips and she gulped down a pungent, salty liquid. The curtain of shadow dissolved, the weakness ebbed.

Tioru said, "Is this enough for one session? Or do you want to go on?"

"I think I'm all right now. I have some questions. For one, are all hybrids hallucinators?"

"No," said Storm. "Some are—well, we call them empaths. They have a peculiar rapport with animals—dolphins, usually, of course. It isn't exactly telepathy, but it's similar. Some are mass-sensitive. Others have a homing ability. There are a number of categories and every hybrid has a talent in at least one. And there are several categories of hallucinators—visual, audio, tactile, even a few who can hallucinate tastes and odors. Some can hallucinate in two or three categories at the same time. Some can transfer, others can't. The visual type is the most common."

Dorthy turned to Squid and said, "What's your talent?"

Squid said, "I don't know. It hasn't showed yet. You can't tell when it will."

"A talent may show itself at almost any age," said Storm. "The earliest known, I think, was ten months after birth. The father is a violinist, and the parents— and some of their friends—began to hear violin sounds at all hours and in unexpected situations. It was some time before they realized that the baby was doing audio transfers."

"How upsetting!"

"Why upsetting?"

"It seems so—so uncanny, and inhuman."

"On the contrary," Storm said. "All these talents are inherent human capabilities and were known long before there were either Tritons or hybrids. The people who had them were known as sorcerers, soothsayers, saints, healers, or miracle workers. In Drylanders they are super-recessive capabilities, as if they were locked up with an extremely complicated lock that doesn't open except under very rare—and unknown—conditions. Hybridizing Drylander and Triton appears to be the combination that opens the lock. That's why I said that, in creating the Tritons, the Drylanders hit the jackpot without knowing it."

Seized by a sudden thought, Dorthy turned to Limpet and said, "Do you have any hidden talents?"

"No!" said Limpet, her eyes widening. "I'm just a Triton. I'm nobody special."

Dorthy said, "I don't agree with that. To me, you and Squid will always be someone special."

She turned a questioning look toward Tioru, who smiled and said, "No hidden talents here either."

Dorthy pressed her fingertips to her temples and closed her eyes for a few moments, then said to Storm:

"I need to think about this for a while and try to absorb it. I don't doubt what you've told me, but it seems unreal, as if it might melt away any minute, like—what did you call it?—like a transfer hallucination."

"You've had all you can take for the present?"

"Yes," Dorthy said. "Do you mean there's more?"

"There's nothing else."

"Then . . ."

She took Squid and Limpet by the hand and said, "Come with me."

The three of them mounted the rocky platform. Standing between the two children with her arms around their shoulders, Dorthy faced the assembled Tritons and said:

"What you've done for me tonight means more to me than you can ever know. I love every one of you, and especially Squid and Limpet. May you find the green deeps at peace."

The response of the Tritons rose in a wave of sound. "And the Dark Waters quiet."

The Tritons rose to their feet and began to move toward the water's edge. Dorthy came down from the platform and stood facing the beach, with the little swells of the incoming tide washing over her feet. She extended her arms on either side and as the Tritons moved past her and waded into the shallows each one stretched out a hand and brushed it against hers.

The near calm in the dark sea offshore was disturbed by the surging and hissing sounds of a flotilla of submersibles rising like surfacing whales from their berths where they had lain waiting on the bottom. Dorthy wondered how they had known when to surface. By thoughts leaping from mind to mind, from hybrids on the beach to dolphins to hybrids in the ships?

When all the Tritons except Tioru were in the water Dorthy turned and faced the sea. The subs had turned on their undersea floodlights so that each one was encircled by a halo of pale green luminous water. The dark shapes of curvetting dolphins and swimming Tritons were visible in the lighted zones. The Tritons began climbing aboard the subs that would return them to their reef homes around the world.

The floodlights blinked out one by one, leaving a swarm of paired red and green running lights, which began to separate and disperse. Dorthy watched as they fanned out over the sea, receding and dwindling. Then she turned and surveyed the beach.

The fire had subsided to a bed of bright orange-yellow coals with small blue flames flickering over them. Beyond it, the blue and white beach rug lay on the sand with the round ivory casket resting on it. Tioru was standing beside her.

He said, "Where do we go from here? How do you feel?"

"I'm not sure just where we go from here," said Dorthy. "And my feelings—right now they're a mish-mash. I'm happy—and I'm scared at the same time."

She walked slowly to the beach rug, seated herself on it, hugged her knees up under her chin, rested her chin on them, and stared at the dying embers. Tioru seated himself beside her and waited for her to go on.

Finally she said, "I'm happy because of what was done *for* me. That doesn't need an explanation. But I'm scared of what happened *to* me. Suddenly I'm obsolete. All Drylanders are obsolete."

"Think about that a little more," said Tioru. "You've been jolted by having to believe the unbelievable. Tomorrow you'll feel differently."

"But this isn't tomorrow, it's now. This is how I feel *now*. What chance do Drylanders have against a race that can hallucinate at will, and who knows what else? We're all on a moving floor carrying us to the gateway to oblivion. 'Drylanders This Way Out. Exit from the Universe.' What else can I think?"

"You can think this," said Tioru. "Look. Suppose the human race had evolved as Tritons to begin with. What would they do about the Dryland world? They'd have to invent Drylanders to exploit it. They need each other—and that's just as true for you and me as it is for Drylanders and Tritons collectively. And we'll need more than that when we start living on other worlds. It's a big universe, and a mere two kinds of human beings won't be able to cope with it. It takes more than two fingers to make a hand."

"Still *more* kinds? That's even worse! A proliferation of *things!*"

"Am I a *thing?*"

"Oh no! Tioru, I'm sorry! I didn't mean that! But it still scares me."

"That's because it's an utterly strange idea. But it won't always be so. Someday all these strange things will be commonplace. You're frightened because your mind is tired. Tonight was just one shock and surprise after another."

"I'm not tired. I'm shaken. I'd feel the same if I returned to Atlantic HQ and found it shattered by an earthquake. Don't you see what this does—to you and me?"

"Probably I don't see what you see."

"It means that we can never marry and have children. We'd be doing our bit to help the decline and fall of the Dryland world. The Triton world too. And I'll have to stand by and watch it begin to happen. I'm honor bound not to tell what I know. Normal Tritons and

Drylanders will be retarded children compared to the hybrids. They'll go the way of the mastodons and the Neanderthals."

"That I don't believe. After we've studied the talents of the hybrids for a few generations we'll know how to develop the same talents in ourselves. Then we'll all be on the same level."

Dorthy knuckled her eyes. Then she said, "I can't think any more tonight. Let's stay here until the fire goes out and forget the problems for a while."

The tide had been creeping up the beach as they talked. A line of foam would surge up the gentle incline, and recede. Then advance and recede again; each time it came a little further. Finally it touched the edge of the bed of glowing coals. There was a hiss, a cloud of steam, and the seaward edge of the fire became a fringe of black, emitting little wisps of vapor.

Tioru said, "Dorthy, I think I know what you're thinking."

"Go on."

"The fire is the world of normal Drylanders and Tritons. The tide's the tide of change. You're watching the end of the world."

"Tioru! You're reading my mind! You do have the talent!"

"I swear before the sea and the stars, I'm not a hybrid and I didn't read your mind. I just know a little of the way it works."

They were silent for a while, and the blackened area inched across the hot coals, hissing and steaming.

At last Dorthy said, almost inaudibly:

"No. No, I can't face it. It's too much. Too many things coming to an end at the same time. All I want to do now is—is to run away and hide."

"No matter what happens," Tioru's voice said in the dusk, "wherever you go, whatever you do, you will hear the voice of the sea, Dorthy. And wherever you hear that voice, you will hear mine too. You are a Triton now. The sea has made you its own. Once you have been down into the Dark Water, you can never come back."

"I know it," Dorthy said. "I . . . know it."

The fire became a thin red line. Then the tide surged over it, and the world was dark and waiting.

## BOOK THREE

## 12   A Strafing Scene

As Biond Smith moved south along the Constitution
Avenue walkway toward Prime Center, he had the dis-
tinct feeling that the asteroid called Flavia was pressing
down on the back of his neck, all the millions of tons
of it, all its jagged edges and melting contours and
frozen bones. He was not surprised. The thing was there,
right between his shoulder blades, almost literally now.

It was on everyone else's neck too; but he could see
no signs of this in the faces that passed him. True,
some of them looked preoccupied, or even worried,
but no more so than they might have been had they
been reflecting their more usual concerns about job or
family. Most of them, also as usual, simply looked vac-
uous, though the approach of Flavia was now public
knowledge. Certainly he saw no signs of terror at all,
which was probably just as well.

All the same, the terror might be there—probably was
there. A human face has a limit to the *amount* of emotion it can body forth. Whether a man is frightened by
an impending catastrophe, or just a sudden attack of
acute indigestion, cannot be inferred from his expres-

sion alone; even the greatest actor must lean heavily upon the context of the play.

Prime Center—the place, not the body—was what had once been the War Room in a section of Novoe Washingtongrad still called the Pentagon, though the office building that had gone by that name had been vaporized, along with most of the old city, in the Third War. The first Prime Center had been built, consequently, in Buchuanaland in southern Africa; later, with many misgivings, it had been transferred to Tetropolis, a medium-sized city of fifty million in the heart of Unistam, formed by the confluence of the old Leavenworth, Atchison, and St. Joseph. Still later, it had been cautiously transferred to Novoe Washingtongrad—but now even that residual caution was proving useless; no location on the Unistam continent was safe from Flavia, and her advent might well prove fatal to settlements and people as far away as Ganymede and Titan.

The walkway veered leftward smoothly around a cubical shrine where, if legend could be trusted, a bearded god named Honest Abe had once been adored, and slid through a corridor mysteriously called Burial Bridge. The trip was very long and Biond loathed it, but obviously the forthcoming disaster was far too great to allow for one of those cozy meetings in Deban Tod's apartment; the whole resources of the War Room were needed now—and they would not be sufficient.

As the walkway speeded up—it now ran across an area called Potomac Gap, one of the many deep-buried sections where the unemployables of UNOC watched 3-V and bred—there was a sudden bray of simulated trumpets from the public address system: Communications Corporation had something important to announce. Biond looked up instinctively, though of course there was nothing to be seen along the roof of Burial Bridge—

it was only something to be gotten across. More about Flavia? Then why hadn't Biond—

"Your attention, please," a voice boomed. It was a human voice, not a computer's, and, furthermore, it was tantalizingly familiar, despite the distortions produced by the corridor echoes. The next moment, however, that minor puzzle was driven completely out of Biond's mind by what the man was actually saying. "Your attention, please. We bring you an important bulletin from the Central Research Council. The Council this morning notified Prime Center that it has discovered a practicable interstellar drive. Plans for the construction of an experimental interstellar vessel will be proposed shortly. A further announcement will be made later today through regular news distribution channels."

The trumpets sounded again, and then the PA system went back to dispensing its usual thin, soothing molasses—the "background music" that had been an ineradicable public nuisance for eight hundred years. Biond did not notice; he was thoroughly stunned.

Even were the report true—and Biond had no good reason to doubt it—this was a crazy time to be announcing it. Certainly it should never have been issued before—indeed, just before—a Full Council discussion. Marg't Splain, he thought, you've got a lot to answer for.


In the semicircular room there was the usual last-minute scurrying of subordinates and technical staff, and an unusually loud hum of conversation. Well, they had plenty to talk about this morning.

Biond settled himself at his desk, before the microphone that, at a meeting as important as this, would make three separate tapes of every word that was said. There were no last-minute memos on the desk, for which he was grateful. He looked around. Deban Tod was presiding again, and he, too, was scanning the desks.

"Are we all here?" he said. "I don't see Dorthy Sumter. Anybody know where she is?"

"You're too late, Deban," Marg't Splain said, her eyes glittering. "Haven't you heard? You've lost your girl friend to a Triton."

Biond shot a quick look at the mike. The red light wasn't on yet; still, the remark was an egregious violation of privacy. Deban Tod, however, merely brushed it off with a proverb, a common tactic of his.

"Nobody owns anybody," he said. "Biond, have you heard anything?"

"Dorthy was in my office yesterday," Biond said. "But by last night she'd vanished."

"Sir," a man said from the floor. Biond recognized him —an SPC regional administrator of some kind. "Chairwoman Sumter is at Great Inagua."

"We'll proceed, then. She was notified, and time is too short to postpone for her," Deban Tod said. The red light came on. "I'm sure we all have a dozen questions about this morning's interstellar drive announcement, but first things first. Flavia is almost upon us. I call upon the Disaster Plans Board. Biond, would you like to preside?"

"No, thank you," Biond said. From the chair, he would be less free to ask questions, especially out-of-order ones.

"Very well. How are the evacuations proceeding?"

"On schedule. Our only problem was a town where there was a family convention going on, complicated by a pipeline jam, but that's over now, thanks to Transcorp and my man McGee."

"And the Tritons? Operation Safeguard?"

"Hung up," Biond admitted. "Or it was the last I heard. I really don't know its immediate status. I was hoping Dorthy could tell us. That may be why she isn't here."

"Or it may not," Marg't Splain said. Biond stared at her. While his attention had been on Deban, Marg't had been joined at her desk by another woman, a young brunette in the white coveralls that were the dress uniform of a Transcorp scientist. She looked familiar, and after a moment Biond realized why—she was Helga Auer, who years ago had been his parawife, until she had been shipped out to some planet or other. Did Marg't know that? It seemed quite possible; in her hour of triumph, Marg't seemed not less malicious, but more.

"Submarine will of course have to administer the project, but the responsibility is yours," Deban Tod said. "We will want an immediate report, please."

"The minute I get one, of course."

"Chen U, what about resources? With all the disruption coming, I assume that the world will have to go on short rations for a while. Distribution is of course Transcorp's problem, but will we have enough food to distribute?"

"Temporarily," Chen U said. "We have stocks for all immediate needs, if, as you say, Transcorp can distribute them. But thereafter the situation will get worse. Marg't's 'one lean year' may be seven."

. "Worse?" Deban Tod said. "I can't see why. As order is restored—"

"I hate to have to admit this," Chen U said. "But . . . you'll remember the change in the standard ration that we approved, back at the meeting just before we'd heard about Flavia. It appears that we were wrong. The new ration does have a substantial side effect on humans. It has, in fact, promoted a major increase in fertility."

"My God," Biond burst out, wholly involuntarily.

"I quite concur," Deban Tod said. "The last additional

disaster we could have wanted. Just how major is 'major,' Chen?"

"The exact figures are still being computed. However, in effect, it means that, despite the loss of life we expect from Flavia, the post-Flavia population will be *up* about three percent."

"That's not much," Biond said, surprised. "In fact, my office calculated almost that much of an increase. It always happens after a big disaster—even a major war. Death makes people breed."

"I mis-spoke," Chen U said precisely. "My three percent isn't a predicted gross increase. It's a rise in the *rate* of increase itself. And it is going on now, before the disaster."

The faces Biond saw, all the way down to the minor technicians, were studies in consternation. The silence lengthened. At last, Marg't Splain said:

"Of course it's unfortunate—"

"*Unfortunate!*" Deban Tod said.

"And it's doubly unfortunate that we weren't able to notify Biond's office in time to revise his calculations. But I suggest that the total situation has changed since yesterday, when we didn't have the interstellar drive. I insist that we talk about the drive now—otherwise all our other Disaster plans may be equally unrealistic."

"If there are no objections—"

"I object," Biond said instantly. "I want to hear about this drive as much as anybody, but first of all, Marg't, on the population jump figures, who's this 'we' you're talking about who should have notified my staff?"

"My office, naturally."

"Why 'naturally'? How did Transcorp get onto it before I did?"

"Probably," Marg't said smoothly, "the same way we heard about Flavia before you did—because we were paying attention."

"Untrue," Biond said hotly. "I heard about Flavia . . ."

And then he recalled completely how he had first heard about Flavia. The sentence died in his throat. Marg't smiled sweetly and said:

"Deban, do I have the floor or don't I?"

Deban Tod looked at Biond, who spread his hands slightly and slumped back in his chair. And my God, I was in love with this madwoman! There was another of Deban's proverbs: *Be sure your sins will find you out. . . .*

"All right. Now rather than attempt to explain the drive myself—which I'm not sure I'm competent to do, anyhow—I've brought along Dr. Auer. She's from the Ganymede project, where the actual work was done. Afterward, we'll both answer questions as best we can. All right, Helga."

The scientist, obviously a little awed by her surroundings and her audience, said hesitantly, "I suppose I had better begin by explaining that we first discovered this effect through what we thought was a malfunction in a new type of particle accelerator we were testing. As I'm sure you know, there's a natural law called the Lorenz-Fitzgerald Effect in which, as a body approaches the speed of light, it gains mass, and at the same time shortens in diameter in the direction of travel. Since at the speed of light the diameter approaches zero and the mass approaches infinity, the law seems to state that no material body can attain the speed of light."

"Hence, no interstellar drive," Deban Tod said. "We're all familiar with this material, Dr. Auer. You can go a little faster."

"Well, then you know that the Effect is easy to observe in a particle accelerator, where particles can be accelerated to quite close to the speed of light. In our new machine, however, we found that there seemed to be a flattening out of the Effect at just about 0.97 of *c*. It was difficult to measure accurately. As you probably also know, Jupiter has an intense magnetic field, and huge van Allen belts in which Ganymede moves. In addition, Ganymede gets sprayed with radio emanation from the parent body every so often.

"After we decided that the flattening-out was real, we modified the original Lorenz-Fitzgerald expression to account for it. This required us to assume that *c* is not an absolute limit, but only a cutoff point in the original equation. Since the new accelerator was theoretically capable of driving a particle to the speed of light, and the limitation seemed no longer to hold, we tried it.

"When we did, the particles simply seemed to vanish, without our being able to find where they were leaving the machine. Even more important, we found that they were reappearing elsewhere in the Project—"

"On Ganymede?" Biond said.

"Yes. We didn't become aware of that until another team complained that it was getting stray particles, despite all possible shielding, which were disrupting another experiment.

"I'll skip all the intervening stages. Briefly, what we believe we have stumbled on here is *experimental* proof that the universe is multidimensional, and that the Lorenz-Fitzgerald Expression is just a local ordinance of our particular four-dimensional segment of it. In other words, the velocity of light is a limit only in a very restricted sense. What it actually is is the *cosmic escape velocity*. Once you exceed it, you pop out of the local plenum into another. You come back into this one as soon as the speed drops, so it should be easy to collimate. As soon as we had this worked out, we called Transcorp, and here I am."

Biond was scribbling furiously, but at this he looked

up. "So in fact you don't have a drive, let alone a 'practicable' drive. What you've got is a theory."

"Well, yes," the girl said. "But the theory is revolutionary in itself, and we feel strongly that we've made a real breakthrough on the problem."

"Do you know whether it would work outside of Jupiter's magnetic field and the other conditions you mentioned?"

"There's no reason why it shouldn't, but of course we'll check that."

"All right," Biond said. "But there's something decidedly odd about the theory too. If $c$ is really the cosmic escape velocity, then it seems to me that you have a ready measure of the mass of the universe. By simple arithemic—maybe too simple—I make it 26,571.4 times the mass of the Earth. That's less than a seventh of the mass of the Sun alone!"

"Not as silly as it sounds," Dr. Auer said. "As a matter of fact your figure is correct, Biond. But you forget that there's a question of density here. The mass of the universe is widely scattered, not all wrapped up in a ball like the Earth's. The result is that, at any point in space where there isn't a large adjacent mass, the velocity of escape—the CEV, that is—is what it would be from a body some 26,000 times as massive as the Earth. That part checks out very well."

"All right. Nevertheless, I repeat, and I call the Council's particular attention to, the central fact here. *There is no drive.* Nor is there any good reason to think that one is imminent. I know Dr. Auer and respect her, but it seems to me that in this case she's simply a dupe—she's allowed her work to be used, to be blown up into something it isn't, and probably won't be for some time to come."

"A disgusting piece of niggling," Marg't Splain said. "The theory is a magnificent achievement and ought to bear fruit very rapidly. Biond's behaving like the amateurs who sneered at Einstein, or Galileo for that matter."

"Every pseudo-scientist compares himself with Galileo, it's one of the marks of the breed. I notice Dr. Auer herself doesn't invite any such comparison. What I object to is not her work, but the announcement. It was made without proper consultation, evidently in the hope of forcing us to approve a *fait accompli*. It is thoroughly premature—to say nothing of being sociologically dangerous, especially during this Flavia crisis. In my judgment it's very likely to interfere seriously with our Disaster planning. I always did think Marg't was dangerously hipped on this subject, but her present behavior is outright paranoid."

"That accusation," Deban Tod said heavily, "is a mistake. It will destroy the usefulness of one of you to Prime Center—it's not immediately apparent which. Consider, Biond, that this discovery may be just what Marg't says it is. If so, its importance is obviously beyond all imagining."

"I don't deny that. I only say that it shouldn't have been announced now—before Flavia arrives—and that the announcement is going to be damaging."

"How do you propose to establish that? Obviously we can't run an independent check of the whole scholium between now and Flavia."

"No," Biond agreed. "But if Marg't is behaving as irrationally on this subject as I suspect she is, a psych test would show it. If she's acting in good faith, she'll volunteer for one."

"Obviously I've just *been* volunteered," Marg't said, in a white fury. "And of course I refuse. No, better still, I accept on one condition—Biond is also to volunteer. He is trying to sabotage me from personal motives—to be precise, vindictive jealousy. I won't specify further—

let the question be put to him in just that form. He knows very well that he wouldn't survive it."

"Now we *are* in a mess," Deban Todd said. "Biond?"

"I refuse. The condition has nothing to do with the problem."

"Nevertheless we can't avoid it now. Since you both, in effect, refuse, and we wouldn't dare to keep you both under these conditions, I am going to have to rule. You should have taken the chair when it was offered, Biond . . . and it doesn't help you that Dorthy isn't here, either."

"In short, you rule against me."

"Yes," Deban Tod said. "We have to allow for the possibility that the drive exists. I think the evidence thus far is slightly in that direction. Furthermore, I don't see how we could replace Marg't with another Transcorp chief this quickly. There are no visible candidates, and no time to call an election. For a Disaster chief, we have McGee. You implied yourself that he is a good man."

"He's the very best on the Board, I wouldn't deny that for a second."

"Very well," Deban Tod said. "I so rule. And I now call a ten-minute recess so that Mr. Smith may make an orderly departure from these deliberations."

Just like that, Biond Smith was unemployed.

## 13  Biond goes Under

Just like that, Biond Smith was no longer one of the effective rulers of the Earth, no longer a Board chief, no longer even a voter, but instead just another of the billions of unemployed—and this on the edge of a world-wide disaster over which he could no longer officiate, or indeed from which he could even protect himself.

Habit took him almost back to his office before he remembered to remind himself that it was no longer his; habit took him back to his apartment, though there was nothing for him to do there, either; unlike Deban Tod and his exotic weeds, Biond had no serious outside interests—disasters had been his hobby as well as his job. Often, academically, he had thought about remedying that, against his inevitable retirement, but somehow nothing sufficiently compelling had ever turned up. At the moment, he hadn't even a wife.

Habit, consequently, also kept him speculating about how Prime Center would function now that it had decided to dispense with his services. Not how well it would function, for an organization as massive as Prime Center might stay in fairly good shape for as much as a decade on sheer momentum, but simply what further changes might come about in the Full Council. McGee would doubtless work out all right; he knew Biond's job as well as Biond had, and probably would prove easier for Marg't and Chen U to manage, for he was more of a politician than Biond had ever been, more accustomed to bending to the winds of change.

He was also more ruthless. If, sooner or later, it became

necessary for him to stand up to Marg't Splain, he would probably win, especially if Marg't's disintegration became more apparent. In the collision between the two, someone less adroit—like Dorthy Sumter—might easily sustain some cuts and bruises of her own, but the executive life had been like that at least ever since Alcibiades (and the odds against a comeback just about as great). Dorthy would just have to look after herself; the nascent power of SPC behind her was very great, if she could ever learn to use it.

In the meantime, it might be interesting to see at firsthand how well people were responding to the Disaster preparations, and how they were reacting to this morning's crazy announcement about the interstellar drive. Not that he had any use for such information now, or expected to; disasters were his hobby, that was all.

And besides, he realized for the first time, it might be just as well for him to start finding out just how the unemployed did fill their time and their lives. Surely not even the most mindless human being could spend sixteen hours a day throughout a lifetime just eating and watching 3-V; and he knew at least in the abstract that huge percentages of the unemployed were anything but mindless—they were just superfluous, which was another matter altogether.

And a good place to begin, he thought, might be Potomac Gap. He had never been in that teeming underworld, or in any section of any city like it. If there was any place in the world that he would find the desperate, it would be there—and no matter that by definition their apartments were no smaller or worse equipped than his or Deban Tod's. In any conceivable society, as in any conceivable apartment building, somebody has to be on the bottom.

Putting on walking shoes bought five years ago for a

vacation that had never materialized, Biond went out to practice tramping.

As he felt he should have suspected, somebody else in Unistam had realized that not even the most piglike Boeotian could spend all his life watching 3-V, and had realized it perhaps as long ago as several centuries—it was no longer possible to know.

The heart of Potomac Gap was an enormous machine—it seemed to occupy several levels and about four square miles—which the people who used it called the Wreck Hall. Its age was indeterminate because it was constantly in motion, rebuilding, adapting, and adding to itself; Biond's guess about its age had been based partly on what he could see of its present rate of growth, and partly on the fact that he had never before even heard of such a device. Evidently its existence had been covered up by layers and layers of the unemployed, and by layers and layers of their unrecorded history, for a very long time. Was it the only one of its kind, or did every city have one, or more than one? The answer to that, Biond was sure, would take more digging into the archives than he could ever expect to get done now.

Perfunctorily, the thing could have been characterized as a games machine—an elaborate, self-reproducing, semisentient penny arcade. But there was enormously much more to it than that. It was full of complicated mechanical games, to be sure, for one, two or a score of players. But one of these was a computerized bourse, where anyone might bet a fixed fraction of his dole against the computer's predictions of next year's output of almost any commodity, or even against the gross UNOC product.

Surely an illegal arrangement—and besides, where did the payoff money come from? Baffled and fascinated, Biond spent several hours trying to outguess the bourse, putting coins into the machine's blinking face until he managed to remember that he, too, was on the dole now. Thanks to his long and sometimes dismal acquaintanceship with how computers thought, he wound up with eleven shares in Transcorp to which he had no right at all, since he wasn't employed by the corporation— or by any other, for that matter. The stock certificate the machine issued him in return for his few tokens and his few moments of calculation looked perfectly authentic, and it occurred to him suddenly that were he to become expert at this game, he might even collar enough shares in Transcorp to *vote* Marg't Splain out of office, without her ever knowing who had done it, or from where.

Unfortunately, only a little additonal figuring showed also that, at this rate, such a strategy would take him about twelve thousand years. Too bad; what a vast joke on Marg't it might have been!

But this was only one of the first of the more elaborate games the Wreck Hall offered to play with its patrons. In another area, the machine was a series of 3-V viewing rooms, which were also theaters, or studios, where people who had learned formal roles, or wanted to ad-lib them, could participate in the plays just as the bourse allowed them to participate in the economy. Biond barely got out of that area with a whole mind; the moment he entered a booth there, mythical Scotland lit up around him, and he found himself storm-lashed, half naked, and declaiming,

> How far's it called to Forres? . . . What are these,
> So withered and so wild in their attire . . .

Totally naked witches, improbably alive and beautiful, closed in on him as he fled, and the one who managed to touch him was no illusion.

The end was not yet. The theaters shaded over into viewing rooms where, ostensibly, what was available for the watching was only the standard news broadcasts. But here again it was possible to play roles, and hence seem to be taking a part in history or even to be changing it. When Marg't Splain came walking and smiling toward him in one of these cubicles—how did the machine know so instantly what the customer most wanted? —he had sense enough to run without asking any more questions.

The news theaters, in turn, blended smoothly into classrooms, where Biond could not tell whether the audience was studying a subject or inventing it. On a 3-V platform, Marg't Splain was saying, "The general theory of the interstellar drive shows that . . ."

He did not stay for the end of that sentence either.

Most disturbing of all—because it was impossible to be sure of it—was the impression all these flickering chambers gave Biond that they were connected intimately with other such machines or complexes elsewhere in the world. Somehow, he was irrationally sure, every participant in every game was modifying every play, subject, event, or statistic for every other player, at least fractionally; and the eleven shares of Transcorp in his pocket did not encourage him to think that the machine dealt solely in illusions.

No, the Wreck Hall's grand game was real—a sort of computer-modulated, yet creative community effort, nearly or wholly fruitless and yet world-wide, going on beneath the surface of UNOC, each oblivious of the other.

The Wreck Hall held him all the rest of the day, and he suspected that it—and the problem it posed—might well have become that obsessive, lifelong hobby he had never found, had it not been for the residual but still compelling pressure of Flavia upon the back of his neck. Whatever the Wreck Hall was doing for or to the world, it was not coping with the wild asteroid . . . though some of its psycho-dramas exploited subjects like love affairs between Drylanders and Tritons, and even more explosive topics that official UNOC fare still shied away from. All the same, all this, though stunningly unexpected, was not what he had come down into Potomac Gap to learn. He tore himself away from the vast, phantasmagoric hypnosis of the machine, and went still farther down into the extinct valley in pursuit of a group of shabby Wreck Hall patrons who had said something about finding something to eat. Most of them looked far less dazed by the machine's programmed deliria than Biond felt; evidently it was possible to build up at least a little immunity. But there was no time left for that now either.

He lost a few of the men he was trailing to a bowling alley or some other sort of gymnasium, but most of them seemed as little interested in such sports as he was; the place was grimy and dimly lit, and looked poorly patronized. Maybe that was only because this was the dinner hour for the 0900-1400 shift—but no, nobody down here had a job at all on any shift, and, besides, the men he was following didn't seem to be going home to eat. They wore the expression of resigned camaraderie of men who would rather die than go home just yet; Biond had never seen it before, but he recognized it instantly.

They wound up in a small refectory, where they sat down at a splintered table and ordered drinks, which Biond—after his encounter with the Wreck Hall—suspected might even be alcoholic. The table was a long one, and after a moment's hesitation, he sat down at it, within earshot, and dialed a standard meal and a kaffina. One of the men looked at him briefly and incuriously; the others ignored him. That was a fair start.

At first their conversation was either dull or incomprehensible, most of the latter apparently revolving around the betting on the bourse. There were frequent references to a man—or a computer?—named Willy, who seemed to be the group's expert at the "numbers game" of outguessing the UNOC economy. Biond spooned in his brit soup and listened carefully, but it began to seem to him that he had been wasting his time.

Then, suddenly, he pricked up his ears. What was this?

". . . going on the damn maneuvers tomorrow."

"You don't catch me going on any maneuvers."

"Why not? It's something to do. Besides, it's the law."

"That's right, Tom. Besides—want to stay here and get hit by a meteor? No sense in that."

"Damn if I think there *is* any meteor. I think the whole thing's just a blind."

"Ah, come *on,* Tom. A blind for what?"

"You heard them announce that star-drive thing this morning, didn't you?"

"Sure. What of it?"

"This is it," the man called Tom said. "I think Prime Center is getting set to ship us all out to some other solar system."

"What's the sense of that? You're out of your mind."

"Look around you. Everybody you see is useless down here—and Potomac Gap isn't the only place in the world like this, you can bet your life on that. Wouldn't UNOC and Prime Center scramble to get rid of the lot of us—make a fresh start, with more elbow room for them?"

"They'd never even get moving on it. Too many people. Otherwise they'd have farmed us all out to Mars and Venus long ago."

"Maybe," Tom said, "or maybe not. Either way, I'm not going to let them practice on me."

There was a short silence, which Biond filled by pretending to eat. He was beginning to feel very ill.

"Tom, wait a minute. Look at it this way. Maybe they're going to use the star ships to take us out of the splash-down on this meteor. Ever think of that? Doesn't it make better sense?"

"Hey, Tom, what about that? Prime Center doesn't bother much with us usually. They don't seem to lie to us much either. Maybe that's just what they're up to."

"All right, suppose that's true. So who wants to go to another planet, anyhow? They've got no right to haul me out of my house and shoot me halfway across the universe. If that's what they're up to, I'll just hole up in the Wreck Hall and take my chances."

"Hmm. I don't know that some other planet'd be any better than this one, come to think of it. They might chuck you out into some Forest and tell you to start digging holes."

"You bet they might. You wouldn't get any eight-room apartment, or any Wreck Hall either. Or maybe any Forest. It'd probably be more like being dropped in a Bio Preserve, full of lions and dinosaurs."

"Dinosaurs are all dead."

"On another planet? How do you know?"

"I'm not so fond of lions, either, come to think of it."

"Maybe Tom's right. One thing's for sure—if they're going to shoot me off to some other planet, I don't see any sense in breaking my back to protect Potomac Gap from some stray rock. The hell with it."

"Sense in that."

"I tell you what," Tom said. "Let's make a blast of it. Collect the women and the kids and go to the Hall till the asteroid thing is over. Two or three days. We can hide out in a dream room. Prime Center doesn't even know they're there."

"You hope."

"Besides, that costs money."

"Well," Tom said, "what's more important—blowing ten credits a head, or winding up in some jungle you never even heard of?"

"Count me in—if I can sell the family on it."

"Me too."

"Wait a minute, wait a minute. Has it come over any of you characters that we don't know what we're talking about? At least, we ought to ask Willy what he thinks."

"Willy doesn't know everything," Tom said disgustedly.

"You think you know more than he does?"

"Well . . . all right. But it ought to be tonight. There isn't much time."

"Tomorrow. No point in *my* talking to Willy if my women won't go along with it."

"Same here."

Tomorrow, Biond knew, would be time enough for them, but too late for him. Trying to be casual, he said, "Excuse me, gentlemen . . ."

It was the wrong form of address. Their expressions froze instantly, and all at once they were inspecting him very closely. As far as he knew, he was dressed exactly as they were, but evidently there was something wrong with him all the same that they could sense.

At last the man called Tom said, "What is it, mister?"

"I was interested in your argument," Biond said. "I'd like to know more about it myself. Could you tell me where to find this Willy you were talking about?"

"Watch it, Tom. The guy looks UNOC to me. For all we know, he's out to arrest Willy for something."

"I used to be UNOC," Biond said frankly. "But I got fired. I'd like to get reinstated. And it sounds like Willy could help me."

To his bafflement, they all laughed.

"Willy?" the man called Tom said. "He can't help himself. You UNOC types can't walk three feet down here without falling on your faces. But I guess Willy'd be glad to see you. You could hold hands."

There was another roar of laughter. Gritting his teeth, Biond left.

The man's name was Willy Naujack, and contrary to the impression the men in the refectory had given Biond, he had never at any time belonged to UNOC.

He was unmarried, and his apartment was an almost continuous clutter of glassware, breadboard electronic rigs, bottles of reagents, ambiguous instruments, and faxes of documents from Bibtek Central, some of them apparently very old. He admitted Biond with the cheerful readiness of a man accustomed to all kinds of callers.

"Sorry about the smell," he said. "It's not garbage, at least—just a rack of thirty-six hour syntheses I've got going to completion. Once I get this project finished I can clean up, but in the meantime, you'll just have to pick your way about as best you can."

"What are you working on?" Biond said. "I thought you were a statistician. This all looks much more like something to do with photosynthesis."

"Oh no, far from it, though it does have something to do with food. But first, Mr. Smith, who *are* you? Not that I'm alarmed, you understand—I'm thoroughly harmless and everybody knows it—but on the other hand, you're not my usual kind of client, so if you want me to satisfy your curiosity, you must satisfy mine. You've got the manner, the tan, the accent of a UNOC man. What's your story?"

Without hesitation, Biond told it; he sensed at once that with this man nothing less than total candor would serve. It helped that Naujack seemed to have heard of him. When it was over, his host sat down on a plastic mushroom and said meditatively,

"I see. I see. Well, Biond, the fact is that I'm not really a statistician, though I use statistics in my work. I'm a biophysicist—an amateur biophysicist. I spent a long time trying to get the Central Research Council interested in what I'm doing, with no luck. They said it was 'highly improbable.' That's the trouble with letting computers make decisions. So then I had to go into it entirely on my own. For that, I needed money—much more money than I could divert from my dole. So I took to counseling all my de-classed friends down here on how to invest in the lottery—the investment game. Either I was lucky, or it's not hard to beat World Resources at these production predictions—take your choice."

"Why didn't you play the game yourself?"

"Too time-consuming. The player has to be on the spot, at the bourse, half the day. But my commissions made me enough money to support my laboratory—the shambles you see here. It's dull stuff, but it works, much of the time, and in addition my neighbors took to asking my advice about all kinds of other matters."

"Then—just what do you do, Dr. Naujack? Where do you live when you're home, so to speak?"

"I'm not a doctor," Willy Naujack said. "And what I do hasn't got a name yet. But about ten years ago, when World Resources announced that it was going to convert food production from photosynthesis to dinosynthesis, I became interested in the problem. Dinosynthesis is an interesting process, but inherently it can't be made much more efficient than its predecessor—ten percent, say. That's worthwhile for WRB to invest in, but I thought there must be something better.

"I thought it would be possible to get right down to basics, to the way the living cell generates energy for itself. It's really surprising how much is known about it already. More than half my work had already been done for me several centuries ago. The basic reaction is what's producing that odor. It's called phosphorylation and it takes place in tiny intracellular organelles called mitochondria. So I suppose you might call what I do mitochondriatics, though I prefer to reserve the term for the process itself."

"You've actually got a process?" Biond said, trying not to let his sudden excitement show.

"Oh yes, I've got a process, though in its present state it has too many stages to be practicable. Even in this clumsy form, however, it's about fifty percent more efficient than dinosynthesis. That's only *in vitro*, of course. Actual production figures are always a little lower than what you get in the laboratory. What I really would like now is a pilot-plant test, but of course that's out of the question. What I've got here is just a smelly hobby. When I'm through, I'll file my results and Bibtek Central will forget them."

"Not necessarily," Biond said. "Would you mind showing me what you've got on paper—figures, flow charts, formulas? I'm not an expert, but everybody on Prime Center has to have some knowledge of such things. And since you're planning to publish anyhow—"

"Why not?" Willy Naujack said cheerfully. He burrowed into a stack of documents on a nearby table and came up with a clipboard, to which about ten neatly hand-lettered sheets were affixed.

Biond read through them, not bothering to conceal the intensity of his interest now. The equations were elegant; the diagrams, in four colors, eloquent and easy to follow. The chemistry was much too advanced for Biond to make much sense of, but he could understand enough of it to see that Naujack was indeed at home in the subject.

He could scarcely dare to believe it. He knew that many of the unemployed were creative in one way or another, and that some even dabbled in the sciences—like Kim Wernicke's friend Dr. Matouf and his silver-fish. But this—this was far beyond anything Kemal Matouf would achieve if he lived two thousand years. It was, in fact, of far greater potential importance than even a *real* interstellar drive could possibly have been.

It meant a job for Willy Naujack, and reinstatement for Biond, if it could just be proven, and gotten through to Chen U. But it meant much more than that: it was, quite possibly, the solution to the forthcoming food crisis, complicated though that would be by both Flavia and the fertility jump.

"I don't want to be too sanguine," he said slowly, "but there's a chance that you've pulled off a miracle here, Mr. Naujack. First, as you say, we'll have to have a pilot-plant test. I think I might be able to get it for you."

"It would be expensive."

"Perhaps not as expensive as it would be if we had to start from scratch. There's a Disaster City out west, named Gitler, that has some equipment that could be modified for the purpose. The man in charge is the senior water engineer. He used to be a subordinate of mine and we were friendly—I helped him with a romance—so I think he'd cooperate even though I have no official status now. Of course we wouldn't be able to start work until after the disaster, but you ought to be on the spot and ready to go immediately after that."

"Whatever you say," Willy Naujack said, his eyes gleaming. "Of course. I can go anywhere—everything I need is on that clipboard. But how'll we get there? We're both de-classed, and all travel has been inter-dicted for the duration."

"More pull, I hope. I'll call McGee, my successor, and put my thumb in his eye for an aircar. Have you got a vidphone?"

"Everybody," Naujack said drily, "has got a vidphone.

The alternative is suicide. It's over there, behind the Craig countercurrent distributor—that thing that looks like a glass pipe organ."

"Thanks. If this doesn't work, we'll try something else."

But it did work; McGee, apparently, did not think it beyond the bounds of possibility that he might be working for his old boss again someday. Within an hour, they were in the air.

And as they flew, a flaming streak arched through the night sky over them and burst like fireworks—another exploding meteor. The sword of Damocles was hanging lower; the thread was fraying.


## 14   The Dove Descending


The evacuation of the Joneses was over, the pipeline had been repaired, the refugee occupation of Gitler was completed. There was now nothing left for Jothen Kent to do but wait in his apartment in the stand-by crew's colony until Flavia should fall.

Jothen was not by nature a philosophical man—engineers almost never are—but he knew that he was waiting also for the end of an era . . . the longest and most peaceful one in all of Earth's history. What post-civilization was going to be like he could not imagine, and he suspected that no one else could either. Eight hundred years of near stasis had left behind no history immediate enough from which to draw analogies. Even the Third War now seemed as remote as the fall of Troy—remote, senseless, and useless.

Oddly, it had been the news that Biond Smith had been fired that had shocked Jothen into this unusually contemplative frame of mind. It seemed to him, quite suddenly, that the total, invariable de-classing of such men was wasteful. Of course, in a world where only the creative artist, the scientist, and the genius-class administrator could find anything of consequence to do —excluding rare technicians like the police, the Forest rangers, and Jothen himself—it was true that UNOC had an almost unthinkably immense reservoir of brainpower upon which to draw. And, academically at least, it made sense to de-class a man totally, rather than just to demote him; if he could fight his way back to his old job, or an equivalent one, he was doubly worth having. A pure case of natural selection; UNOC didn't dare risk men who, once broken under pressure, were content to stay broken. The stakes were too high, the alternatives too readily available.

Academically; but when you, personally, saw a man like Biond Smith go Under, it was nevertheless damn disquieting. Well, that was part of the selection pressure too. Jothen wished there were something he could do for Biond, but the system forbade it. Once you were down, you were out. Unless you worked for one of the corporations, you couldn't even vote—and even then, only within the corporation.

In a way, it was vicious; but it had worked. Eight hundred years were hard to argue against.

To stop himself from circling futilely over Biond's predicament—brooding made Jothen acutely uncomfortable—he tried again to call Kim at Starved Rock. Once he and McGee had worked free of the Jones Convention, he had found the vidphone circuits jammed with other Disaster Plan calls, and of course Jothen had no access to the Earthwave system—that was for Prime Center and other corporation HQs alone. But this time, to his great relief, he got through.

His relief was short-lived. Kim's voice was frightening —at once quite toneless, and with a jangling undertone of extreme tension. He said, "Are you all right?"

"Quite all right."

But she was dissembling. All the ground that had been gained between them at the Barrier-hilthon seemed to have been lost; she sounded like a stranger. Worse, she sounded as though if anyone touched her she would shatter, like a Prince Rupert's Drop.

"I've been worrying about you," he said carefully. "We had a terrific traffic jam here, and then all the lines were tied up—"

"Oh, I was wondering."

"Didn't Biond tell you—"

A brief tic jerked at the corner of her left eye.

"I haven't talked to Biond," she said. "Anyhow I can't, now. He's gone Under."

"Yes, I know. But before, he was wondering about the Preserve, and hadn't heard from you. I thought that when you'd reported, he'd tell you about what happened over here . . ."

Suddenly, the Prince Rupert's Drop flew into a thousand pieces. Kim began to cry, soundlessly, hopelessly. Her mouth working, she said:

"I . . . had nothing . . . to report. That's all."

"Kim, Kim, what is it? Do you mean that you didn't destroy the Preserve?"

"That's what I mean," she said. "How could I? All these helpless animals, all these beautiful woods and deserts and lakes—they're our heritage, from long before the world was sterilized. We'll never see them again any more—not any more. How could I destroy them? Who'll protect them, if I don't? That's what I was supposed to do! Don't they have as much right to live as all those useless people?"

She was weeping uncontrollably now. Appalled, Jothen said, "But Kim—if the Preserve is breached—"

"I know," she said bitterly. "I know. I didn't expect you to understand. It's up to me. Good-bye, Jothen."

The image of Kim collapsed into a gray plane. So much for communication! Jothen, swearing helplessly, grabbed at a china pomander—the only small, hard object in the entire apartment—and threw it at the blank vidphone screen. The screen smugly and safely bounced it back at him across the supersoft carpetment.

Kim had broken too. And when McGee—that ward heeler!—found out about it, she, too, would go Under . . .

The apartment computer chimed.

"Shut up," Jothen snarled. Then, irrationally, "What is it?"

"You have callers, Mr. Kent," said the computer in its fruity, flute-like voice. "A Mr. Willy Naujack and a Mr. Biond Smith. Shall I admit them?"

"I don't know any—wait a minute. Did you say *Biond* Smith?"

"Yes, Mr. Kent."

"Great seas and stars. Of course, let them in, you flaming idiot—let them in!"

Biond explained the situation crisply and rapidly, with some help from the rather diffident Willy Naujack. Jothen, with his standard engineer's suspicion of anyone who did not belong to his own trade, was a little put off by Naujack, friendly and unpretentious though he seemed to be; but he knew that he could trust Biond—and besides, here was something that Jothen could *do*, something that would bail him out of all his morass of useless, half-hearted philosophy.

"No, not yet, I'm afraid," Biond said, as if reading his

mind. "All I really want you to do for the moment—all you *can* do—is put us up, until Flavia's landed. After that, there'll be lots to do, if there's anything left to do it with. But first, we're just going to have to sweat it out. Incidentally, I'd just as soon Prime Center didn't know we were here."

"Of course. But Biond, at least we could plan—there are two or three idle line systems we could use, depending on which you think best."

"There's no time left. We were damn lucky to get here at all. Flavia is going to hit in—let's see—yes, just at 0336, if the last prediction I saw was accurate, and I think it was. That's twenty-four minutes from now. Better turn on the vidphone and we'll see what we can see. I wouldn't want to miss this for anything."

"Well, but—all right."

Willy Naujack said softly, "Dear friends and gentle hearts . . . let us compose ourselves, for our time is now at hand."

"Amen."

As the deformed lump of spoiled planetary fragment that was Flavia crossed into cis-lunar space, black dots that were men jetted away from her and vanished into the indifferent darkness. Only a target beacon was left to show that there had ever been anyone there at all.

The mass was uglier than ever now, for the men had left it sculptured with jagged points, sharp edges and long gouges, carefully calculated to generate the maximum amount of air friction without inviting a splitting of the main body. That would wear her away some, at least.

The Moon came to life. From the crater Aristarchus leapt an intense blade of blue light—a laser pulse, driven from a monocrystal sapphire. The pulse lasted only a tenth of a second; as a result, for a few seconds both ends of it could be seen, a widthless ribbon 18,670 miles long, glowing in the Earth's magnetic tail.

Then it struck. Flavia's surface was already hot from sunlight and from preliminary friction with the first faint traces of Earth's outermost atmosphere; and the laser light, in addition to being blastingly hot itself, was also intensely actinic. The asteroid's moonward side melted, and then seethed with chemical reactions. A glowing tail streamed away from her—free radicals, driven by the solar wind.

Another laser bolt followed. Flavia was perceptibly smaller now, and more lopsided.

Another bolt—and the last. The next one would have been pointed too directly at the Earth to have been risked.

Everything that could have been done was done now. Glowing sullenly, Flavia plunged down toward the southern tip of Hudson's Bay, pushing ahead of her a growing pile-up of plasma already fifty miles in diameter.

The final average diameter of the asteroid was one and one quarter miles.

In Jothen's apartment—and all over the Northern Hemisphere—the vidphones almost at once produced a shower of snow and quit; the Earthwave system was still functioning, but Jothen's only access to that was in his office. However, it wasn't needed. Through the big picture window in Jothen's living room, the predawn sky was already glowing. The glow sank slowly, as if the sun were setting instead of rising—but at the same time it was growing brighter.

On the roof of the level below, the leaves of the Forest rustled uneasily, and gradually began to stand out from each other like the metal tongues of an electroscope. For an instant Jothen thought that they, too, were glowing and that tongues of delicate flame were reaching out from the tips of the branches and the tops of the trees. But almost at once the sky was too bright to make sure of it.

In an appalling silence, the light sank toward the horizon, seemingly only eighteen miles away across the Missouri flatlands. By now it was as bright as the sun, though it was still only a point with a faint ring around it—the ball of plasma. The effect on the surrounding landscape was eerie, making everything look like a model in a toymaker's window. No one in recorded history had ever seen a landscape lit by a point-source before.

A faint roaring noise, like a distant waterfall, began to shake the air, the Forest, the window, and then the floor itself. As it grew, the false sun set, leaving behind a colossal aurora, like a fanfare of searchlights.

"Down!" Biond shouted hoarsely behind him over the swelling clamor. "Fireball! Down, quick!"

He was too late. Magnificently, horribly, the new false sun rose, a peculiar reddish yellow. Jothen threw both arms over his eyes and turned his back, but he could feel the heat of the thing beating against his neck and shoulders.

When he dared to look again, nothing was left to see but a sort of roiling chimney of dimming orange, thinner than a pencil—it was, he knew, a good forty miles in diameter—topped with a tiny mushroom stitched with slivers of lightning. Then that, too, faded, leaving his eyes swimming with greenish afterimages.

But the noise continued to rise, and now the wind was rising with it. The leaves began to flutter and fly from the trees. Then the trees themselves were bowing, all directly away from the light, as if worshiping the city.

The sky turned black. Seconds later, it erupted into the last of all imaginable thunderstorms. No—not thunder—exploding secondary meteorites. But the lightning display was also blinding and incessant, like the final moment before Noah's flood.

Then, gradually and inexorably, the whole Earth began to rumble and shake. Rising from the floor of the universe, the monstrous groan of a planet's agony became a *basso profundo* scream.

The city shuddered continuously. At last the window—the dependable, indestructible glastic—split from corner to corner and fell inward in a shower of shards. A hot blast of ozone hit Jothen like the prow of a tube-train. In a last shock of horror and despair, he felt himself slammed against the far wall, clawed uselessly for cover, and was battered into an aching silence.

They awoke slowly, Jothen could not tell how much later, except that it was still dark. It was also completely quiet; the storm, evidently, was over, though the air still stank of ozone, plus a strong odor of crushed green plants.

Jothen stood cautiously. His entire body was a solid mass of pain; he felt as though he had been pounded with hammers for hours. He groaned involuntarily.

At once Biond's voice said, from somewhere nearby:

"Jothen? Is that you?"

"I think so. Are you all right, Biond?"

"Pretty battered, but I don't think anything's broken. You?"

"All right. Where's Willy Naujack?"

"Here," Naujack's voice said immediately. "I was just sitting here enjoying listening to you two. I didn't think I'd ever hear anything again. What a tremendous racket!"

Jothen took a tentative step. Something crunched under his feet. At the same moment, the lights came back on; somebody in Gitler had gotten the emergency circuits going.

"Ah, that's better," Biond said. "Now if the vidphone's just back in order, maybe we can find out what's happened to the rest of the world. *We* were lucky, that's for sure—but we were pretty far away from ground zero."

"With all that ionization, I'll bet the vidphones will be out for days," Naujack volunteered.

"Okay, but first—hello, what's this?" Biond had taken a step toward the vidphone, and had been rewarded by the same crunching noise Jothen had noticed. He looked down.

The entire floor, the furniture, the ledges, everything was littered evenly with small pellets, ranging in size from pieces like gravel to bits smaller than sand grains. Biond bent and brushed the floor with his palm. Jothen and Willy closed in to look with him.

On his palm, the smallest bits glittered in the light: minute silvery spherules. "Nickel-iron?" Willy Naujack said.

"Can't be anything else. Evidently our friend out there was vaporized completely. I wonder if there's anything left of the Northwest at all?"

For the first time, Jothen took time out to look closely at his friends. They were a mess, no doubt about it—completely filthy, covered with bruises, and with drying cuts from the flying glastic here and there. Biond had one over his left eye—that had been a near thing. Jothen knew he could look no better. Biond was right; they had been very lucky.

"How much radiation do you suppose we took aboard?" Willy Naujack said.

"Not very much, I hope," Biond said "We were a long way away from the plasma cloud, and the fireball should have been less radioactive than that, not more.

All the same, before I was fired I'd already ordered post-Flavia blood tests for all survivors within line-of-sight distance of the ball. We figured on a lethal dose anywhere within a hundred miles of the impact. And no doubt we're going to see a lot of radiation sickness—and a *whole* lot of mutation."

"Could the nuclear bombs they used in the Third War have been as bad as this?" Jothen said. "They blew up whole cities—"

"Nothing like this," Biond said flatly. "The worst of those was rated at an explosive force of about a hundred megatons. Flavia ran about *fifty million.*"

There seemed to be nothing left worth saying after that. After a moment, however, the silence was broken by a muted, irregular buzzing, from the direction of the window. They all turned.

Something black and about the size of a handball was coming in through the shattered pane. It buzzed slowly and with a sort of comic dignity directly across the room, making all three of them dodge, and ran squarely into the far wall. Caroming off this, it zoomed diagonally away, ran into the next wall, and fell to the floor.

They all stared at it. "Good heavens," Willy Naujack said. "What on Earth *is* that?" Neither he nor Biond, however, made any move to go nearer to it.

Jothen had seen things like it before, and it aroused in him a sickening suspicion. Carefully, he walked across the floor toward it and knelt. The thing was now climbing slowly up the wall.

It was a large, clumsy black insect, with a wicked-looking pair of mandibles.

"That," Jothen said slowly, "is a beetle—an ancient North American species, called, I think, a June bug. They had them at the Starved Rock Bio Preserve."

"But what's it doing here?" Willy said, in a voice both

alarmed and aggrieved. The beetle seemed to upset him more than Flavia had.

Obviously it upset Biond, too, but for better reasons; he had leaped to the obvious conclusion. "Jothen," he said, "didn't Kim destroy the Preserve after all?"

"No," Jothen said, "I'm afraid she didn't. And this means that it's been breached."

"And all the surviving critters are loose—in the Forest?" Biond said, almost in a whisper. "No, that can't be. It can't be. There's some other explanation, Jothen."

"Have you ever seen anything like *that* before?"

"No," Biond said. "Not out of a bottle. But Jothen, if it's from Starved Rock, how did it get here so fast? It doesn't exactly fly very well. Maybe it got out some other way—like your friend's silverfish, what's-his-name, Dr. Matouf."

"It could have gotten here very easily," Willy Naujack said interestedly, prodding the climbing beetle with the end of a stylus. "Blown here on the shock wave, for instance. Like all these little nickel-iron particles."

"That's obviously the answer," Jothen said. "Biond, there's no ducking it. Starved Rock has been broken open."

After a long pause, he added, almost to himself, "I've got to go there."

"You can't do that," Biond said. "We need you here. We have to get started setting up Willy's pilot plant."

"I can't help that. I've got to go to Kim. Besides, Biond—don't you see? We won't be able to keep the Forest, keep a controlled ecology, if we're back in an age of wild insects, birds, and so on. And what good's a new food process without crops for raw materials? We have to know just what's been let loose, first, and whether or not anything can be done about it."

"I suppose that's true," Biond said reluctantly. "And

I ought to find that out myself. Besides, Jothen, you can't go alone."

"I'll go too," Willy Naujack said.

"Nothing doing," Biond said instantly. "You're our only source of knowledge on the new process, if it can be made to work after all. As of the moment, Willy, you're perhaps our most valuable natural resource."

Willy sighed. "All right," he said. "But be careful."

"We will. Jothen, what about power for the aircar? I suppose we can get a full charge for it here, but that won't last all the way to Starved Rock, and we've no way of knowing whether we can get a recharge along the way. We may well wind up grounded."

"In that case," Jothen said grimly, "we'll walk. I don't think the Forest is off limits any longer."

## 15   A Walk in the Paradise Garden

In the chill of the predawn twilight, between four and five o'clock, Jothen and Biond climbed into the aircar. Several other, larger machines huddled dispiritedly on nearby pads, tipped and skewed by the shock wave, but there was no traffic. Their own machine had been slid along the vitrolith about fifteen feet, but seemed undamaged.

"You'll have to fly this thing," Jothen said, his voice unconsciously muted. "I'm no pilot."

"I'm not what you'd call an expert," Biond said. "But

the autopilot grid is all fouled up with static and snow. We'll have to fly by contact and hope."

Jothen shivered slightly in the morning chill. "Do we really need all this gear we're taking with us?"

"Maybe not. But we're almost sure to be grounded—maybe at night." Biond started the lift fans. "There's not' a lot of it. Headlamps, compasses, stun guns, food bars, canteens."

The plane lifted uncertainly, and headed northeast over Missouri. The greater stars were still visible overhead, and the slender sickle of a crescent moon rode above the band of aquamarine light that lay along the eastern horizon. Far southward, the rotating St. Louis beacon, still defiantly alive, swept its triad of beams—fiery crimson, brilliant white, sapphire blue—rhythmically across the lower sky.

The land lay blanketed under a ground-hugging layer of mist, softly luminous in the dawn. The upper terraces of cities rose out of it like islands. As the daylight mounted higher in the sky, the sea of mist became agitated, heaving and rolling like some monstrous sleeper resisting nightmare. Almost immediately, it seemed to Jothen, the sun came up like a ball of hot iron. Thermal currents tattered the mist, and then it was gone.

Under the coppery-orange sunlight falling almost horizontally across the landscape, the woolly carpet of the World Forest took on a strange, theatrical color of intense verdigris. The irregular, sponge-like contours of the close-set treetops and the angular, terraced city structures were thrown into high relief, casting deep blue shadows. Eastward lay the Mississippi—a ribbon of molten brass in the fiery light, all of its meanderings smoothed into the great sweeping curves of a series of artificial lakes formed by a staircase of dams.

Every dam was a river-spanning city, swallowing the

river on one side, disgorging it on the other. Straight ahead was Hannibal; Quincy was visible northward; to the south, Luziana.

Jothen peered curiously down at Hannibal as they approached it. The city was formed of hexagonal pyramids, fitted together like the cells of a honeycomb. But the comb was no longer patent. The northerly wall, where it lay across the river, had been breached by a jagged, gaping notch. The dislodged material had slumped into the river in a huge mound of rubble. Steam or white smoke was rising from the breach, and from numerous vents among the trees on the adjacent terraces.

Biond banked, edging the plane nearer the broken wall. Shortly, Jothen could see a swarm of people and machines working on the rubble slide and in the cutaway interior revealed by the break. Twinkling bluish-white stars indicated metal-cutting laser beams at work. Green medicopters were constantly arriving and departing.

"That's a nice mess," Jothen said. "What could have happened?"

"Who knows?" Biond said wearily. "An explosion, maybe—or a temblor. Or a secondary. Or all three. At least it looks like McGee is on the ball."

"Why wasn't Hannibal evacuated?"

"We had to put the boundary of the evacuation zone somewhere. In this case, evidently we guessed wrong. But from here on up, everything is depopulated—the computers have the towns to themselves."

Jothen was not listening. His eyes had suddenly fixed on a sight as nearly mythological as a dragon. He pointed mutely.

High above Hannibal, two huge birds soared on motionless wings. At the ends of the wings, feathers curved up and diverged like outspread fingers. The creatures rode the thermal updrafts in great leisurely curves, rocking slightly. The aircar passed within two hundred feet of one of them, close enough for Jothen to guess that it had a wing spread of six or seven feet. Then it veered suddenly, wings at an angle, and shot past them on the left. It was coal black except for its head, which was red and naked. The car flinched under Biond's hands.

"What was *that?*"

"God knows."

They droned on, finding nothing to say to each other. After a while, a belt of clouds and stormy low-level turbulence loomed ahead. Biond inched the car skyward until it was above the cloud deck. This got them over the thunderstorms well enough, but the terrain below vanished. By the time it was visible again, they were just crossing the Illinois River.

Biond lost altitude and scanned the ground, frowning. Finally he said, "Dammit. I'm lost."

"Follow the river," said Jothen, consulting the map. "It will take us to Starved Rock, walking or flying, without bothering about staying on a straight course."

Biond said, "No, that'll waste time and power. I don't want to walk any farther than I can help."

They flew over a quarter-mile-wide swath that had been cut through the Forest by harvesting machines and which now was planted with neat rows of young trees. A flock of small, dark-colored birds that had been foraging on the ground took flight as the aircar approached.

Jothen looked at the map again.

"When we crossed the river," he said, "we passed near a smallish town—about five million, I'd say. The name on its airfield was Avana. But it should have been Peoria—if we'd been on a northeast course all along. So we're off course and must be heading almost due east. There's a big city looming up on the skyline, off to the left. Swing over that way and see where we are."

The city's name was printed in gigantic orange letters

on the flyport airfield: BLOOMINGTON. The flyport was deserted. The radar dish was motionless. No aircraft were parked on the field.

"We're about fifty miles south of the south boundary of the Bio Preserve," Jothen said. "So we *were* going east before you veered up this way."

Biond said, "At least we know where we are and can start checking the landmarks again."

Some miles north of Bloomington Jothen said, "I've been watching the treetops. Judging by the way they're bending, the wind is from the west, so we must be drifting east."

Biond groaned and said, "I'll try to compensate, but it will be guesswork. Just hope that we don't drift too far."

Then he added, "Our ammeter reading is going down steadily. We won't fly many more miles. I'm going down near treetop level. There's a city coming up on our right. Can you read the name on the airfield?"

"Looks like Gridley. Yes, it is Gridley. Nothing's stirring at the flyport."

Soon the sound of the motors grew fainter, then faltered and ceased. The aircar nosed downward and plunged into the trees with a loud crackling and snapping of branches and came to rest with a crunch, tilted at a steep angle. They broke the grip of the conforming seats. The glastic windshield was unbroken. Except for some blue sky directly overhead, all they could see was leaves—narrow, pointed leaves growing in paired rows along both sides of long whip-like stems.

With some difficulty they scrambled up the steeply sloping floor into the rear compartment to get their guns and canteens, and discovered that the exit door was jammed against a tree limb and could not be opened.

Jothen said, "Now what do we do?"

"We go back to the cockpit and blow off the canopy," Biond said.

They slid down the inclined floor into the cockpit; Biond pressed the canopy eject button. With a loud bang and a puff of smoke, the canopy somersaulted into the air and fell with a crash into the trees some distance away. This was followed by a loud chorus of guttural voices crying, "Krah! Krah! K-k-k-krah!"

"What under the stars was that?" asked Biond nervously.

Jothen said, "I haven't the slightest idea, but I'm glad we brought guns."

The aircar had lodged about fifty feet above the ground. The two men climbed down to the lowest limb with the guns and canteens slung over their shoulders. Here the ground was still ten or twelve feet below them. After casting down the guns they hung by their hands and dropped.

While Jothen stood dusting himself off, Biond looked up into the canopy of foliage. "These trees look like something tropical—palms or tree ferns. They must be a Genetics Board project."

"They grow all around outside of the Bio Preserve," Jothen said. "I forget what they're called—paradise tree, tree of heaven, something like that."

"All right," Biond said, hitching up his gun and canteen straps. "We'd better march. It sounds like some of the things around here aren't all that heavenly."

Jothen looked about dubiously. The forest floor was carpeted with a thick mat of coarse grass that grew in overlapping rosettes. Overlaying the grass were withered ailanthus leaves and a clutter of the whip-like leaf stems. Little saplings, offshoots of the tree roots, thrust up everywhere.

Overhead, the creaking and crackling of the aircar as it sank slowly into its nest of trees grew gradually to a volley of snapping and splitting sounds. Both men dodged aside and looked up. The car's angle of tilt was growing steadily steeper.

"Look out," Jothen said. "The damn thing's going to—"

In a fusillade of breaking branches, the car lost its last support and plunged to the ground with a rending smash. Somewhere inside, a few sparks snapped. All around them, the voices broke out again: "Kra-a-ah! K-k-k-aah! Kr-a-a-ah!" There was a tumult of flapping, invisible wings.

The cries receded into a dubious silence. Mopping his brow, Biond consulted his compass and moved off, Jothen at his heels.

As they trekked, Jothen became gradually aware of a puzzling medley of little sounds rising from the matted undergrowth: rhythmic elfin chirps, whirs, clicks, ratchetings, drawn-out *zings*. They were always just ahead, behind, or to the side, never where he was. It was as though the two men were pushing forward inside an eerie bubble of stillness.

The ailanthus trees were planted in a precise checkerboard pattern, making endless aisles in every direction. They were a good sixty feet tall, and so close together that their upper branches interlaced, forming green arcades shot with slanting sunbeams. The leaves surged together softly in the wind. Now and then, a falling frond seesawed silently to the turf. The tiny, enigmatic sounds only made the over-all hush seem more cathedral-like.

Despite his urgency, Jothen began to feel more and more bemused. He still knew where he was going, and approximately why, but as the hours passed he became less and less sure that he cared. It was as though the forest exhaled some invisible narcotic, half isolation and half quietude. There no longer seemed to be any such

hing as UNOC, or a megalopolis; the very proposition
seemed faintly ridiculous.

After what seemed a long while, the chirping began
to be joined by a strange, remote sound, a reedy trum-
peting somewhere in the far reaches of the heavens.
Jothen looked up, but could see nothing but the inter-
locked fronds. Biond stumped on regardless. They had
come to a wide, cut-over swath, planted with rows
of knee-high young trees, and broken into humps and
hollows by the passage of tree-planting machines. The
soil was full of tough, projecting tree roots from a previous growth, and Biond was watching his footing carefully; but Jothen found it impossible to ignore that high,
imperious summons. He stopped and looked up again.

For a moment, just passing out of view, he saw a flock
of birds flying in V formation. They were so high that
he could only barely make out their slowly flapping
wings and long necks.

The sweet honking voices dwindled, wild, free, and
thrilling. Jothen's soul seemed to rise out of his marrow
after them; he was astonished to discover that there
were tears misting his vision. Probably just the brightness
of the sky; after all, he had flown himself, often enough.
But in his heart the ancient Icarus, of whom he had
never heard, stirred and would not be stilled.

After that came the sadness. Where were they going?
Where could they go? How could they live out there
in that smashed and sterilized world?

"Come on," Biond said irritably. "Are you going to
stand there all day? Let's move."

Reluctantly, Jothen resumed walking. He promptly
tripped over a root and fell, scratching himself considerably. Biond helped him up.

"Watch your feet after this."

"Oh, shut up."

Near the middle of the clearing Jothen felt something

soft and light graze his cheek; another brushed past his
nose. Then a bit of white fluff floated down and
settled on his arm. Others were sailing past all around
him. He examined the one on his arm and saw that
the white fluff was attached to one end of a minute
stalk, thin as a hair, with a tiny, pointed brown seed
at the other end.

"What do you make of this?" he asked Biond, holding
out his arm.

Biond peered at the little object and said, "I've never
heard of a flying seed but I'd guess this is one. The air
must be full of floating seeds and spores."

"We're still miles away from the Rock. How could
they travel so far so soon?"

"Remember that blast of wind after Flavia struck? I
carried that beetle all the way to Gitler."

There were still more of the airborne seeds aloft,
sunlit white dots against the blue. Jothen's attention was
wrenched away by a harsh, high-pitched scream, followed by a muffled drumming sound. About one half
mile away a herd of animals burst into the clearing in
a cloud of dust. They wheeled and headed straight
for the two men.

Biond started to run for the grove on the side of the
clearing ahead of him. Jothen followed, promptly stumbled over a hummock, and fell flat. While he was scrambling to his feet Biond went down; by the time Biond
was up Jothen was down again. In spite of the alarming
loudness of the pounding hoofs, thudding like a thousand drums, Jothen felt a fleeting amusement. His amusement speedily vanished when he discovered that his
belt had been firmly hooked by the crooked, protruding end of a buried root. He was pinned down.

He glanced sideways and saw that the stampeding
animals were horses, of all sizes and colors. They had
fanned out into a ragged phalanx extending nearly a

the way across the clearing—an avalanche of tossing heads and manes, glaring white eyeballs, flashing teeth, sleek bodies, and galloping legs surging toward him in a boiling dust cloud filled with flying tufts of grass and fragments of seedling trees. He shouted to Biond.

The vanguard of the horses reached Biond before Biond reached the trees. They opened their ranks and passed around him on both sides. Jothen turned toward the oncoming stampede. A long-legged roan was almost upon him. Preposterously he raised an outstretched hand and shouted, "Stop! Stop!" Then he buried his face in the dirt, covered the back of his head with his hands, and waited for the end.

The drumbeat of hoofs ended only inches away. There was a split-second cessation of the sound, as if the horse had been annihilated. Then came a heavy thud, the drumbeat resumed on the other side of him, and receded. The horse had jumped over him.

He raised his head slightly and peered with one eye. Another horse vaulted over him. And another. And another.

The air was full of choking dust. Was it all over?-No! There was a second wave galloping out of the dust-haze. This one was different. Some of the horses were striped black and white from nose to tail. They passed around him. Then there was one more, a big white stallion. It leaped over him, the backward stroke of its hoofs showering him with dirt when it hit the ground and sprang forward.

Jothen raised himself halfway on his hands and glared after the white stallion. Then he noticed the marks on the retreating white rump—four parallel, diagonal slashes, fringed by down-flowing rills of scarlet.

*Claw marks?*

Biond stumbled toward him, white-faced under a grimy coating of dust.

271

"Jo! Are you all right?"

"Yes." He disengaged himself; it was absurdly easy, now that the need had passed. "I caught my belt on one of those damned tree roots."

"I thought you were right on my heels all the time."

"Wish I had been. Can't we take a break? I'm parched."

"Sure."

In the shade of a grove on the other side of the clearing, they peeled off their tunics—both were sweating, as much with terror as with heat—sat down at the base of a tree, and drank noisily. After a while they felt calmed enough to try a food bar. Biond yawned.

"I couldn't agree more," Jothen said. "We haven't slept since—when? Before we left Potomac Gap, anyhow. If we don't knock off, we may just drop dead instead."

Biond nodded and they both stretched out on the matted grass. Despite his exhaustion Jothen couldn't sleep. After a while he said, "Biond?"

"Urghh."

"That white horse."

"What about it?"

"It had four long scratches on its rump—still bleeding. Like something had taken a swipe at it. Whatever did that may be still around. I think we ought to stand watches."

There was no answer. "Biond?"

This time, Biond responded with a soft snore. Resignedly, Jothen propped his back against the tree and cradled his stun gun in his lap.

The shafts of sunlight that slanted down through the aisles became more and more oblique, and began to dim. Jothen began to shiver; from being too hot, he was now unaccountably becoming chilled.

He awoke with a yelp of terror, but there was nothing anywhere near him; the Forest had not changed, only become darker. The noise brought Biond awake, mumbling.

"Whassa malla?"

"Nothing. Nightmare, maybe. Listen, Biond, look at the light. We'd better move out. We overslept."

"All right."

Within what seemed only a few moments, the light became so faint that they had to put on their head-lamps. Even so, they came within an inch of walking over a small cliff—a twenty-foot drop, retained by a vitrolith wall.

"Contour terrace," Biond said. "Ought to be a ramp somewhere, to get to the next one."

The darkness became total. They walked with infinite slowness, the light cast by their lamps surrounded by shadows and mystery, haunted by ever louder and more numerous chirps and trills. Overhead, only an occasional star shone through the leaf canopy.

The noises grew louder; not just whispers now, but grunts, croaks, screeches, whistles, and once a spine-chilling noise like heartbroken laughter. Just ahead of their lights, something scrambled abruptly and charged away into the blackness.

Then, suddenly, their way was blocked by a solid vitrolith wall. They played their light beams up along its face, but the top was invisible. It was too high, in any event, to be just another contour terrace wall. It had to be the side of a city—which one, it was impossible to guess.

"I'm dry," Biond said. "And the canteens are empty."

"Let's move west. We might find a conduit."

"Fat chance. They're all underground."

The wall proved to be built in a series of zigzags, each straight section about a mile long. On the last leg of a W, they heard a steady rushing noise and suddenly pushed forward with eagerness; but it was only a blast of warm air, pouring from a series of louvered openings at least thirty feet in diameter. No light shone through the louvers.

"Bound to be water somewhere on the other side," Jothen said.

"Sure, and if we bust in, we'll have a computer watchdog on our necks. These evacuated cities are lethal—they have no sense."

The compass said they were now free to continue northward. The city vanished behind them almost at once. After a while, they came to a second cut-over clearing. Here the starlight was brilliant, and in addition there were dim flutterings of an auroral glow in the sky, the aftermath of the ionospheric turmoil created by Flavia. On the other side was another terrace wall, and again they had to search for a ramp.

It seemed to Jothen that there was a smoky odor in the air. He sniffed.

"I smell something too," Biond said. "Something scorched."

"Yes, and something else—something foul."

The smell became stronger as they went farther. There was a bluish haze in the air now; the beams of their headlamps became more sharply defined. Then they found their way blocked by a *cheval-de-frise* of fallen trees. There seemed to be no way through it; it cut through the Forest as straight as a ruled line. A break in the barrier, created by an intersection with a cut-over swath, aroused their hopes briefly, but it, too, was barricaded; an embankment of heaped-up earth, rocks, and tree fragments—like a levee about twenty feet high—lay across the clearing.

"We'll have to climb for it."

They began scrambling up the slope, sometimes on

all fours, their feet slipping and sliding in the loose earth. It felt warm, and gave forth an unpleasant garlic-like odor.

They reached the top of the embankment and recoiled from the stench that met them. They were looking into a tremendous trench, at least two hundred feet wide and fifty feet deep. Coils of bluish vapor were rising from it. It was strewn with tree fragments, some glowing and smoldering, others actively burning. The straight trench extended away in both directions farther than the beams of their headlamps could reach.

Something was advancing along the bottom of the trench, far away on their right, something that throbbed and crunched and hissed. At every hiss one of the small fires went out. It was furnished with three spotlights—one that shone downward directly ahead of it and two that were constantly moving and searching on either side. One of these roving beams leaped ahead and fixed itself on Jothen and Biond just as they were turning to retreat down the embankment away from the insufferable odor.

They stumbled and rolled down the slope, then withdrew to level ground.

"Whoever is driving that machine must have spotted our headlamps," said Biond. "We'll just wait here. They'll be investigating in a few minutes."

The noise drew nearer, paused, then resumed, but at a slower tempo, as if the machine were moving laboriously. The beams of both headlamps were directed toward the top of the embankment. A dark rectangular structure heaved itself above the crest of the heaped-up earth; then the three spotlights appeared. Two converged on Biond and Jothen, the third continued to shine straight downward. The rest of the machine rose into view and became identifiable as an eight-legged pedicar. It paused on the crest of the rise and directed a jet of foam into the trench, then began to pick its way cautiously down the sloping earth. Its "feet" were flattish domes four feet in diameter, their undersides studded with short, blunt spikes.

It strode toward the two men, then halted, towering over them. A light came on in the rectangular cab, there was a click, and a window slid open. Two green-uniformed Forest rangers leaned out.

One of them called down, "What in the name of all that's holy are you doing out here?"

"It's a long story," said Biond. "We're trying to get to the Bio Preserve. Our aircar crashed not far from Gridley."

"You mean you walked from there?"

"Yes."

"Great stars! Well, just keep going in the direction we came from. It isn't far. We'd pick you up and take you there, but we have to put out these fires and we can't call the ranger station and have them send someone after you because the radio isn't working."

"I think we can make it," Jothen said. "But tell us one thing. What knocked down the trees and gouged out that trench?"

"It was either a hunk of Canadian rock or a piece of Flavia. Whatever it was, it's loaded with arsenic minerals. Smell that odor? It's arsine gas—deadly if you breathe too much of it. The rock came in almost horizontally, clipped the Preserve, and dug that groove in the ground. Don't come close to it again, if you want to stay alive."

"If it's so deadly, how do you survive?"

"The cab's gastight and smoke proof. By the way, did you see any animals?"

"A few," Biond said.

"Doubt that you'll see any more around here—because of the gas. But watch out."

"Thanks."

The two rangers withdrew into the car and the window closed. The light in the cab went out. Like some animal, the pedicar wheeled around, crunching at every step, labored up the slope, descended into the trench, and disappeared. Jothen was sorry to see it go; it was a reminder of a more familiar world.

As they recovered from its light, he was astonished to see traces of dawn on the sky. Without a word, the two men resumed marching.

And just at full daylight, the Forest ended, and they were staring at the ruins of Starved Rock.

## 16   "... but we shall all be changed."

The original Starved Rock—named for some incident in pre-Unistam history of which no record survived— had stood on an island where the Des Plaines and Kankakee rivers joined to form the Illinois, and the Bio Preserve had simply been extended outward from it, using the Rock as the core of its central ziggurat, and leaving the rivers as they were. Situated only fifty miles southwest of Chicago, it had been judged imperative that its contents be destroyed, but unlikely that the structure itself would sustain really heavy damage.

Both of these calculations had now come to grief. Kim had not destroyed the contents; and as Biond and Jothen emerged from the Forest at the Preserve's southwestern edge, the original Rock reared blackly before them into the sky, thrusting up from a colossal, smoking jumble of twisted and riven beams, tumbled vitrolith, and shattered glastic. The Preserve had been proof against any ordinary earth shock, even a severe one; evidently it had taken a direct hit by a secondary meteorite, not one of the earlier, smaller ones such as had nearly panicked the Joneses, but a fragment of the Earth itself blasted out of the crater when Flavia struck. On the Moon, as the "bright rays" showed, some such secondaries had been hurled halfway around the satellite, and others had been thrown free of lunar gravity entirely; even on Earth, the distance from lower Hudson's Bay to northern Illinois was not extraordinarily far for one to be thrown.

The outcome could have been worse, Jothen thought. The thing had not missed Chicago by much, and the city was a much bigger target. Somehow the thought did not comfort him a bit.

With the utmost caution, the two exhausted men worked their way northward around the ruins. Biond seemed to be swearing continuously under his breath, but Jothen could not find the heart to say a word; his tongue seemed cloven to the roof of his mouth, half by thirst, half in fear.

Gradually, it became evident that the destruction had not after all been total. Only about a third of the Preserve, all on this side, was in ruins. The rest of it ranged from slightly damaged to apparently intact. Jothen pointed silently; Biond nodded and they moved closer, more cautiously than ever.

The sections that were actually, not just apparently, intact were easy to identify: they were opaque from the outside, the glastic revealing nothing but a solid wall of greenish-gray mist. Evidently, whatever Kim's original intentions, the impact of the meteorite had set off automatic safeguards, which she had omitted or had not known how to circumvent. Whatever the reason, the intact sections were now filled with gas.

"I hope the staff had enough warning to get into pressure suits," Biond muttered. "That stuff is wicked— an out-and-out contact poison, and corrosive to boot."

"Why did it have to be so drastic?" Jothen asked through stiff lips.

"Because we wanted it to kill *everything* in there, even things that don't breathe, right down to the soil nematodes and the bacteria. The basic ingredient is thiolutin, a protoplasm poison, besides surfectants, potentiators, and I don't know what all else. A vicious gas."

"No wonder Kim hated to use it. Look, there's an area where it seems to have been pumped out again. Do we dare go in there, or will stray traces of the stuff kill us?"

"It's safe. The mist is an indicator. Only a measured amount is released, according to the amount of protoplasm contained in the area. When the mist clears, that means it's all been used up."

"Charming," Jothen said. "Well, here's an entrance. We might as well try it. If we can find one of the staff, we just might learn more about what we're up against."

"Lead on. You know the place better than I."

Probably this had once been true, but the moment they were inside the entrance Jothen realized that it was no longer. Because of the destruction, he could not now guess even what geographical area of the Preserve this section had belonged to; and of internal clues there were none left. Before them, what had once been an exotic and idyllic haven, an enclave containing some last survivors of a long-vanished world, there now loomed nothing but an empty cavern containing nothing but a few meaningless foot bridges, galleries, gullies, stony outcroppings. Nothing moved here any longer but the vanes of a few rain machines, turning idly as though they had just finished spraying down the area. Others stood silent and obviously damaged, towering over the devastation of their pocket universe like impotent metal gods.

Except for the occasional bare rocks, the cavern was floored, to a depth of several inches, with a gray, acrid slime of which Jothen could at first make no sense at all. Then, with a shock, he realized what it was—the dissolved remains of every living thing the section had supported—every animal, every insect, every tree, every blade of grass . . . as Biond had said, right down to the soil nematodes and the bacteria. They had all been slain; and it was more than likely that the world would never see many or most of these species again.

And of course the very fact that they had been successfully destroyed showed that they need not have been; their section had not been cracked. Yet it had been impossible to predict that, and the alternative—the one Kim had taken, however inefficiently—of letting all survive and trusting to luck had not proven to be any better a solution . . . except, possibly, for the escapees.

Appalled, Jothen looked back and forth, up and down, utterly at a loss; and for once nothing more practical seemed to occur to Biond. Confronted with a perfect specimen of his hobby, the former Disaster chief could only mutter:

"This tells us nothing—and we can't go into the next section, that's still full of gas. Any ideas, Jo?"

Jothen shook his head. At the same time, he realized that a gargoyle head, like a mouthless skull, with huge black discs of eyes in an indistinct face, seemed to be staring at him through the glastic divider nearest him. When he blinked and looked again, it had vanished into the poisonous mists; but a moment later, an airlock nearby began to cycle.

Both men retreated a step as the valve opened and a
figure in a pressure suit emerged, carrying a tank with a
flexible hose and a flared nozzle. "Jothen!" it said.
"Biond! What are you doing here? I mean—I'm glad
you're alive—but it's very dangerous here—the gas, the
ruins . . ."

Jothen stepped forward, but Kim waved him off
with her free hand. "I'm not safe to touch. And there's
more of the gas in this tank," she said. The familiarity
of her voice made her look all the more ghostly in the
protective suit. But she sounded almost normal, except
for an overtone of shock and horror, for which she
could scarcely be blamed. Jothen felt a wave of relief.

"Are you all right?" he said.

"I guess so. But Jothen—oh God. I was going to say
it's all so awful, but the word—it doesn't begin to say
what I mean."

"There are no words," Biond agreed gravely. "But
just what do you think you're up to now, Kim? Put that
damn tank down before you do more damage."

She put it down promptly. "I won't hurt you," she
said. "I'm really all right now. If you're going to say it's
too late, you're right."

"I wasn't. It's what you're doing now that I'm interested in."

"Let's go outside so I can take this suit off. Then I
can talk better, and you'll both be a lot safer. This would
be a ridiculous time to have an accident."

They followed her out, leaving the Preserve to its
death agonies. She did not stop until she reached the
margin of the Forest. Then she shed the suit, emerging
looking sweaty, wan, and dirty, and the most beautiful sight Jothen had ever seen.

"All right, shoot," Biond said.

"It's very simple," she said, sitting wearily down on
the turf. They were glad to follow her example. "I was

crazy to hold back on killing off Starved Rock, and I realized it the moment I saw the asteroid actually falling. I guess I hadn't really believed in it before, not really. It . . . scared me. Of course I know it scared everybody, but the thing is, I hadn't been scared before, not enough, anyhow. By then it was too late. When I came to after the southwest wing was smashed, I found that the automatics had cut in. I still don't know how much of the population got out into the Forest—"

"Quite a lot," Biond said.

"I suspected that, but I couldn't be sure—there was so much destruction. So I thought that the least I could do was to go through the intact sections, the ones that were still sealed, and make sure that the rest of the sacrificing was thorough. I was just finishing that when I saw you. I was startled, but—but I'm glad to see you both . . . especially you, Jothen. There's . . . a lot that I was wrong about. But you, too, Biond. I'm ready to take my medicine."

"I think you've already taken it," Biond said gently. "Both immediate and condign. Even if you hadn't, I no longer have any power to punish anyone, and I think McGee is practical enough to shrug his shoulders and take the situation as it stands. Yours wasn't the only error made in the world in the last few months, or the last few centuries either, Kim."

Kim's eyes misted. Jothen said, "You're damn decent, Biond."

"I'm conservative," Biond said, shrugging. "The world is going to need every skill it can muster for whatever this next era is going to be like. There'll be mysteries and rigors both, and in abundance. To be legalistic now about small failures would be suicide, if we haven't committed it already."

There was a distant rustling and tramping in the

Forest behind them. It grew louder. "Hello," Jothen said unnecessarily, "somebody's coming."

They all stood up, feeling both embarrassed and relieved. Just out of sight, something in the Preserve creaked, rang, and collapsed.

Dorthy Sumter came out of the Forest. Behind her was a party of Tritons, headed by Storm and Tioru, in heavy flying clothes that doubled very well as hiking outfits.

"Dorthy!" Biond said. "What—how on Earth . . ."

Dorthy laughed. "We were looking for you," she said. "And for Kim and Jothen, too, for that matter. We called Gitler, but a man named Naujack told us you'd come here. So we got a twenty-passenger copter from Transcorp and came after you."

"Not by telling Marg't what you were up to, I'll bet."

"Marg't was in a white rage," Dorthy said, with a rather cat-like smile. "In fact, I think she's a little mad. Half the time she was accusing you of a dozen different crimes—including something called treason, which I never heard of—and then she'd begin ranting about taking off for Alpha Centauri right away. Even Chen U was shocked. I insisted that we get you back—I said I'd take you into my corporation if Prime Center wouldn't go along with me. McGee sided with me right away. He thinks very highly of you, Biond, and I don't think he liked being your replacement."

"Probably not. I hadn't thought of it before, but he wouldn't like being top dog in anything—it leaves him no place to pass the responsibility. He's a born second-in-command."

"That's pretty much my assessment. Anyhow, he was no trouble, and Deban Tod is a little beholden to me, in addition to being a very fair man. When Marg't saw she was outvoted, she hissed and spat and tore up the carpetment until Chen U had to take her out, and

I don't think she'll be back. The result is, Prime Center is still functioning, but the balance of power is with me now. And we need you—all three of you. With the mess the world is in, we can't afford to waste any talent, not any longer."

"I'm happy to hear it," Biond said gloomily. "But—maybe I'm just exhausted, Dorthy, but to tell you the truth, I don't think the mess is remediable—not any more. If there was ever any hope of solving the population problem, it should have been tackled no later than the twenty-first century—even if it had to involve something mildly oppressive, like compulsory sterilization injections. I told Marg't that, back before we even knew about Flavia, but she wasn't listening to me even then. Sure, it would have been difficult, choosing the candidates, and choosing the people to choose them. As soon as you start talking about human reproduction, everything turns out to be sacred.

"But we never even tried to face up to the difficulties. Instead, we ducked them—in the name of humanitarianism. We let ourselves be sold on the notion that we could never have too many people, not even if they were standing on each other's feet. And we threw everything we had into just one effort—to accommodate *everybody*, and not just adequately, but in luxury.

"Well, we made it for a while, quite a long while. But it was bound to break down sooner or later. If it hadn't been Flavia, it would have been something else, now or later. It turned out to be now, that's all.

"And we've had it. From now on, it's going to be guns, starvation, and tyranny—and we brought it on ourselves."

"Surely it can't be that bad," Jothen and Kim said, almost simultaneously.

"You two," Biond said, "have lived in isolation almost all of your lives, one in an artificial wilderness, the other in an empty city. You know the facts as well as I do—but you haven't had to live with them. But you'll see—you'll see."

"We have little to be proud of," the Triton Storm agreed unexpectedly. "Except our humanity, and the fact that we did try—however futilely. But we did after all keep the peace, and contrive abundance for everybody, for eight full centuries, which is a record."

"And there is still hope," the Triton Tioru added. "There are two races of men now. There is hybrid vigor. And there is, of course, the sea."

Jothen stared at the two Tritons, startled and baffled. Kim looked as taken aback as he felt, though Biond simply looked doubtful.

"That's a major beginning, anyhow," Dorthy Sumter said. "It's another reason why I was able to oust Marg't Splain, and even get Chen U's help doing it . . . even though I'm a relative newcomer to Prime Center. For the foreseeable future, all our hope lies in Submarine Products—and with the Tritons."

"We're going to move Prime Center to Great Inagua," Tioru added. "It was hit by a tidal wave, but it stood up under it very well. And making an SPC regional headquarters the hub of the world ought to be a forcible reminder of where we have to turn now."

"I have to concur," Biond said thoughtfully. "But still, the sea isn't after all our only hope. In addition, there's mitochondriatics—never mind what that is for now, I'll explain later. And of course there's hybrid vigor. I hadn't thought of that, but it's been gone from the world for a long time, and we've needed it. And there's the mutations that the fall of Flavia is bound to provoke. All disorderly and unpredictable, like the sea itself—but we never really did have our order imposed upon nature, we were only fooling ourselves. Eight centuries of self-hypnosis . . .

"But they're over now. Too bad the awakening had to be so brutal, but obviously nothing less gentle would have served. Now, the Biological Preserves are broken and obsolete, the monotonous old World Forest is doomed, new life is let loose in the world. Who knows what might come of it? Listen!"

They all listened. Very distantly, something inhuman called. Nearer, something else answered.

No one seemed willing to break the murmuring silence. Slowly and thoughtfully, one by one, they began to walk back into the Forest toward Dorthy's aircraft and Great Inagua.

At last there was no one left but Storm. He paused to look back in the direction of the ruins of Starved Rock Preserve, his ebony face enigmatic except for his mechanical, slow-falling, and—perhaps—meaningless tears.

Then he, too, was gone, and the world was ready to begin.

71

SCIENCE FICTION from the GREAT YEARS

| | | |
|---|---|---|
| *01570 | **Alien Planet** Pratt | 75¢ |
| *02938 | **Armageddon 2419 A.D.** Nowlan | $1.25 |
| 06713 | **The Blind Spot** Hall & Flint | $1.50 |
| 07690 | **The Brain-Stealers** Leinster | $1.50 |
| 07840 | **A Brand New World** Cummings | $1.25 |
| 27291 | **The Galaxy Primes** Smith | $1.25 |
| 52831 | **Metropolis** Von Harbou | $1.25 |
| 53870 | **The Moon Is Hell** Campbell | 95¢ |
| 70301 | **The Radio Beasts** Farley | $1.50 |
| 70320 | **The Radio Planet** Farley | $1.50 |
| 75431 | **Science Fiction—The Great Years Part II** Pohl | $1.50 |
| 75894 | **Sentinels from Space** Russell | $1.50 |
| *84331 | **The Ultimate Weapon** Campbell | $1.25 |
| 87182 | **War Against the Rull** Van Vogt | $1.50 |

*Available wherever paperbacks are sold or use this coupon.*

45C